"Don't touch me," Liliana said, her eyes flashing with scorn.

"Don't even come near me. You stink like a . . . like a *peasant!*"

Hu Morgan was a proud man, and Liliana had finally said one thing too many. His lips tightened, his brow lowered and his gaze burned into hers. He grabbed her arm, pulling her to him. "You are my wife," he said coldly, "the way Mott is my dog and this is my house. Don't you *ever* say such things to me again. Do you understand?"

Shocked and truly frightened by the fierce intensity in his dark eyes, Liliana couldn't speak. She had forgotten the incredible power Hu had exhibited on the tournament field.

He was a warrior. A brave, passionate man, almost savage. Dear God, she had wanted such a man for her husband—but she had not truly understood what it was she had wished for. . . .

Dear Reader,

June's *Unicorn Bride*, by Claire Delacroix, is truly a big book. This sweeping medieval tale tells the story of Lady Alienor, a young woman betrothed to a man veiled in secrets and legends.

Popular author Margaret Moore brings us the latest installment in her Warrior series, *A Warrior's Way*. Awarded an estate for his valor, knight Hu Morgan is doubly pleased to acquire a wealthy wife in the bargain. However, the lady in question is decidedly less enthused about the match.

Jonathan Harris and Polly O'Neil make an unusual pair of lovers in *Timeless*, by Western author DeLoras Scott. Jonathan has been given a second chance in life and love, thanks to Miss Polly, but she soon begins to wonder exactly who—or *what*—he really is.

Laurel Ames creates another romp set in the Regency era in *Homeplace*. Masquerading as a boy in order to keep her inheritance, Justine Mallory finds herself in trouble when her handsome guardian decides to make a man out of her.

And keep an eye out for the *Promised Brides* Historical short-story collection, with authors Mary Jo Putney, Kristin James and Julie Tetel.

Sincerely,

Tracy Farrell
Senior Editor

Please address questions and book requests to:
Harlequin Reader Service
U.S.: 3010 Walden Ave., P.O. Box 1325, Buffalo, NY 14269
Canadian: P.O. Box 609, Fort Erie, Ont. L2A 5X3

MARGARET MOORE

A Warrior's Way

Harlequin Books

TORONTO • NEW YORK • LONDON
AMSTERDAM • PARIS • SYDNEY • HAMBURG
STOCKHOLM • ATHENS • TOKYO • MILAN
MADRID • WARSAW • BUDAPEST • AUCKLAND

ISBN 0-373-28824-7

A WARRIOR'S WAY

Copyright © 1994 by Margaret Wilkins.

Printed in U.S.A.

MARGARET MOORE

confesses that her first "crush" was Errol Flynn. The second was Mr. Spock. She thinks that explains why her heroes tend to be either charming rogues or lean, inscrutable tough guys.

Margaret lives in Scarborough, Ontario, with her husband, two children and two cats. She used to sew and read for reasons other than research.

Chapter One

Hu ap Morgan ap Ianto mumbled a string of eloquent Welsh curses and shifted slightly as the blow fell.

"Not wise to abuse the smith, boy," his friend Elwy chided. "Not when he's the one got to get the helm off your head."

Hu heard Elwy's deep, rich laugh and frowned as much as he could in the confines of his helmet, which had gotten so battered during the tournament that he couldn't remove it. The straw padding tickled his nose and made breathing difficult.

The smith hit the helmet again.

"Going to get a good ransom from that knight, for this," Hu muttered.

"Providing we can get that thing off you. You might have to spend the rest of your days as Hu the Helm."

Hu grunted as the smith hit again, reflecting that Elwy would probably make jokes on his deathbed.

"I told you it wasn't fitting right—*o'r annwyl!*" Elwy exclaimed with a low chuckle. "Here she comes."

"Who?"

"You know. The girl that's made you lovesick."

Hu shifted again. He never should have told Elwy he thought Lord Trevelyan's daughter the most beautiful girl he had ever seen. "I'm not lovesick."

Nonetheless, for the first time he was rather glad that his helmet was stuck. No one could see him blushing.

"She's coming this way, and she's got her maidservant with her."

"She is not, you liar."

The smith hit the helmet so hard that Hu cursed forcibly in a language the man would understand.

Then, to his shame, he heard the sound of women's laughter. Embarrassed laughter. Oh, God, he knew that laugh! He had strained to hear it throughout the feasting last night, when he had also tried not to stare at Lady Liliana Trevelyan."

"Good day, gentlemen."

Oh, God's *teeth!* It would have been better if he had been knocked unconscious.

"Good day, my lady," Elwy said respectfully.

Hu didn't say a word.

"I'm sorry about your friend," Lady Liliana said. "Is he going to be able to get it off?"

"Aye, my lady," Elwy answered.

Lady Liliana's voice was soft, as Hu was sure her skin would be. He was pleased that she cared enough to inquire about him, but he found himself wishing he had been wounded. Nothing fatal or maiming, just something a little more . . . awe-inspiring. That would be better than having to sit on a stump with his head on an anvil like a chicken about to become dinner.

"Perhaps he should have left the field sooner."

"Hu never leaves a fight, my lady."

Hu? Would Elwy never learn to use his proper title, especially at times like this? They were both knights, albeit landless ones.

"So I saw," she replied. "I was most impressed during the tournament. I hope we shall have the pleasure of his company at the feast tonight. He deserves a fine meal."

"We're both looking forward to it, my lady."

After a few minutes that seemed like hours while the smith continued to work, Elwy said, "They're gone."

"Good." Hu sounded annoyed, but he wasn't as angry as he might have been. Lady Liliana Trevelyan had spoken well of him.

"If you'd give me a hand, sir, I think we can get this off," the smith said gruffly.

"About time," Hu muttered as Elwy and the smith took hold of his helmet and pulled. The helmet popped off like the cork from a keg of ale.

Hu drew in deep breaths of air, happy to be out of the stuffy confines of the padding. "God's teeth! That's better."

He rotated his shoulders and flexed his stiffening muscles. It would be good to get his chain mail off, too. He glanced at his plain black tunic. Muddy, but not torn. Thank the Lord for small mercies!

Elwy laughed. "You look like you could use some ale," he remarked in Welsh. "And you smell like you need to wash."

Hu glared at his friend. "I don't smell." He frowned. "Do I?" It was bad enough Lady Liliana had seen him like that, but to think he stank, too!

"Not bad," Elwy said. "The smith stinks worse."

Hu glanced at the muscular smith and thought it was a good thing Elwy was making his insults in Welsh. "I'll be back with some coins in a few minutes," he told the man in Norman French. "Many thanks."

The smith smiled and began to gather up his tools. As they walked away, Hu made a slight gesture with his hand, and his dog, Mott, who had been sitting patiently beside the stump, trotted ahead of them.

"Never thought I'd see you tongue-tied near a woman, boy," Elwy said with a chuckle.

"Who was it? I couldn't hear anything clearly."

"Liar."

Hu frowned with mock displeasure, but didn't bother to reply. He was thinking about Liliana Trevelyan. The way her golden hair rippled and gleamed in the sun. Her lovely green eyes, like the first leaves of spring, and the way the skin at their corners crinkled when she laughed. The little dent in the top of her lip that he wanted to touch. The slight swell of her breasts above her narrow waist. She made his heart beat as fast as it did before a joust.

By now they had reached their tent, which had been set up in a meadow not far from Lord Trevelyan's huge castle. Hu ducked inside and washed, determined to look his best at the feast tonight.

Hu and Elwy had come to take part in a tournament and hoped to win some ransoms from other knights. Baron DeLanyea, the Welsh lord for whom they had been squires, had gladly knighted them when their time as squires was at an end, but he could not provide them with estates. However, they were young and strong and well-trained, and the baron had had little doubt that they could do the rest themselves. They thought so, too.

Hu was also blessed with other things—handsome features, curling dark hair, fearless black eyes and a muscular body. Women stared at him quite shamelessly, and not a few came more than willingly to his bed.

Elwy, on the other hand, was as dark and homely as a demon. He had, however, a sense of humor and a fine singing voice that stood out even in Wales. In this he was able to feel superior to Hu, for Hu, unfortunately, was an oddity among Welshmen in one respect. He sang, so Elwy said, like a dog howling at his master's grave. Nor did Elwy lack for female companionship, for with his jokes and songs, he was able to charm women despite his big nose and bigger ears.

The two had been friends since childhood. That was how Elwy knew that Hu *never* left a fight until he won.

But he didn't know why.

"He's very handsome."

Liliana turned to her red-haired maidservant as the girl bustled about tidying the large chamber. Draped over the bed and chairs were several gowns, and Liliana tried to decide which to wear to the feast that evening. "Maude, you think any man in chausses who isn't already married is comely."

Maude giggled. Maude often giggled. Too often, perhaps, and too easily, but she was the closest thing Liliana had to a friend.

"Well, that Hu Morgan is, and you can't deny it. His friend may not be, but he certainly has a nice face.

And they both got good legs." Maude's blue eyes twinkled mischievously.

"Maude!" Liliana moved a gown out of the way and sat down in the carved oak chair. She stifled a yawn. She had been awake early that morning. It wasn't often her father allowed her to watch any part of a tournament, and she hadn't wanted to miss a moment of this one.

And a good thing, too. She wouldn't have seen Hu Morgan defeating two famous knights—and getting his helmet stuck on his handsome head. Last night she had been impressed by his good looks. Today she had been even more impressed by his battle prowess. He seemed extraordinary, until she realized he couldn't get his helmet off. That made him seem much more... approachable.

"Well, they do have fine legs." Maude grinned slyly. "I saw the way you looked at Hu Morgan when he was at the smithy—and the poor fellow sitting there like a horse being shod."

Liliana shared a giggle over the memory. She also hoped laughing would mask the fact that she was blushing. Hu Morgan did have the best legs she had ever seen, as well as the finest shoulders. His entire body was marvelous, but not nearly as marvelous as his face. Before falling asleep she had laid awake for several minutes picturing him in her mind.

But it wouldn't do to let Maude know that.

Another maidservant poked her head in the chamber door. "Excuse me, my lady, your father wishes to see you."

Liliana nodded. It was probably something to do with the feast tonight.

Since her mother's death when she was a little girl, Liliana had come to do the honors as lady of the manor more and more. At first, trying to act as mature as she could, she had maintained a somewhat forced dignity and aloofness. Now cool composure was natural for her when she was in company.

She sometimes wondered if that was why people seemed almost afraid of her.

"I have decided to wear my green gown, the dark one," she said to Maude as she paused at the door and gestured toward her finest gown of rich silk brocade with golden threads woven through it.

"Yes, my lady."

Liliana wanted to look her very best tonight. After all, it was expected of her.

Lord Trevelyan paced the floor of the great hall, unmindful of the several servants laying fresh rushes and herbs in preparation for the evening's feast. The trestle tables still lay against the walls, but would soon be set up and spread with fine white linens and flower petals. From the kitchen corridor delicious aromas drifted to his nostrils. As always the feast would be lavish, so that was not what brought the lines of worry to his brow.

Apart from the ever-present concern about the acts of King John, which always caused much disgruntled discussion when noblemen gathered, he was troubled by the news that there was a band of outlaws living— and stealing—at the farthest outskirts of his vast land holding. It was rumored that they were Welsh, disaffected men who held the Normans and their laws in complete contempt. So far, they were only a nuisance, but their leader was said to be a man capable of compelling other dissatisfied tenants to follow him. Trevelyan knew he would be wise to ensure that the manor on the edge of his lands was held by a strong knight.

He was also concerned about Liliana. Alfred Beaumare, whose daughter was married to a man twenty years her senior, had made yet another comment about Liliana's age and a sly remark concerning her spinsterhood, with the unspoken implication that somehow Trevelyan had managed to raise an unmarriageable daughter.

It was true that Liliana should have been married a few years ago, but surely nineteen wasn't *that* old. She was beautiful enough to still have her pick of many suitors.

Perhaps he *had* spoiled her a bit, but she had been left motherless so early in life . . .

Lord Trevelyan heard the rustle of skirts and turned as Liliana walked toward him down the length of the great hall. She wore a lovely gown of patterned linen in a deep red color, with elongated cuffs on the sleeves and a slightly raised hem to reveal the pale silk chemise beneath. A girdle of supple black leather was tied about her slender waist and hips, the ends dangling nearly to the floor. Her bountiful blond hair was coiled close about her head and covered by a veil of silk that matched her chemise.

Yes, she was a beauty, with her mother's golden hair and expressive green eyes.

But there was a hint of stubbornness about her full lips that had never belonged to her mother.

He had to admit that something of his nature resided in his daughter. Maybe that was another reason he let her have her way in so many things. Too often his parents had tried to reign him in, to his great resentment. He had given his daughter a freedom he had not had until his parents died.

Today, he decided, he would try a different method. He would see what a little strong talk would do.

"Father, you wished to see me?" Liliana asked with a smile.

"Sit here," he replied, pointing to a chair. She complied, and he sat beside her.

"Is something the matter?"

He cleared his throat. "Liliana, I've decided it's time you were married."

"Again?" she asked with a lift of her eyebrows and a merry smile on her rosy lips.

He frowned. "I mean it this time. There are several fine noblemen here for the tournament. I've decided you must choose one of them."

Liliana's lips pressed together. He knew what that meant.

"I won't brook any arguments, Liliana. I've made up my mind."

Liliana looked at her father and recognized the stubborn set of his jaw. He meant it! This time, he actually meant it!

Usually he gave in to her if she persisted enough, but not when he got that look on his face.

She gazed unseeingly at the intricate tapestry on the wall behind her father.

This day had to come eventually. She had heard the rumors that were beginning to be told about her. Averil Beaumare made sure of that. People were saying Liliana Trevelyan was beautiful but cold. That she thought no man good enough for her. Even that she didn't like men and might be...unnatural.

She had often told her father that she would marry when she met a man she wanted for a husband. She had even considered one or two, but always decided against them.

Where would she find a husband who would give her the freedom her father allowed? And was it too much to ask that he be young, and preferably not as ugly as a boar?

"What about Sir George de Gramercie?" her father asked quietly.

She shrugged her shoulders. He was nice enough, but he was not a man to inspire passion. On the other hand, he was steward to one of her father's oldest friends, so he would be busy much of the time. He might be willing to let his wife "help."

Her father named another lord.

"He's too old."

He named another.

"He's as fat as a rainwater hogshead."

And another.

"He drinks too much."

Another.

"Everyone knows no serving wench is safe from his lecherous advances."

Her father frowned with exasperation. "Liliana, this is your final chance. If you don't make a choice today, I shall make one for you."

She could hardly believe it. He was absolutely serious.

"What about Hu Morgan?" he asked after a moment.

Her gaze went back to the tapestry. Hu Morgan couldn't be accused of not inspiring passion, with his physique and handsome face. And he was young, too. But...

"He doesn't have any land," she protested halfheartedly.

"I'll give him some."

Liliana eyed her father warily, especially when his face began to look rather triumphant, as if he had just concocted a wonderful plan.

"There is a manor at the far border of my property that has been rather neglected of late," he said. "A young Welsh—ambitious fellow like Morgan would be an ideal choice to take charge of it. Provided he would swear allegiance to me."

She frowned. "And offering your daughter would no doubt make his acceptance more certain."

"Not unless she is willing." Her father leaned forward, his face full of compassion. "Liliana, I have known Hu since he came to one of my tournaments when he was a lad. He's a fine fellow. I don't think you could do much better."

As the idea of becoming Hu Morgan's wife settled in her mind, her heart began to race. Last night she had watched him whenever he was talking to someone else, and she had to admit that he excited her as few men had. To be sure, he was a rather uncouth Welshman, but then he would be more likely to defer to her superior knowledge of Norman ways.

"Very well, Father. I suppose *some* choice is better than none at all."

* * *

Hu stared at Lord Trevelyan as he sat in his vast, well-appointed hall, not daring to believe what he had just heard. "You . . . you're offering me a manor?"

"Yes. The last man who held it for me died recently. It will require some repairs, I believe. Charles was not, shall we say, an ambitious fellow. However, I'm sure you could manage to make it quite prosperous and comfortable. It's not a large demesne, but the land is good. You would have to swear allegiance to me, of course."

"Yes, my lord," Hu said slowly, still not quite sure he could believe his own ears. Land! His own land! What he had been dreaming of, planning for, working for ever since he had left Wales. Lord Trevelyan was a just man and a fine lord. He could ask for little more. "I would be honored to serve you."

"I should tell you that there have been rumors of outlaws nearby. Welshmen, it is said."

"If they break the law, they must be punished according to the law," Hu said solemnly. He had no sympathy for malcontents. He had made his way in the world of the Normans. So could any man, if he truly wanted to.

"There is one other condition . . ."

Hu waited, hoping that the condition would not be one to make him refuse.

"I would be honored if you would consider marrying my daughter."

Dumbfounded, Hu could think of nothing to say except a feeble, "Oh?"

"Her dowry would help to improve the estate."

"My lord, I'm . . . I'm overwhelmed," he said after an awkward pause, although that was obviously true.

Lord Trevelyan smiled. "You're a fine young man, Hu. I would be pleased knowing she had such a husband. This way, too, she will be near me. I love her very much."

Hu's riotous thoughts and jumbled emotions settled down rapidly. There was no mistaking the implied threat in Lord Trevelyan's voice. If he mistreated Lord Trevelyan's beloved daughter, her father would not care that she was legally her husband's chattel, and he would have to be answered to.

Of course Liliana Trevelyan was beautiful, and he had wanted her since he had first laid eyes on her, but what else did he know of her? Not one thing.

But if he didn't marry her, he wouldn't get the estate.

Hu almost laughed out loud. What was there to think about? Only a fool would say no. "I would be honored, Lord Trevelyan."

The older man smiled and Hu thought he sighed with relief. "Good. The wedding will take place in, say, a month's time?"

God's blood, a month would seem like an eternity.

"I have no objections," Hu said. He felt rather proud of himself for managing to sound so calm.

Chapter Two

Liliana stared glumly out the narrow window of her bedchamber.

It was her wedding day and it was pouring rain.

"You'll have to wear a cloak, that's all. It could be worse."

Liliana turned to Maude with a sour expression. "Oh? Just how?"

"Well, you could be ill. Or burning with fever. Or the groom could be..."

"What? Too busy?"

Maude frowned, and Liliana knew the girl wished she had kept quiet about the groom. Ever since the feast four weeks ago when her father had announced her betrothal and the date of the wedding, Hu Morgan had spent all his time at his new estate.

There had been a horrendous thunderstorm a few days after Hu left Castle Trevelyan, with high winds that had caused much damage. She had excused his absence then by supposing he had repairs to oversee. But when he still hadn't come to visit her by the third week, her resentment began to fester.

"Now, my lady, don't look like that," Maude cajoled. "Your father said the hall needed some work. And that storm was terrible. Maybe the roof blew in. He's probably making sure things are ready for you, like a good bridegroom should."

Liliana snorted in a most unladylike fashion.

"My lady!"

"Well, is it too much to expect your future husband to make some effort to visit? I might be a leper for all the attention he has paid to me."

What Liliana didn't say, but certainly felt, was that she was not used to being ignored. By anybody.

She turned away from the window. Of course it would rain like the Biblical deluge on her wedding day, too. If it weren't for her father's grim determination to see his daughter married at last, she would refuse to go through with the ceremony, regardless of the money already spent on preparations.

"Don't tug on your gown like that! You'll ruin it." Maude caught the expression on Liliana's face. "My lady," she added respectfully. ·

Liliana let go of the intricately embroidered sleeve and walked over to a small table where a chalice of wine sat.

"Be careful, my lady!"

She gave Maude a black look. "Have you packed my combs?"

"Yes. Everything but your clothes for the journey tomorrow, and your finest silk shift . . . for tonight."

Liliana tried not to blush at the mention of the wedding night. But not from any knowledge of what was to come, unfortunately.

Liliana was very aware that she was woefully ignorant of what was expected of a bride on her wedding night. Her father had always made it clear that he considered such matters unfit for polite conversation in his hall. Since Liliana spent all her time occupied with tasks in or around the hall itself, she was never privy to more earthy discussions concerning human nature.

Even now, she was tempted to ask Maude—*Maude!* who couldn't be trusted to keep a secret if her life depended on it—what happened between a man and a woman when they slept together. How did they make babies? Was it pleasant? Did it hurt?

All Liliana had been able to ascertain by the most undignified method of listening to servants' gossip was that it involved kissing, and some part of the man's body entering a woman's. But what part? And where?

Was it better to admit her lack of knowledge to Maude or to her new husband? Liliana opened her mouth to speak—then heard the clatter of hooves on the cobblestones in the courtyard. Maude rushed to the window, and Liliana joined her.

Yes, it was Hu Morgan, leaping down from his horse and splashing unheeding through puddles toward the chapel.

"Well, he's not late," Maude said, her relief obvious until she caught Liliana giving her a sidelong glance. Her next giggle was rather strained.

"Don't think you have to spare me," Liliana said, keeping the relief from her own voice. She had begun to worry that he might not arrive at all.

"Let's get your cloak on. I'll hold your skirts up out of the wet."

"A very fine, dignified bride I'll look," Liliana muttered.

"You don't want to get this lovely gown muddy, do you, after all the time we worked on it?"

There was a knock at the door. Maude opened it to reveal Lord Trevelyan. He wore his finest tunic of blue and green brocade, and his long, iron-gray hair touched his shoulders. He looked every inch the nobleman, and Liliana was suddenly filled with even more determination to look every inch the nobleman's daughter.

"Ready, my dear?" he asked softly.

Liliana lifted her chin. "Ready."

Hu shook his head, sending droplets of water flying about the chapel. His dog, Mott, who had already shaken himself dry, sat at his master's feet unmoving.

"Do you mind?" Elwy asked as he brushed the drops from his clothes.

Hu grinned and adjusted the belt about his knee-length black tunic. "Sorry." He rubbed the toe of one boot against the back of his other leg, then repeated it for the other boot.

"All right. Not excited or anything, are you, boy?"

"You're just jealous."

Elwy sighed. "Right you are, there. Why, if I had your nose, she'd be marrying me."

"Huh!" Hu smacked at his clothes with the damp gloves he had just removed, looking down at the mud that had spattered on his chausses. He frowned. He had planned to get himself some new clothes for the wedding, but he had needed to buy some more nails for the barn. Then he had hoped to get to Lord Trevelyan's castle the day before the ceremony, but the new bed was late arriving. Hu had stayed to make sure it was constructed properly.

"You're as jumpy as a ram in the spring, man."

"Shut your mouth."

"Oh, Holy Mother. What's this?" Elwy plucked at something on Hu's head.

With a curse, Hu's hand flew to his hair. Then he saw Elwy's broad grin.

"Do I or do I not have nits in my hair?" he asked ominously.

Elwy's smile disappeared. "God's wounds, nervous you are, if you can't take a joke."

"You—"

"Shush! Here they come!"

Later, neither Liliana nor Hu remembered much of the wedding ceremony. The priest was old and mumbled, Liliana was desperately trying to look dignified, and Hu was all too aware of his muddy, disheveled appearance.

Things did not improve at the wedding feast. It was, like all Lord Trevelyan's feasts, a very extravagant meal. Servants brought food spiced with the best, most expensive herbs, including several roasted chickens, a whole roasted boar and sauced mutton. The bread was made of the finest flour, the wine came all the way from France, and the fruit had cost a small fortune.

Liliana noticed none of this. All she could think about was that she was married, joined for the rest of her life to this man at her elbow who was quickly and loudly getting very drunk. This man who had even brought his *dog* into the chapel, the very dog he was feeding from the table with meat from his plate.

It wasn't enough that he hadn't once come to visit her since their betrothal. No, he had to completely humiliate her by jesting loudly in his stupid language with his ugly fool of a friend. He seemed completely lacking in dignity and any idea of the proper conduct of a nobleman.

Barris Beaumare, fat and nearly ancient at forty, sat on her left. His wife, Averil, sat on his left, far enough away so that Liliana didn't have to talk to her or listen to any snide comments. Judging by the behavior of the groom, Averil would have plenty of things to comment about, too.

Nonetheless, the sharp-eyed, wasp-tongued Averil was still all too likely to notice anything amiss between the newly married couple, so Liliana fought to keep her displeasure from her face.

And she was beholden to Averil for one thing. Try as she might to hide it, Averil was jealous. It was something to have a moment of triumph after enduring Averil's smug, superior airs for the past few years.

When Barris left the table for a moment—probably to be ill outside, Liliana thought with disgust—Averil leaned closer, a sly, knowing smile on her face. "I envy you your wedding night," she whispered, but still loudly enough for the groom to hear.

Although she looked at Averil, Liliana knew that Hu had heard and had turned their way.

Averil feigned embarrassment, while Liliana blushed to the roots of her hair. She sat as if frozen. She couldn't have faced Hu Morgan at this moment for all the money in the kingdom.

Instead she smiled at Averil, hiding her embarrassment as best she could—and her sudden overwhelming desire to ask Averil what she meant. "I trust it will be as pleasant a wedding night as yours," she said sweetly.

A flash of displeasure came to Averil's pale blue eyes. She had never bragged about her husband's looks or manners. How could she? But Liliana had had to listen over and over again to accounts of Barris's vast wealth and huge estate, so perhaps it was only natural that she would strike at Averil's weakest spot.

Barris returned, settling his corpulent body into his chair. Liliana hoped he felt too ill to talk anymore.

She reached for her goblet, and her arm brushed against Hu's muscular forearm. She didn't dare look at him, and when she raised the goblet, her hand trembled. She quickly set down the wine and placed her hands in her lap.

She was behaving like some foolish child. Why should she react this way to Hu Morgan? She had known many young, handsome knights, and some had been relatives of the king.

Of course, she hadn't been recently wed to any of those young men...

Hu said something to her father, who was seated on his other side, and both men shared a companionable chuckle. Liliana suddenly had the rather uncomfortable sensation that she was the victim of a conspiracy.

She lifted her chin a little higher. Maybe her father and Hu Morgan were priding themselves on a fine alliance. Perhaps they thought she would have nothing further to say on the matter, now that the ceremony was over.

If that was the case, they were both going to find out otherwise.

Hu watched Liliana out of the corner of his eye. She was as cold and stiff as a corpse. Had been, ever since the wedding.

She was probably angry at him for not coming to visit her after the betrothal. He had wanted to, but Lord Trevelyan had not lied when he said the manor needed some work. The manor house was practically falling down in places, the barn was missing a roof, and he suspected the local tenants had been making off with bits of the outer wall for their own use. The tremendous storm had caused more damage, and lightning had struck the mill.

Hu had ordered the mill to be repaired at once, for it was the most important. When that was well in hand, he had set some men to fixing the barn. His tenants and the reeve, obviously used to being left on their own, had grudgingly obeyed, but he could never be sure they would do as they had been told unless he or Elwy supervised the work.

One day he had gone to the nearest large town, leaving Elwy in charge. There he had bought some livestock with most of the money he possessed.

In his childhood he had been a shepherd, and he thought he could make a fine profit from raising sheep, to add to the incoming tallage the tenants would pay. He had also bought several hens, a rooster, some cattle and pigs.

Hu took another gulp of the wine. Fine wine it was, too. Not that he really liked wine. He preferred ale. But it seemed Normans put great store in wine, so he would drink it.

The week before the wedding, he had tried to get some work started on the manor house. Originally it had had two levels, the bottom for storage and the upper one for the great hall and living quarters, but the wooden flooring had apparently rotted in several places and finally caved in. The roof had been in terrible condition, too. At least he had managed to get that patched, and had the beams that would hold up the new floor inserted over the corbels. However, that was all they had been able to accomplish.

In desperation, he had set aside an area at the far end of the lower level for his bedchamber, and he thought it not uncomfortable. In the spring, they could lay a new floor, and the upper hall could be improved.

He took another gulp. This really was the best wine he had ever tasted—and if he was drinking, he couldn't be expected to talk much. At home, his French sounded fine, but here, almost totally surrounded by Normans, he couldn't help feeling that he sounded like some kind of peasant.

His wife—his wife!—reached out for a piece of fruit. For a moment he ignored Lord Trevelyan's reminiscences and glanced at her again. She looked like an angel in her white gown embroidered with gold around the V of the neck, which offered a tantalizing glimpse of the swell of her breasts. Slim, graceful hands emerged from wide cuffs that reached nearly to the floor. Her lovely hair was just visible under the thin white veil, and her pale cheeks flushed with a maidenly tinge of pink. It was clear Liliana had no need for cosmetics. She was naturally beautiful.

When he had taken her soft, slender hand to put on the wedding band, she had trembled, as had he. She was trembling again now. With anticipation?

He grinned. No doubt she was nervous, probably about the night to come. Most virgins were a little hesitant, he thought as he felt a familiar pleasant tightening in his loins.

Well, he had been with lots of women. He knew how to make the coming experience as enjoyable for her as it would be for him.

He continued to sample the wine as the musicians arrived. The tables were taken down, and a space cleared. After what he thought was a most gallant bow, he stumbled through the first dance with Liliana.

Dizzy and grinning like an idiot, he mumbled that he had not much practice at such things.

"Obviously," Liliana replied peevishly. She glared at him, but all he saw was that she was looking at him with her lovely green eyes.

"It is getting late," she said through clenched teeth. "I believe I shall retire." *And spare myself further humiliation,* she thought.

"Fine idea, fine idea," Hu muttered, taking yet another gulp of wine, not noticing that he spilled some on the white cloth covering the table. "I'll join you shortly."

Liliana shot a look at her father that plainly said, "Are you *quite* pleased?" before she marched off to her bedchamber. It had been decided—by Hu and her father, without asking *her* opinion—that she and her new husband would spend their first night together in her father's home. Tomorrow they would travel to her husband's estate.

Maude trotted along behind her, trying to keep up with Liliana's angry strides. When they reached the bedchamber, Liliana slammed the door shut. "He is— he is *intolerable!*" she exclaimed, pacing the room.

"He's your husband."

Liliana's look kept Maude quiet as she helped her mistress disrobe. She took the lovely white gown and folded it carefully, putting it in one of the chests that stood ready for the next day's journey. Then, with a half-frightened glance at Liliana, she lit a brazier. It was not yet winter, but it could get cold in the night. Especially if one was wearing . . . nothing much.

"Leave me," Liliana said impatiently.

Maude nodded and went out quietly. She had things of her own to prepare, for Lord Trevelyan had agreed to let her go with Liliana to her new home.

Liliana, dressed in the shift she had worn beneath her gown and not the special embroidered silken one, began brushing her hair with hard, furious strokes. After a few minutes, the strokes slowed. Then stopped.

She frowned as she glanced over at her bed, where Maude had drawn back the sheets and coverlet. If Hu Morgan expected to find her waiting patiently in the nuptial bed, he would discover he was sorely mistaken.

Liliana was still sitting there three hours later. She had heard her father's footsteps go past, so she knew he had retired. Then she had listened to the drunken singing from the hall below, her anger smoldering the whole time.

At last loud male voices approached her door, and she stood up, crossing her arms.

The door crashed open and her husband came reeling in, barely able to stand. His dog followed him inside and stayed when Hu turned and shouted at his friend in that abominable Welsh, then kicked the door shut. He almost fell over when he turned to face her.

"You are drunk," she said slowly and deliberately.

"Not much," he slurred, trying to wink but failing.

"Get your dog out of this room."

He frowned. "Mott sleeps where I do."

"Then you may enjoy *his* company on your wedding night, because I am leaving."

She began to walk past him, but he grabbed her arm with surprising strength. He pulled her close, close enough that the stench of his breath assaulted her nostrils. "You're my wife."

"For the present, although you seem to think I am some stupid country wench happy to wait for your attention."

She glared at him defiantly. She wasn't afraid of a man so drunk he could hardly stand. She lifted her arm and pointed at the door. "Get out of here—and take your dog with you!"

He didn't move except to shake his head. "Oh, no. You're my wife and this is our wedding night."

She pushed him away. "Sot! Drunken oaf! *Welshman!*" Humiliated, she infused the last word with all the anger and venom she could muster—which was quite a bit.

In the next instant he grabbed her by the waist, lifted her up and threw her on the bed. He stood in front of her, and for the first time she was afraid of him. Of the anger in his eyes. Of the strength of his body.

Then he blinked, moaned and fell on the bed, his chest over her legs.

For a horrifying moment she thought he was dead, until she heard his deep, heavy breathing.

He was asleep.

Liliana kicked him off her, and he rolled to the end of the bed. She was tempted to kick him again so that he would land on the floor.

If this was the usual behavior of young grooms on their wedding night, all her uncertainty about her duties in her husband's bed had been completely unjustified.

With a final angry glance at the slumbering man, she lay down, yanked the covers over her head and tried to sleep.

Hu's head felt as if the smith was pounding on it again. From the inside. With a low moan, he sat up.

Then he saw Liliana. She wore a gown of plain green fabric. Her hair was confined beneath a wide crown of stiffened cloth, a green veil and chin band. Despite the bright color, she looked as severe as any nun from a strict convent.

Liliana. His wife. Sitting on a chair, staring at him with a look of utter loathing.

He could vaguely remember her in this room last night. She had been wearing something white that clung to her shapely body. They had argued ...

Somehow, between his faulty memory, the look on her face and the fact that he was fully clothed, he suspected they had not consummated the marriage.

"I am going to speak to my father," Liliana said fiercely. "I want this marriage annulled."

Hu stared at her. "Why?" he asked, not willing to believe what he heard.

"Because you are a drunken oaf. I want nothing more to do with you."

She meant every word she said. Hu Morgan had acted no better than the worst sot in the village. She would not spend the rest of her life with him.

She meant it even now, when he looked at her with sleep-tousled hair that made him seem boyish and vulnerable. Even now, with that questioning look on his handsome, roguish face.

She lifted her chin a little higher. Yes, she meant it, she told herself.

He stood up and tugged his wrinkled tunic down. "I'm sorry."

Her eyes widened. "It's rather late for apologies now. You have completely humiliated me."

"I didn't mean to. Truly." He gave her a winsome, questioning look. "The marriage *can* be annulled, I suppose?"

How contrite he seemed! And even rather wistful. Was this the same man she had seen in the tournament, his expression hard and determined, who had fought for hours without fear or giving quarter?

"Yes," she said softly, then she straightened her shoulders. She realized she was beginning to regret his state the previous night as he stood there, the laces of his tunic undone, exposing his muscular chest. She must not weaken now.

But was it so unusual for a man to get drunk at his own wedding? Perhaps he wasn't used to her father's fine wine, which was rather strong. She had seen older, wiser men get drunk quickly when they first tried it.

He was looking at her.

She stood up. "I'm sorry, but I think it's for the best. I'll ask my father to let you keep the estate. After all, you've sworn allegiance to him."

"I've sworn allegiance to you. As my wife." The look in his black eyes sent a thrill of some unknown emotion through her body.

He took a step closer. "I am truly sorry. I acted like a fool. Will you...could you...give me another chance?"

Chapter Three

"Very quiet you are, man, very quiet." Elwy grinned at Hu, who sat slumped in his saddle like a sack of turnips. "Tired, no doubt."

Hu gave him a weak smile, thankful that he was feeling better, at least physically.

Shifting his somewhat stiff shoulders, he was glad he wasn't wearing his heavy mail, although they were both well-armed with swords and daggers. Hu also had his bow slung over his shoulder and a quiver of arrows tied to his wide leather belt.

He glanced over his shoulder. Liliana, wearing a beautiful cloak of soft blue wool the color of the sky at dusk, rode behind them. After her came the cart loaded with her belongings and dowry. Her maid sat on the cart's rough wooden seat beside the elderly driver who looked half-asleep.

He stifled a sigh of relief. For an anxious moment back in Lord Trevelyan's castle he had been certain that Liliana would indeed seek an annulment. And apparently with some cause.

He had been a fool to get drunk like that. If she ever

asked, he decided he would tell her it was a Welsh custom. Something, anything other than the truth.

Which was that he was a lowborn fellow, and all the battle prowess in the world couldn't make up for that.

"Thinking I'll follow your example," Elwy said thoughtfully.

"What?"

"Thinking I'll find myself a rich wife. That's the way to do it, all right."

"Oh."

Elwy gave him a sly wink. "God's blood, man, you're near death. I notice the wife's not talking much, either."

"It's a long ride."

"Right. Whatever you say, Hu." Elwy spoke again after a moment of silence. "Her maid's a pretty little thing."

"You think any woman who laughs at your jokes is pretty."

"Well, that shows they're smart, too."

"I thought you just said you were going to marry a wealthy woman."

"So I am, but I have to pass the nights till then, don't I?" Elwy gave him a broad wink and began to sing, his rich, deep voice echoing through the forest.

Dafydd heard a man's laugh and crept closer to the road. It was his job to keep watch for strangers passing through the forest, especially richly dressed strangers without many soldiers to protect them.

Cautiously he pushed aside a bush and saw two men and one woman mounted on very fine horses. Behind came some servants and a covered cart. Unless he misjudged the bulges under the cloth covering, the cart was filled with chests of goods and furnishings.

Perhaps one of the men was the new lord they had been hearing about, the one given the manor at the edge of Trevelyan's holding.

Dafydd crept a little closer and noticed the short Welsh bow the good-looking one carried. He stared in amazement, for no Norman would ever deign to use such a weapon. Indeed, they held any kind of bow in general disrespect, as they did the people they had so ruthlessly subjugated.

Could it be true, then, that the new lord was a Welshman? It didn't seem possible, not if Trevelyan had married his daughter to him.

But that bow...

The ugly man began to sing, and Dafydd's mouth dropped open in amazement at the familiar tune.

Ivor had to hear about this.

Liliana stopped looking at Hu and glanced around nervously. They were traveling through a forest, and she felt rather frightened. After all, there was only Hu and his friend, herself, Maude and Old John, and the cart was full of clothes, linens, dishes, some fine furniture, candles and even silver coins. They would make an easy target for outlaws.

She had heard the rumors of such men living in these very woods, but her father seemed to set little store in such talk. Perhaps she was worried for no reason. Hu had refused her father's offer of an armed escort, and her father hadn't insisted. He would have, if he thought she was in danger. Obviously he believed Hu and his friend with the ridiculous name capable of defending them.

Above, the sky was filled with gray clouds. She wondered if they would arrive at Hu's estate before it began to rain again. They had been traveling since morning, and it was now nearly dusk. The trees were still dripping from yesterday, and the road was little more than a muddy path.

Her gaze returned to Hu and the short bow slung across his broad back. She had heard that Hu Morgan was a fine archer, but knights used lances and swords, maces or battle-axes, not a weapon relegated to foot soldiers.

In some ways he was very different from the noblemen she had known all her life. Perhaps that was part of his charm.

To think she had been so determined to annul the marriage, only to surrender when he looked at her...that way. Her thoughts and feelings had been in a tumult ever since. One minute she was determined to leave him, the next she wanted him to take her in his arms.

Maybe it was true, what men said. That women were all weak, frail creatures. She hadn't really believed it before, but perhaps she hadn't met the right man.

Suddenly Hu's dog ran off through the woods. Before she realized what was happening, Hu had reined in his horse and reached for his bow. In the next instant he had yanked an arrow from the quiver at his side, cocked it in his bow and fired. The arrow flew through the air and struck something on the ground.

A moment later, the dog came trotting back, a coney between its teeth.

Hu turned to his friend and fired off a spate of Welsh before dismounting and picking up the rabbit. He pulled out his arrow and, she noted with some disgust, wiped the animal's blood on his chausses. Then he looked at her, a wry grin on his handsome face. "Dinner," he said with a wink.

He didn't wait for her to reply, but remounted, tied the carcass to his saddle and slung his bow over his shoulder.

No, he definitely was not like the men she had known all her life.

When they began riding again, she was hard-pressed to keep from staring at him. He had shot so suddenly and completely without warning, his movements swift and sure and not without a certain grace. She had little doubt that the rumors of his archery prowess were not fabrications.

As they continued on, Hu spoke quietly with his friend, and she had the unhappy sensation that she was being excluded. Again.

Maude was giggling behind her, listening to Old John recount some foolish tale.

Liliana shifted in her saddle and told herself she didn't need anybody to talk to.

After several minutes, she realized Hu's horse was slowing. Soon he was beside her on the narrow road. "It's not far now," he said casually.

She glanced at him surreptitiously. The air was chilly, but he didn't seem to notice it. He wore no shirt beneath his leather tunic, so his bare arms were exposed to the cool air. His lean, muscular bare arms.

She stared at her horse's head, suddenly embarrassed by the heat that coursed through her veins.

"I missed the harvest, of course," Hu said, "and not a good one it was, judging by the little grain in the barn. Thinking that more of the harvest went to the villeins' crofts than should have. I got a fine bargain on some cattle, and pigs, too, from a widow."

"Oh." Liliana couldn't muster much enthusiasm for crops or the villeins. That was for the steward to worry about. "Tell me about the servants for the hall."

Hu hesitated a moment before answering. "I've got a woman to do the cooking. Her name's Sarah. She's a Saxon."

"I speak their language."

"Oh? Good."

There was an awkward pause.

"I've bought some chickens, too," Hu said. "They look a little skinny to me, but the price was too good to pass."

Liliana frowned slightly. Did he really think she wanted to hear about thin chickens?

What she would really like to hear about was *him*. Where was he born? How did he come to speak Norman French? How did he get to be a knight?

How did he really feel about her?

"It's just around the next bend." He nudged his horse and went ahead.

It was a good thing he did, because that way he couldn't hear her shocked gasp as she pulled her horse to an abrupt halt when they rounded the corner.

What once had been a fine, if small, manor was now a crumbling ruin. The outer wall was literally falling down, with several stones missing. She could see the wattle-and-daub manor house through a gaping hole in the wall. Most of the roof had obviously been repaired in the last month, and the walls looked as if people had been throwing rocks at them.

There were other buildings, too, of various sizes and in various stages of decay, except for what she was sure was the barn. It was as large as the manor and in obviously better repair.

Her husband apparently cared more about his livestock's accommodation than that of his own wife.

Hu looked at her over his shoulder, a wide grin on his face. "Needs work, I know. But we'll soon set things right."

Liliana clenched her teeth. How could they do this to her? Didn't her father know how badly this estate was ruined? How could he let her marry the man who lived here? And how could Hu Morgan think any woman would gladly get down off her horse to live in that...that hovel! If it hadn't started to rain, she would have turned her horse around and ridden straight home, let Hu look at her as he would!

But it did start to rain. Hard.

Liliana pulled up her hood and noticed with an angry frown that Hu didn't wait for her, but rode on without even glancing at his bride.

She followed Hu and his friend through the barn door and was pleased that she had at least made it to shelter before her cloak was soaked through. When she dismounted and threw back her hood, she realized they were not alone.

About twenty men in the barn babbled and laughed and slapped Hu on the back while she stood there, ignored. Hens scratched in the dry dirt floor, cattle lowed from stalls at the far end, a horse whinnied, Hu's dog tore around like it was possessed by an evil spirit, and from the nearest pen came the unmistakable odor of pigs.

This was not the welcome she had envisioned as the newly married wife of a lord.

After a few minutes, Old John and Maude rode in, the cart dripping profusely.

Then, finally, Hu looked at her.

"These are some of my useless friends from Wales. They're the best builders in the world. Baron De-Lanyea sent them when he heard about my marriage and..." He paused awkwardly.

"And that your estate obviously needs the best builders in the world?" she finished, her voice tinged with sarcasm.

Which apparently was completely lost on its intended recipient, for Hu's face broke into a wide smile. "Exactly! Wonderful, it is!"

"Wonderful," Liliana muttered, pulling her damp cloak more tightly about herself as Hu turned to his acquaintances and went off into a long string of Welsh.

Maude giggled as Elwy, the only man there with any conception of courtesy at all, it seemed, helped her from the wagon.

Liliana went toward the cart. Everything was probably drenched. All her clothes, all the linen. Everything.

"Go on to the hall," Hu called out. "We'll be there soon."

Liliana marched outside and proceeded to stomp through the muddy courtyard until she realized she was splattering her clothes. Then she began to pick her way around the puddles carefully.

She went up the steps that led into the hall. On the threshold she stopped and stared. The floor above the lower level, which was usually used for storage, was missing, except for the broad supporting beams. Instead, there was scaffolding with a ramp leading down to the ground level.

She would be living in a *storeroom?* In a place with a dirt floor and, she could see as she went down the ramp, a long, makeshift hearth in the center. Benches stood near it. Trestle tables were up against the wall, and there was a screen at the far end.

A wizened old woman she assumed must be Sarah stood near a door at the other side of the room. The way to the kitchen, perhaps? The old woman dipped in some kind of acknowledgment and grinned toothlessly.

Liliana sank down on the nearest bench. They had a toothless hag for a cook! Probably she used frogs' eyes and newt legs in her potions! And where were the rest of the servants? Why weren't they all here to greet her? Where was Maude with her things? She needed dry clothes.

She looked up at what would eventually be the main hall. The last light of day came in through three narrow windows. The walls were drab and bare and had last been whitewashed years ago, if at all. There was no paneling of any kind, not even where the dais would be.

Liliana began to shiver and shifted closer to the fire. She pulled back her skirts a little to let her feet dry.

Maude finally came in, shaking her cloak. "Good Lord above, I'm nearly wet to the bone!" She looked at the ramp, then at the beams and up to the roof. She giggled. "Well, they got the roof on anyways. Elwy says most of it blew off in that storm." She caught sight of her mistress's face and hurried toward her. "Old John's bringing your things right away. It took some time to find the right chest. I told them how to pack the cart, but nobody seemed to listen."

Liliana scowled. She certainly knew how *that* felt, and she could well believe that no one had considered the packing of her goods to be important. They had all been thinking of the wedding feast, no doubt.

Old John came in carrying the chest that contained the fine bed linen she had made for her new home. "Where's this to go?"

"There." The old woman suddenly spoke, pointing at the screen at the far end of the room.

Liliana's eyes narrowed and her lips pressed together. Hu Morgan expected her to sleep there? To consummate their marriage with a group of men not thirty feet away? It was outrageous!

Maude, with a worried glance at Liliana, proceeded to follow John down the room. "Bring the carved oak chest next. She needs dry clothes." They disappeared around the screen.

Hu came in, and behind him his gaggle of Welsh friends. He bounded down the ramp as if he thought it great sport and tossed the dead rabbit at Sarah. "Here—we'll have that for dinner tomorrow." She took it and went out.

He turned to Liliana with a bright smile that quickly turned to a frown. "Aren't you going to take off your cloak?"

"No. I'm cold."

He grabbed a log from a pile near the door Sarah had gone through and threw it on the fire. "There now. That'll be better." He spoke to his friends jovially, and they all began to chuckle. He sat beside her as the men, shoving and laughing, began putting together the tables for the evening meal. Hu joined in their conversation, and stretched out his long legs so that his feet were nearly in the fire. As his clothes dried, it became very obvious that he had been around the livestock. Especially the pigs.

Liliana kept her lips pressed firmly shut, although there was plenty she wanted to say. She didn't think it dignified to point out the inadequacies of her husband's preparations in front of others.

Maude and John brought in another chest, casting wary looks at her, but she still didn't say anything. Maude would know how to arrange her things.

Sarah came in shortly after with meat, bread and ale. Liliana would have liked to refuse, but she was too hungry. It had been a long journey, and they had only stopped once. Maude finished her work and joined some of the men at a far table, giggling and smiling the whole time, which did nothing to assuage Liliana's mood. John at least kept his mouth shut and simply ate.

The food was surprisingly good. Liliana smiled at Sarah when the woman brought more fine, white bread. Perhaps it would be a wise idea to keep her as cook, and a little courtesy would not be amiss.

Clearly it was going to be up to her to demonstrate proper manners. Her husband seemed to believe manners unnecessary in his own hall.

After the meal, Liliana stood up. "Good night, my lord," she said coolly.

Hu gave her a grin that did nothing to lessen her anger. "Is it that late?"

"I'm tired from the journey."

"Oh, yes. Good night." He spoke to his friends again, and they began exchanging knowing looks and sly winks.

Liliana frowned as she marched down the hall. Apparently he was planning to spend another night carousing with his friends. He would probably get drunk again, too. Well, this time she would not be so forgiving. She would go home to her father and have the marriage annulled, no matter how contrite Hu Morgan looked.

She stepped around the screen. Some attempt had been made to prepare quarters for her, and, judging from the untidy way it had been done, Maude must have thought that she wouldn't have to work as hard now that they were not at Lord Trevelyan's castle. She would soon learn otherwise.

But for now, Liliana was tired and angry and she simply wanted to go to sleep.

The only furnishings in the area were her chests of belongings, a small table with a basin and ewer, a single brazier and a huge bed. A very huge bed. Sloppily made with her linens.

There was a burst of harsh laughter and some snatches of song from the men in the hall.

She heard a noise behind her and spun around. Hu came toward her with an impudent smile on his face.

Liliana crossed her arms. "Do you expect me to sleep right here?"

"Why not?" His grin was devilment incarnate. "No place else but the barn, I'm afraid."

"I will not be humiliated in such a way. It isn't fitting."

He didn't move, but his grin turned into a slow smile. She was the most beautiful woman in the world, and spirited, too. He had never wanted a tame, docile woman for a wife. "I know it needs some work—"

"*Some* work? This is no better than a pigsty!" She glared at him. "Take me home."

His eyes narrowed. "You are home."

"I will not live in this place."

"You're my wife and you live with me."

"No, I'm not and no, I won't!"

Hu was acutely aware of the sudden silence that had descended on the other side of the screen. To think that only moments ago he had been accepting the congratulations of his friends for his beautiful wife— who was, as yet, not his wife.

"I said, take me home!" Liliana demanded.

He would not be humiliated, not on his own land. Not before men he had known since childhood.

And there was more to the anger that grew in him as he looked at her. She had already hurt him more than she knew. He had seen the revulsion and disappointment on her face when she first saw the manor, forcing him to see it with her eyes. She could never know how wonderful it looked to him, despite its condition, simply because it was *his*.

With swift strength he picked her up and dumped her on the bed.

As she scrambled to her feet, the veil fell from her head, letting her golden hair tumble around her shoulders while her face flushed with anger. "How dare you!"

"You are my wife."

She edged away from him toward the front of the screen. "This is barbaric. I won't . . . let you, not with all those men right here."

"They've gone by now."

"What?"

"They've got other places to sleep."

"Then . . ."

"Then we're all alone."

Maude's giggle came from the other side of the screen. "Excuse me, my lady, please."

She gave Hu a scornful look. "Yes?"

"Where do you want the rest of your things?"

Hu went around the screen and took the chest from the giggling maidservant. "You sleep in the kitchen with Sarah for now. Understand?"

"Yes, sir. I certainly do, sir."

He came around the screen.

Liliana hadn't moved. "Don't touch me," she said, her eyes flashing. "Don't even come near me. You stink like a . . . like a *peasant!*"

Hu Morgan was a proud man, and Liliana had finally said one thing too many. His lips tightened, his brow lowered and his gaze burned into hers. He grabbed her arm, pulling her to him. "You are my wife," he said coldly, "the way Mott is my dog and this is my house. Don't you *ever* say such things to me again. Do you understand?"

Shocked and truly frightened by the fierce intensity in his dark eyes, Liliana couldn't speak. She had forgotten the Hu Morgan she had first seen in a tournament, forgotten the incredible power he had exhibited on the field, forgotten that he was not some nobly born gentleman used to treating women like sacred objects.

He was a warrior. A brave, passionate man, almost savage. Dear God, she had wanted such a man for her husband—but she had not truly understood what it was she had wished for.

Hu pushed her onto the bed. Then he was on top of her, holding her arms, his face inches from hers.

His mouth came down on hers, firm and strong.

She had never been kissed that way before. It was possessive and persistent, a warrior's kiss. So different from the few tentative kisses other men had bestowed on her when she had allowed them such a liberty.

His insistent tongue pushed until her mouth yielded and his tongue entered its moistness.

What was he doing? She struggled beneath him, twisting and trying to push him off. Was this the consummation? Was this the way a man took possession of a woman and made her his wife?

She stopped fighting as his mouth left hers to trail along her cheek. She tried to still her pounding heart. When his hold upon her arms loosened, she drew in a great, deep breath.

Passionate longing thrilled through Hu as he pressed soft kisses to her cheeks. This beautiful woman with the flashing eyes was his wife, or soon would be in the most complete sense. He would forgive her insults, for obviously she could not know that she was wounding him deeply. He had been angry with her, but not for long. How could he be, when she felt so right in his arms? Her mouth was tender and soft as the spring bud of a flower. She had been unwilling, but probably no man had ever dared to do more than touch his lips to hers, if even that much. And perhaps he should have bathed...

He lifted his head and looked at her. A smile played on the corners of his mouth.

Then Liliana raised her hand and slapped his face as hard as she could.

Chapter Four

"**G**et away from me!" Liliana cried, her voice filled with anger and indignation. "Get out, you—you..."

Before she could strike him again, Hu grabbed her arm. "Don't," was all he said, and all he needed to say.

He stared into her eyes, knowing that for once, he had underestimated an opponent. Then, as he gazed at her, he saw that beneath the anger, she was afraid.

Afraid of *him!*

At once a memory flashed through his mind of a sobbing girl, and shame, and a solemn vow never to terrify a woman again. He dropped her arm and moved off her.

Disgusted with himself for giving in to his anger and his selfish passion, he stood up.

"Get out, you *Welshman!*"

A pillow hit the screen beside his head, but that was not why Hu turned slowly to face his wife. "I *am* a Welshman, and proud to be one."

Liliana scrambled to her feet, her disheveled hair falling about her like a golden waterfall. "I said, leave me!"

"I am not your servant, Liliana." Hu fought a twinge of regret that the first time he used her given name, it should be with such cold deliberation.

He would forget how much he wanted to wed her. He would ignore the pangs of desire that tore at him still. He would not even look at her eyes to see if he had only imagined her fear before. "Understand this, Liliana. I am your husband." He walked toward her. "I could throw you down on that bed and do whatever I wanted to, and it would be my right. I could even beat you. But God help me, I won't. I made a promise once never to take an unwilling woman, and I intend to keep it. Tomorrow, you can do what you like. You can go home to your father, if that is what you want."

Liliana stared at his dark, angry eyes as she backed away. Her legs struck the bed, and she could go no farther.

"But I won't give back this land," Hu continued. "I kept my end of the bargain. You can tell *that* to your father."

Liliana looked away. If Hu Morgan had kept his end of the bargain, he must have consummated the marriage. She was truly his wife. Did he honestly think that now he could simply send her home?

Liliana lifted her chin. She felt the tears burn in her eyes, but she would have died rather than let Hu Morgan know he could hurt her with his words.

"Go away," she said slowly, glaring at him with a look that had terrified servants for years. She had surprised him, that much she could tell. Obviously he had expected her to slink away like some dismissed underling.

"I'll leave you this time because *I* chose to," he said. "And I won't come back to your bed until you ask me to."

"That I will *never* do."

Hu grinned coolly, looking like the very image of temptation. "Think again before you say such things to me. Women have begged to be in my bed."

Liliana smiled with defiant scorn. "I am Lady Liliana Trevelyan—"

"Morgan."

She continued as if he had not interrupted. "And I will *never* beg."

Her husband's face remained annoyingly impassive. "We shall see. Good night. *Norman.*"

Liliana was glad to see him go. He had been rough and cruel. He had consummated the marriage with no regard to her innocence in these matters which, if he was so vastly experienced as he had implied, he should have been able to guess.

She was glad he would never trouble her in such a way again. Never, because she would never beg, not for his favor or any other thing.

She was Lady Liliana Trevelyan—Morgan, damn him—whose family had been nobles since before the Conquest. No one, not even her husband, had the right to speak to her the way Hu Morgan had.

She sat on the bed and decided she would not give him any measure of triumph by returning to her father. Now that they were truly husband and wife, he could indeed claim that *she* was at fault if she went home.

How Averil would gloat! In her patronizing way she would try to find out everything that had happened, and then embellish it and gossip about "her dear friends, the unfortunate Morgans" for weeks.

That would not be the worst, though. Liliana could also imagine the disappointment in her father's eyes. He had been so pleased about this marriage.

Of course, Hu had seemed even more pleased, but perhaps he had been pleased to get this land and her dowry. She had not thought of that before, but why else would he consummate the marriage and then so quickly suggest she return to her father?

Liliana drew in a deep, ragged breath and covered her face with her hands. Of all the thoughts raging through her mind, this was the worst. This had been the nagging doubt she had tried so hard to suppress even before her wedding day, when Hu had not come to see her.

That he had not really wanted *her*.

All her life, people had deferred to her and flattered her and tried to win her favor, from the lowliest scullery maid to the highest-ranking visitor. But she had never been sure if anyone truly liked her, Liliana, herself.

When their betrothal had been announced, Hu had looked so pleased, and he had gazed at her with what she had assumed was passion. No man had ever made her feel the way he did.

Had she imagined what she had wanted to see? Had it been greed shining in his eyes?

She had wanted . . . hoped . . .

Perhaps too much. What did she know of Hu Morgan, after all? That he was a landless knight from the remote northern part of Wales. That he was handsome. That he seemed honorable and gentlemanly and that he had looked delighted when her father announced the betrothal.

Stupid, foolish, conceited girl that she was, she had dared to believe he was delighted because of *her*. She suddenly felt older and wiser and very sad.

No, she would not leave here. She was Hu Morgan's wife, of her own volition. She would abide by her choice.

She had been weak once, in accepting him as her husband. And she knew, when she faced the truth in her own heart, that he had the power to make her weaken again. She understood that now, and she would guard against it.

Liliana awakened when she heard someone moving around. She kept still, but opened her eyes. The window high above let in the faint light of dawn.

It was Hu. He seemed to be searching for something in a small, battered chest beneath the window—and he was completely naked.

Liliana had never seen a naked man before. Hu was turned away from her, but she was able to observe his long legs, lean torso, broad shoulders and sinewy arms. She felt a flush of heat as she stared at his well-muscled body. She was, it seemed, nothing but a weak woman, after all—at least at a time like this.

Then he pulled out a pair of breeches and began to turn toward her.

Quickly Liliana closed her eyes. She had already seen enough to know that with his handsome face and superb body, Hu Morgan was as magnificent a man as any girl could ever hope to marry. If only he had truly wanted her, the way she wanted him now!

During the night she had asked herself if it was any wonder that he was proud, or capable of fierce emotion. What else could she expect of a man who fought the impassioned way he did?

Yet the morning after their wedding, he had seemed so contrite and boyish. It was hard to believe, remembering him then, that he had married her only for land and money.

As for the consummation of their marriage, she had realized it hadn't been completely unpleasant, although she had been too shocked to feel much pleasure. It had all happened so fast!

But she had also remembered that when Hu had looked at her afterward, he had smiled. Not with triumph, but genuine warmth.

She peered out through her slightly open eyes, her body hot and her breath quickening. If he spoke to her, she decided, she would answer. Maybe he would kiss her again, this time gently, and she would let herself enjoy it ...

He reached into the chest and pulled out a tunic. When he put it on, she could see that it was like a rag, drab and full of rents and holes.

She frowned. *This* was the tunic of a knight?

Well, he wasn't overly wealthy. She had known that. Her father had provided her with plenty of silver for her own use. She would have some new clothes made for him.

Perhaps she had been wrong to carry on so about the hall, too. It was not his fault the manor was in such a state. Charles de Monteclare, the former lord, had been notoriously lax in his duties and supervision.

Hu glanced at her and, surprised, she closed her eyes and held her breath, waiting for him to speak.

He whistled for his dog and marched away.

Liliana sat up, trying hopelessly to subdue the disappointment flowing through her. He had not even tried to see if she was still asleep. Clearly he was completely uninterested in her.

If that was so, he truly would not care if she stayed or went, as long as he had his manor.

Upsetting as the truth was, she faced it squarely. His main motive for marrying her had, after all, been gain.

And what had she done? Feigned sleep like a frightened child. Created excuses for his rude discourtesy, and actually felt guilty for her hasty words.

Disgusted with him, and with herself, she climbed out of the bed. She should be pleased she had provoked him, otherwise she might still be living in ignorance.

She had to decide how to proceed. She would not let Hu Morgan learn how devastated she felt knowing that she was no more to him than any other chattel. Her father often said it was wise to be patient and wait for an adversary to make the first move. So, for the present, she would act as if all was well.

Despite her resolve, however, she felt a pang of bitter disappointment that she must consider her handsome husband her enemy. But she did.

She looked down at the woolen gown she hadn't bothered to remove. It was a wrinkled mess, and she was sure she looked like a hag. *That* must not be. Hu must have no cause whatsoever to believe he could affect her in any way.

She would show Hu Morgan how true nobles behaved, and that she would not be content to continue living in a storeroom.

Hearing noises on the other side of the screen, she realized the rest of the household, whatever that comprised, must also be rising. Maude would soon arrive, no doubt giggling.

Liliana tugged at the knot in the lacing of her dress until it gave way, then loosened the bodice enough to allow her to remove the gown. She left it in a heap and hurried to one of the chests, where she knew Maude had packed a dress suitable for daily wear. She managed to get it on before she heard an all-too-familiar giggle.

"My lady?" Maude called from behind the screen.

"Yes?" Liliana replied, keeping her tone calm as she ran her fingers through the tangled mass of her hair. Maude came around the screen.

"I need some help with this gown," Liliana said brusquely. She presented her back to Maude in an effort to dissuade the girl from asking questions. She didn't know and couldn't imagine what excuse Hu might have given for his absence from the bedchamber last night, but she wasn't ready to have Maude speculate on the state of her marriage.

Maude did as she was told with relatively little chatter, for Maude. Liliana learned that apparently the size of the village around the manor was increasing as it became known that a new, young lord had arrived to oversee the land. Some spoke of thieves and outlaws, and there were rumors of a growing band of Welshmen intent on driving the Normans from the border lands.

"How long before Mass?" Liliana asked, her tone somewhat peevish.

"Time enough to brush your hair and put on a wimple, anyway, my lady," Maude said deferentially. She sighed wistfully as she looked at the jumbled bedclothes. No wonder her lady was out of sorts.

She probably hadn't slept all night.

Hu knelt down in the chapel, waiting impatiently for the Mass to begin. He had several things he wanted to do today, the first of which was eat. He hadn't touched much of his food last night, anticipating...

He shifted uncomfortably, and not from the cold, uneven floor of the small stone building. The last place he had expected to sleep on his first night in his own manor with a beautiful bride was in a pile of hay behind the barn.

His proud, stubborn, oh-so-fine-she-can't-be-touched bride. Or rather, his bride until she went back to her doting father. She probably already had her cloak on, and was no doubt ordering her maid to load her baggage on the cart.

Let her go. He had the dowry and the estate. No man would fault him, not when she had refused him his rights as her husband. He would damn well tell Lord Trevelyan so when Lord Trevelyan sent for him, as he surely would.

Maybe his home wasn't as fine as the one she was used to, but he had never told her otherwise. He had assumed—foolishly, he knew now—that her father would tell her the state of the place. He had also assumed that she had not found that a reason to refuse to marry him.

God, he was a fool! And worse, a weak-willed, lovesick fool, who even now couldn't stand the thought that Liliana was going to leave him. He had tried to convince himself he was upset because of the humiliation of having his wife leave after two days of marriage, not because Liliana apparently found him so crude and uncivilized that she couldn't stand to be near him.

Elwy, nearby on Hu's left, glanced at him with a sly grin and leaned closer. "Marriage going to be the death of you, isn't it? Getting more sleep, you need to be."

Hu shrugged, barely keeping a scowl off his face.

Suddenly he heard the rustle of garments, and out of the corner of his eye he saw Liliana kneel beside him on his right. He glanced at her, to see her smile as demurely and dutifully as any man could wish.

What in the name of the saints was she doing here? Or did she wish to insure that his humiliation was accomplished with a greater audience?

The Mass proceeded. Portly Father Alphonse took longer than usual, his words slow and somewhat pompous. No doubt he wished to impress the new lady of the manor.

Hu realized the lady of the manor was so close to him that he could brush her soft, slender hand with his fingertips if he shifted ever so slightly...

He glanced at Liliana again, and this time he saw that she looked tired and pale despite her proud carriage and haughty manner. Perhaps she had spent nearly as sleepless a night as he had.

Finally the Mass ended. He stood up, and Liliana did, too. He hesitated for a moment, but she said nothing, so he turned to go. Then he felt her hand on his arm. He tried not to reveal surprise or pleasure or anything at all, aware that Elwy and several other people from the manor were watching.

"I would like to meet the rest of the servants of the hall," she said softly as they walked out together.

"You've met them," he answered, his voice brusque as he fought to hide his confusion. If she was planning to go back to her father, surely she wouldn't ask about servants. "Sarah and your maid. I can spare no others now."

She frowned just a little, her brows pulling down ever so slightly. "That will not do."

Hu did not want to have an argument in so public a place, so he said nothing and began walking toward the overgrown orchard. He felt her resistance, but he wasn't going to stop. Mott trotted along behind.

The people went about their business, and soon Hu and Liliana were alone beside a huge, hoary old apple tree. The scent of ripe apples filled the air, and the ground was covered with wormy windfalls.

Liliana pulled her hand from his arm. "I must have more servants, and money to pay for tapestries and furniture for the hall."

"No," he said warily. "I cannot afford to spend money on luxuries."

He gazed at her steadily. For years he had practised maintaining an inscrutable expression before a fight to confuse his opponent. His expression was inscrutable now.

Liliana's was not. She crossed her slender arms and glared at him. God's wounds, he had seen such a fierce look before, but never from a woman. "I shall simply have to spend some money," she said defiantly.

Hu didn't know what to make of her. He was not quite willing to believe that she wasn't leaving. "I need all the gold and silver we have to repair the buildings and the mill, and buy feed for the winter," he finally said.

"I will use my own silver, then, that my father gave me."

"It all belongs to me now."

"What?"

"As your husband, all your money and all your goods—"

"*Some* is still mine. It was in the marriage agreement."

With a mighty effort he kept his surprise and uncertainty from his face. He had assumed that everything came to the husband on marriage, but he certainly had no knowledge of the legalities. He could no more read than he could fly, so he had stared at the marriage contract, then signed his name, which was the only thing he could write.

It might very well be that Liliana was correct, but he would sooner walk across glowing coals barefoot than ask her.

Father Alphonse could read. He would have to find some excuse for the priest to look over the marriage contract.

"I meant," he replied gruffly, "that I will not provide for more servants out of *our* money. Of course you may use your own in whatever manner you see fit." He wondered just how much money he had parted with. "I shall be meeting with all the villeins today. You may chose some female servants then."

"I would also like to be introduced to the bailiff, and then the steward. I should discuss some household matters with him."

Hu reached out and twisted an apple off the tree. "I don't want a steward. I plan to be in charge of my own affairs," he said matter-of-factly before biting the fruit.

Since he couldn't read and write, he would have no way of knowing if a steward was cheating him. With Elwy's help, he could manage with coins and notches on a stick to keep account of the animals.

The apple was sour. He spit out the piece in his mouth and tossed the rest away.

Liliana's fine nose wrinkled in disgust, and Hu suddenly had an overwhelming urge to belch or scratch himself. If she wanted to think him loutish, he could give her plenty of cause.

"But you must have a bailiff, at least, and a reeve," she said after a moment. "You can't do all those duties, too."

"Elwy will be my bailiff and act for me. I'll keep the present reeve for the villagers unless I see reason to do otherwise."

Liliana nodded. "As you wish. Now, if you will excuse me, I must go." She turned away.

"What are you going to do?" he demanded, determined at last to be sure of her intentions.

"I am going to eat," she said calmly. "Then I will ask Father Alphonse about the alms, and later today I will chose my servants."

He watched her walk toward the hall.

She wasn't leaving him. Part of him was relieved, and another part was suspicious. Last night she had been so angry, so cold, but this morning, she was acting like the obedient little wife. He didn't understand—and he didn't like that.

Frowning, he picked up one of the windfalls and threw it down the orchard, where it splatted against a tree.

"So rich you are, you can waste your crop?" Elwy's voice boomed out from behind the tree. "Almost got me in the face, Hu—and then I would have had to beat you."

"You could try," Hu replied grimly.

Elwy's eyes narrowed for an instant, but then he smiled. "Look you who's come to visit."

A fine voice started to sing an old shepherd's song. Hu hurried forward. "Gareth!"

"None other," the young man said in Welsh as he came to stand beside Elwy.

Hu was indeed happy to see his friend. Like Hu, Gareth had been offered the opportunity to become a squire, but he had refused. He needed to be free, he said, and he found the confines of armor too restrictive. So, while Hu and Elwy had been studying weapons and fighting, Gareth had been listening to the older shepherds. While Hu and Elwy had practised their riding, Gareth had been studying the innards of a sheep to find out what had killed it.

"Brought the best wedding present of all from Baron DeLanyea, me," Gareth said jovially.

"He's already given me fifty Welsh sheep," Hu said with some surprise. "And sent the workmen."

Gareth's merry brown eyes twinkled with delight. "What's the baron got the very best of?"

Hu stared at the youth. "Not one of the rams?"

Gareth frowned, and Hu tried not to feel disappointed. Baron DeLanyea's rams were wonderful creatures.

"No, Hu," Gareth said slowly. "Not one—he sent *three*."

He laughed at Hu's shock. "Yes, he did. And they were three of the biggest brutes I ever seen. Quite a time I had, let me tell you. That's why I didn't get here yesterday. Had to take my time with them, see?"

Elwy slapped Hu on the back. "What a thing! We'll have the finest flock yet!"

"Not even seen all the sheep, me." Hu sounded like a man not quite awake. He was simply, completely astounded. He and Elwy had checked the rams from nearby flocks and seen at once that they were inferior to the stock the baron kept. The backbone of any flock was the rams, so they had mournfully concluded it would be years before their flock would be anything to take pride in. That would change now.

"Did the sheep all get here?" Gareth asked.

"They got here," Elwy said. "They're near the barn. Come on."

Hu began walking quickly toward the pen that contained the flock. The masons, stonecutters, quarrymen and laborers who had come from the baron's castle looked up from their work on the wall and called out greetings as they went past.

The Welshmen who had brought the sheep were already gathered at the pen. Mott barked and capered about the enclosure as if he was a puppy again—or back home in Wales. Gareth's dog, an older beast, watched Mott's antics with what appeared to be disdain.

"Sorry the baron was that he couldn't come himself," Gareth said. "But he's not going anywhere much with a broken leg."

Hu frowned at Gareth. "Broken? What happened?"

"Fell off his horse chasing a fox, poor man. His old nurse give him proper hell for it, too. He sends his best wishes."

Hu nodded, reflecting that he might need all the good wishes he could get when it came to his marriage. "When do you have to go home?"

Gareth smiled. "I don't—that is, if you want me. The baron thought you'd be needing someone who knows what he's doing with them sheep."

"As if I wouldn't, eh?" Hu asked with a touch of a annoyance, but he was too delighted to be insulted by the baron's seeming lack of confidence.

"Well, a lord now, ain't you? Got more to think of than sheep. Since I got no family left back there, I thought I'd try living farther south."

Hu sighed softly. Right now, being a simple shepherd had a certain appeal. "The baron wasn't angry you left?"

"I trained up your cousin, Iowerth. He's daft, like all the Morgans—" Hu punched his arm, and Gareth smiled "—but quick enough. Besides, I told the baron if ever he needs me to send for me."

Hu nodded his approval. With three DeLanyea rams, fifty sturdy Welsh sheep and Gareth overseeing the flock, he couldn't be happier.

Well, he thought as he caught sight of Maude hurrying to the hall with a bucket of water, perhaps he could. But he still had time to mend things with Liliana—if she wanted them mended.

"Aren't you going to invite the man into the hall?" Elwy asked suddenly. "He wants to see your wife," he added with a broad wink.

"Of course. Please, Gareth and everyone, let's go eat," he called out.

When they entered the hall, Hu could hardly believe his eyes. There were trestle tables set up along the wall, and one—at the end nearest the screen—was spread with a brilliant white cloth. Father Alphonse was there, and some of the men who were not out at the barns or working on the wall. Food, lots of food, was already on the table.

Liliana rose from her seat behind the table. She wore a lovely gown of green that matched her eyes and fit her slender curves to perfection.

Her gaze ran over Hu, and he realized he had on a very old, very shabby tunic that was certainly good enough for wearing around the livestock, but must look terrible to her.

In fact, however, Liliana was marveling at how noble Hu looked despite his ragged attire. Remembering the sight of his naked body that morning, she turned away to hide her flushed cheeks and to try to still her rapidly beating heart.

"This is Gareth," Hu said as he sat beside her. "He's a shepherd." He said the last word defiantly, as if daring her to complain that he was letting a shepherd sit at the high table.

She smiled and nodded at their guest. "I bid you welcome, Gareth," she said softly to the young man taking a seat beside her husband.

Maude, seated at a table below, stared unabashedly at Gareth. Well, for once, she wasn't giggling, Liliana thought, and although that was a relief, Liliana didn't like Maude's boldness. It wasn't polite. It wasn't dignified. She would have to speak to Maude about such behavior.

Father Alphonse mumbled a blessing, and the people began to eat.

Liliana looked around the hall. Many of those present were babbling away in what had to be Welsh, including her husband and Gareth and Elwy, who was seated on the other side of her. The three men were carrying on an animated conversation as if she was not even there.

Liliana frowned as she leaned back and looked at Gareth. He was about the same age as Hu and Elwy, she thought, but not nearly so handsome as her husband. He seemed uncomfortable at the table, and said little. Well, a shepherd surely wasn't used to such fine things.

"Gareth," she said politely, "I hope you had a good journey."

The men's conversation halted. Hu turned to look at her as he had in the orchard, when she had no idea what he was thinking.

"He only speaks Welsh," he said bluntly.

Liliana tried to suppress the blush that she felt creeping up her face. "I'm sorry, but no one thought to tell me that." She smiled sweetly. "I shall have to learn your language, as I have Saxon and Latin, so that I can understand you and your friends.''

Hu's expression changed, and she thought he understood that she was not pleased at being excluded. ''I didn't think a fine lady wanted to learn about blowflies and woolly kidney,'' he replied coolly. ''But I shall have to have Gareth tell you all about them—when you learn the language.''

Before she could say anything more, he pushed back his chair. ''We're going to the meadow now. I'll return for the noon meal. The villeins are going to pledge to me afterward. If you're willing to pay to keep more servants, you can choose them then.''

Chapter Five

Hu stood in the corner of the muddy courtyard, wondering where in the name of the saints Liliana was. Most of the villeins had arrived long ago, and he had already finished hearing their oaths of loyalty.

He had been surprised by the large number of newcomers until Elwy explained that more and more laborers were arriving every day hoping to be given a piece of land to work.

Elwy, in his position as Hu's representative, had allowed as many as possible to make their allegiance to their new lord. The manor would need not only the rent the cotters would pay, but also the labor they could provide to restore the manor to prosperity. And the more populous their village, the less likely outlaws would be to linger in the area.

"But," Elwy had complained morosely, "there's not a one of them with a daughter or sister worth looking at twice, more's the pity."

Now, however, all these people milling around the courtyard were getting impatient. Hu wanted them to at least see his wife—the woman who had been so insistent that she needed more servants, but now, when she had the chance to pick them, was nowhere to be seen.

Elwy sauntered toward him. "Going to stay here all day, boy? There's work to be done. Wanted to get that beam up in the loft—"

"We are waiting for my wife."

Elwy, taking note of the hard line of Hu's mouth, wisely sauntered away again.

Hu crossed his arms, then uncrossed them, aware that everyone was watching him expectantly. Was this some little game Liliana was playing to embarrass him? Or perhaps she had finally understood that they had more important things to spend their money on than unnecessary servants.

Or maybe she didn't have very much money at her disposal.

Somehow he doubted that. Lord Trevelyan's castle was well-supplied and well-kept. Surely Lord Trevelyan had given Liliana plenty of money of her own, if the dowry was any indication.

He had been worried about his wife's possible extravagance, but a new thought took shape in his mind. Maybe Liliana intended to hoard her money. He scowled. He detested miserliness and the smallness of spirit it implied. It occurred to him that a little generosity on his part might not be amiss, either.

His expression grew into a sly grin. If Liliana didn't arrive soon, he would pick some servants himself. That would not only show Liliana that he didn't plan to dance attendance on her, but that he could not be faulted for meanness.

At that moment, however, Liliana arrived, walking through the outer gate with Father Alphonse. When she drew near, Hu spoke quietly. "I trust you had important business with the priest. We've all been waiting."

She smiled at him prettily. "Patience is a virtue, dear husband."

Liliana faced the waiting people as her husband introduced her. There were not many, she thought, considering the size of the manor. Father Alphonse had very kindly escorted her around the village and told her at great length everything he knew—or surmised—about everyone. He was concerned about the new villagers who were arriving daily. "And no one knows a thing about them, my lady. Or not much."

He was worried, too, about the Welsh outlaws reputed to be lurking in the forest.

Liliana, however, had dismissed most of the priest's fears. The manor needed more people to do the necessary work, and as for the outlaws, she could only hope that if there *were* any, they would go away. What she *had* paid attention to was the gossip. She needed to know as much as she could about the villagers, not only to decide who might make good servants for the hall, but also to discover how much money in alms she might have to give out. Her father had provided her a generous sum for her personal use, but if she had to pay for her servants' food, gifts and clothing, use her own money to make the hall comfortable and provide for her own needs, well, she would have to be very careful.

She detested having to hoard her money in such a manner, but she knew she had a tendency to spend too freely, especially for clothes or fine furnishings. Her father always said one chair was as good as another.

Liliana felt, though, that a finely crafted chair of strong, solid wood was better than something knocked together in a day. And if the chair was carved and well-polished, wouldn't it look nice in the hall? And wouldn't you feel better knowing you were sitting in something so carefully and finely made? It would impress your guests and villeins, too. A chair could be so much more than simply a thing to sit upon.

Unfortunately, it seemed Hu shared her father's opinion of furniture and clothes, although now he was wearing his fine, plain black woollen tunic. She had begun to fear he had a touch of miserliness about him when she saw that he had spent on his barns before his hall, and that he frequently wore nothing better than a rag. She hoped she was wrong.

She looked out over the crowd of milling, anxious tenants, but she had already decided whom she would take for servants. None of the pretty girls gossiping and whispering by the well. They would spend too much time flirting and talking instead of working. None of the women shifting impatiently. She valued patience in a servant, for such people would take the time and care to do a job well the first time.

A tall, big-boned young woman, decidedly unattractive, stood off alone in one corner of the courtyard, watching everything. Father Alphonse, so happy to be helpful, had mentioned this girl, whose name was Jhone. An orphan, he had said, a quiet, polite young woman, surely doomed to spend all her life without marrying. It was obvious that Father Alphonse, despite the necessity of loving all God's creatures, wondered what God had done creating such an ugly creature as Jhone. Liliana, however, saw the intelligence in the young woman's eyes. She thought Jhone would do very well, indeed.

Liliana had noticed two other girls who would also make good servants. They stood still without fidgeting, and never looked at the men.

Liliana signaled for Jhone to come forward. "You will work in the hall," she ordered.

Jhone looked surprised, and justly so. It was quite an honor. Then Jhone smiled. The smile was sincere, but slightly wary, and Liliana knew she had chosen well. This girl knew her place, and knew that she was being given a chance to rise above it without really knowing why. She was intelligent, indeed, and probably would not fawn and flatter.

Liliana gave the same order to the other girls she had selected, who told her their names were Dena and Osyth. Osyth was the elder, and Liliana judged her to be nearly thirteen years old. Dena was slightly younger.

"Are you finished now?" Hu demanded.

"Yes." She looked at him, and he was rather pleased that he had worn his best tunic for the swearing, then displeased that he felt so pleased. After all, he couldn't spend the rest of his life worrying about what Liliana thought of his clothes, of all things.

He gestured to a tall man standing nearby. "This is the bailiff, Ralf."

Liliana nodded in acknowledgment, but she felt an immediate aversion to the man. He was thin everywhere, from the skinny strands of lank hair on his forehead to his narrow eyes to his bony ankles. He bowed, but never took his gaze from her face.

The introduction over, Hu announced that everyone could go back to work. Ralf slunk off toward the gate.

"You may go home and collect your things," Liliana said to Jhone and the other girls, who nodded and walked away. The two younger girls spoke in quiet whispers. Jhone said nothing.

Liliana turned and realized that Hu had already gone. Trying to suppress the disappointment that she wished she did not feel, she went into the hall.

Hu was inside. Alone. And waiting for her, it seemed. "Where were you?" he demanded.

His voice was low but firm, and he stared at her intently, but she didn't look away. "With Father Alphonse. He's quite worried about Welsh thieves who've been—"

"I know about them. I'm sure they won't bother us. Why did you keep everyone waiting? That was rude."

That he should try to tell her about rudeness! She kept the slight annoyance out of her voice when she answered, "I told you. Patience is a virtue. I wanted to know who has patience."

"Including me, is it?" He frowned, and one dark curl fell on his forehead. He looked like a petulant youth, not the lord of a manor. A very attractive petulant youth, whose lock of hair she wanted to brush into place.

"No, my lord. I've seen that in you already." She smiled slightly. "I watched you wait out your opponent in my father's tournament."

She was pleased that some of the tension left Hu's face and told herself it would make him more likely to listen to what she had to say next. "I think you should find another reeve."

His eyes narrowed, and all trace of boyhood fled. "Why? Ralf's been the reeve here for years."

"I don't trust him."

"Why not?"

"He was too forward. He never lowered his eyes."

"*I* trust a man who looks you straight in the eye."

"He doesn't know his place. He's not afraid of you, or me, or our authority. He will probably rob you," Liliana finished firmly. She had been choosing her father's servants for years, and her instincts were usually infallible.

All Hu knew, however, was that his wife, who looked even more beautiful this afternoon despite his best efforts not to notice, was trying to tell him what to do. Again. "Ralf stays as reeve until *I* see reason to make it otherwise."

He expected her to protest, but she didn't. She simply said, "Very well, my lord. I must see to the evening meal now."

"And issue more commands?"

"What do you mean?"

"You didn't ask that woman and the girls if they wanted to be your servants. You just told them they would be."

"They are villeins. They should be pleased at being chosen."

"Lady Roanna would have asked, not commanded."

"And who, may I ask, is Lady Roanna?" Liliana inquired, sounding calm but fighting an overwhelming rush of jealousy.

"My former lord's wife—and a very kind, generous woman."

Liliana raised one eyebrow. "As you say, I am not Lady Roanna."

"Obviously."

"Are you quite through criticizing me?"

"Why those three?"

"I dare say you are looking for fault in my choice. Well, if you will, you will," she replied evenly. "I am not sure how much money will be needed to finish the manor in a proper way, or how much we shall have to give out in alms, or pay for food, so I thought I should see what could be accomplished with three competent servants in addition to Maude and Sarah. I selected Jhone because she seems old enough and sensible enough to do what she's *commanded*. Also, she has no family to miss her presence.

"The two younger girls will not have to be paid, and they'll eat less, too. Still, they are old enough to work and young enough to learn to do things the proper way." She crossed her graceful arms. "So, my lord, what is wrong with my choices?"

She waited calmly while Hu struggled to think of something to reply. Short of admitting that her reasons were excellent or reiterating his displeasure at the manner in which she had indicated her selections, there wasn't much.

"Nothing to say, my lord? Then if you will excuse me, I believe I must go to the chapel and give thanks for a miracle. It seems I have done something that meets with your approval."

With that, Liliana swept past him and out the door to the kitchen.

Hu frowned as he went toward the screen at the end of the hall. He didn't understand her. Not at all. One minute she was the consummate arrogant noble-woman, the next she seemed to defer to his authority. Then she reverted to true Norman form, treating the tenants like slaves who should be willing—no, ea-ger!—to do as she commanded.

Maybe it was time she learned just who gave the or-ders in this hall.

Lying in the big bed, Liliana sighed as she pulled the fine woolen blankets over herself. Her linen sheets were clean and soft, too.

She was exhausted. She had spent a long time walking around the village with Father Alphonse that morning, hearing about what he had done and wanted her to do and about the troubles facing the village. He seemed to have years of gossip to impart, too.

Tomorrow she would have to begin to instruct Jhone and the other girls.

She snuggled down even more. The bed seemed enormous for two people, let alone one. Not that she expected Hu to try to join her again. He surely knew that she didn't want that.

No, not at all.

She needed to sleep. She didn't need to waste any time fending off unwanted advances, even if the man making the advances was her husband. He had found some place to sleep the night before. He could do so again. Alone.

At least, she assumed he would be alone.

What did she care what he did, as long as he didn't bother her? She would simply ignore him, as she had done at the evening meal. Nonetheless, it had seemed an interminable time, and she had been very glad when it was over. Now Hu and his men were still in the hall, singing and talking and laughing.

All she wanted to do was sleep. She didn't want to think anymore, about Hu or the work that needed to be done around the manor, or her father, or anything at all.

If only the men would be quiet!

She closed her eyes and finally began to drift to sleep, vaguely aware that the men didn't seem quite so noisy.

Something jumped on the bed. With a squeal of alarm, Liliana sat up—to see Mott lying across the end of the bed. On her finest blanket. "Get off," she snapped, pushing the dog away with her feet.

He landed on the floor, but stood up and wagged his tail, looking happy as only a dog can.

"Get out!"

"I've told you, Mott sleeps where I do."

For the first time Liliana saw Hu standing at the edge of the screen. He began to come closer. She strained to see his face in the dark as she pulled the coverings up to her chin. "Don't you touch me!"

He halted.

"Take that animal and go!"

"Aren't you forgetting that this is my hall, Liliana? This bed is mine, too. I do not intend to spend another night in a haystack."

Liliana inched toward the wall, holding the sheets tighter. She knew from the tone of his voice and his stance that Hu Morgan meant what he said.

"But...but these are *my* linens!" she said desperately. Her heart was pounding in her chest, and her feelings were a confused jumble. She wanted him to go—or stay—but she didn't want him to touch her—or maybe she did...

Suddenly, without a word of warning, Hu reached out and yanked the coverings from the bed, sending her tumbling to the floor. Her protests were muffled by the blankets, and then the feather tick after he ripped that from the bed and tossed it onto the pile. "There. You may have your precious bedclothes."

Liliana pushed her way out of the mass of cloth and stood up. "How dare you! How dare you treat me this way!" She was too angry to be intimidated by Hu's presence or the fact that she wore only her shift.

He crossed his arms, his feet planted wide apart, his brow furrowed as she glared at him.

"You *are* a peasant!" she cried, not caring who heard her. "Those linens cost a lot of money and now look—"

"If I am a peasant, dearest wife, what does that make you but the wife of a peasant?" He came close to her, so close that his nose was nearly touching hers. "I am going to sleep. On *my* bed. Naturally I would be pleased if you—and your fine linens—were also on my bed, but if not, it doesn't matter. A *peasant* is not used to luxuries anyway."

"I would rather die than sleep with you!"

"Then you may sleep wherever you see fit, my lady." He didn't turn away, but began to strip off his tunic.

Liliana abruptly turned away, flustered and confused and so filled with what could only be lust that she was ashamed of herself. Surely she couldn't be so weak willed!

She was trembling, too, and she told herself it was from the cold. Oh, dear sweet Lord, she was nearly naked!

Not daring to look to see what Hu was doing behind her, she reached down and grabbed a blanket, which she wrapped around her shoulders.

After what seemed an age, she heard the bed creak. Cautiously she twisted to see her husband wrapped in his cloak and lying on the bare ropes of the bed. His dog lay beside the screen.

He didn't look very comfortable, but he didn't speak to her, and she wondered if he was already asleep.

Not that it mattered. Not that she cared. If he wanted the bare bed, he could have it!

She dragged the feather tick over to the wall as far away from the bed as possible, lay down, pulled the sheets and blankets over her and tried to fall asleep.

When Liliana awoke the next morning, her head hurt as badly as the time she had had a terrible fever. She sat up slowly, every joint in her body as stiff as an ungreased wheel. She couldn't remember ever having spent a more uncomfortable night.

She moved her head from side to side and pressed her cold fingers to her temples. That helped a little. Perhaps a ride out in the fresh air, with nothing to trouble her, would make the ache go away.

She heard a movement near the bed and glanced up to see Hu, who was completely dressed. He just stood there and looked at her.

"What?" she demanded querulously. "Are you planning to tell me that the floor is yours, too?"

He frowned as he walked to the end of the screen, signaling for Mott to follow. "You are very lovely when you're asleep," he said coolly before he left, "and your mouth is shut."

Disgruntled, Liliana got to her feet. She had never felt more utterly wretched in her life. Maybe she should consider going back to her father. At least he would provide a decent bed. And he would understand that all this wasn't her fault. Surely she could swallow her pride...

She heard the servants stirring on the other side of the screen. Hu jovially called out something in Welsh. She heard his friend answer, and they both laughed loudly.

Swallow her pride? Let Hu Morgan have the triumph? Never, not while she had breath in her body!

She looked at the pile of linen on the floor. She hadn't heard Maude's giggle yet, but the curious maidservant would surely be here soon.

What had transpired between herself and her husband must not become food for gossip among the villeins. Quickly she wrestled the large, cumbersome tick onto the bed. She picked up the sheets and tried to get them on properly, but she had never made a bed in her life. After several frustrating attempts, she stepped back to survey the result.

Not good, but at least it was better than a pile on the floor. She grabbed the blankets and tossed them on the end of the bed.

She hurried to a chest and pulled out the first dress she came upon. It wasn't one of her best, but still rather fine, considering she was living in a hovel. Nonetheless, she pulled it on quickly.

And just in time. At that moment, Maude called from the other side of the screen. When she came around it, her blue eyes widened and she giggled as she looked at the disheveled bed, the blankets that had slipped off onto the floor, and Liliana. "Ooh, my lady!" she whispered. "Again? What a husband!"

Liliana tried to keep her face inscrutable. "Are Jhone, Dena and Osyth here?"

"Yes, my lady."

"Good. I will set them some tasks, and then I want to go riding."

"It's wet out, my lady."

"Raining?"

"No, but—"

"I will go riding. By myself."

"But my lady, you should have an escort—"

"I won't go far. *And I want to be by myself.*"

"Where's Gareth?" Hu asked Elwy when they reached the stables.

"Gone to check the upper pasture." Elwy looked at Hu shrewdly. His friend was tired, that much was obvious, and perhaps to be expected in a new husband. But there was something in Hu's eyes that Elwy didn't like, although he couldn't quite put his finger on it.

"Oh. I'll leave that to him. Where are the sheep?"

"Out at the lower pasture."

"Ah. And Ralf? I want the rest of the barn roof on today."

"He's here, and the men are fetching the thatch. Grumbled a bit, but he got them under control soon enough."

Hu grinned and went toward his horse. "I thought he would be a good reeve."

Elwy decided he must be imagining things. This was more like the Hu he knew from boyhood. "Think somebody's made a mistake," he said solemnly.

"What?" Hu demanded.

Elwy paused awkwardly. "Me, I meant," he explained. "If I want a rich bride, there's not many to be found around here."

Hu began to saddle his horse. "Maybe you're better off unmarried," he muttered.

"What's that?"

"Nothing. Going to meet my neighbors, I think."

"Is that why you got your second best tunic on, then?"

"Of course."

"What's your lady going to do today?"

"I don't know."

"Ah. Shall I go with you, or do you want me to stay here? Maybe I'd better stay. There's those thieves we've been hearing about—"

"They won't come here once they know there's a knight in the manor," Hu replied. He glanced over his shoulder, a slight grin on his face. "I'd be glad of the company, El."

"Right." Elwy hurried to fetch his saddle.

"Perhaps we'll find a rich neighbor with a daughter or sister," Hu said lightheartedly when Elwy returned.

"Didn't think of that," Elwy answered. His tone was just as light, but now he was sure something was wrong. Try as Hu might to hide it, all his good humor had fled, leaving him sullen and quick to anger.

As Elwy saddled his horse, he tried to figure out what might have happened to upset Hu. It couldn't be the manor, or the state of it. Hu had frowned when he first arrived, but the next minute he was full of plans for fixing things. At the time, he had seemed happy to be having to start almost from the beginning.

It had also been obvious that Hu was delighted by the idea of wedding Lord Trevelyan's beautiful daughter. Why, he had been smitten ever since he had seen her. Elwy had never seen a happier bridegroom.

That Liliana Trevelyan was vain and proud was plain enough to see. Well, she had every right to be. But she had wanted Hu for a husband. That had been apparent from the moment the betrothal was announced.

Of course, Hu had been somewhat the worse for drink on his wedding night, but Elwy knew Hu well enough to be sure that his wife couldn't complain of an unsatisfactory lover. Why, wasn't it only two months ago that overly friendly little maid of Lord Murcott's wife had told anyone who would listen that Sir Hu Morgan was the best lover she'd ever had—and then gone into precise detail? Even Elwy had been impressed. No, that surely could not be the trouble.

He remembered how Hu's wife had looked when they first arrived here. She hadn't been too pleased, but he had put that down to the rain and the mud, and of course this place wasn't quite what she was used to.

Hu would have told her his plans by now, surely. She
must understand that Hu had every intention of making this manor the best possible, and that he had the
determination to do it.

Hu had been angry yesterday when she made everyone wait for her. Maybe that was it. Maybe he had
complained to her about it, and she had been upset.
Perhaps it was, after all, just a little lovers' quarrel.

Elwy wondered if she would try to make peace first.
He hoped so, because he knew from long experience
that Hu never would. It was his friend's greatest flaw,
this unwillingness to forgive, but it hurt no one so
much as himself.

"Are you ready?" Hu asked, his voice tinged with
uncharacteristic impatience.

"Yes." Elwy climbed into the saddle. *O'r annwyl*,
he thought as he climbed into the saddle, let his wife
make peace, and soon!

Liliana's mare moved slowly along the narrow road.
Liliana's aching head was finally beginning to feel a
little better, but it had been a long morning. She had
spent most of it explaining to Jhone and the girls what
she expected of them every day. Special tasks that
needed to be done, such as whitewashing the walls of
the hall, hanging tapestries and sanding down the
rough tops of the tables, would have to wait for another day.

She pulled on the reins to halt her horse. She was in
the wasteland near the edge of the forest, just beyond
the hay meadows. The river wound away slowly on her

right. Behind her she could see some of the villeins working in their tofts at the far end of the village.

She lowered her hood and looked ahead at the forest. Father Alphonse believed that at least one band of outlaws, and possibly more, hid in it.

Now, in the bright sunlight of a late summer's afternoon, it seemed safe and quiet enough.

"Nice-looking animal," Ivor said to his companion in quiet Welsh. They were both perched in the branches of a tall oak, watching the road below.

"Which, the wench or the horse?" Dafydd whispered back.

"Either one—but I'd rather ride the wench!" Ivor grinned. "Poor girl looks lost."

Dafydd laughed softly before speaking again. "That's the new lady of the manor."

"Riding all by herself? Not likely."

"I'm sure of it," Dafydd insisted. "And she's too beautiful for a servant. I told you it was true, about a knight coming back. I seen him, too."

"Is it also true, then, that he's a Welshman?"

"Not sure."

Ivor's lips curled with disgust. "He's a traitor, if it's true."

"*She's* not Welsh. Saxon, maybe, or Norman."

"Way she's sitting that horse, like she's got a board up her back, I'd give you good odds she's Norman."

"With that yellow hair?"

Ivor turned to Dafydd with a leer. "Man could get lost in hair like that, eh?"

He started to climb down from his perch as the woman nudged her horse toward the forest. "Let's find out."

Chapter Six

"Hsst!" Dafydd pointed to a pair of riders coming through the forest toward the manor.

Ivor scrambled quietly back onto the branch and frowned at Dafydd as they both realized the men were carrying on their conversation in Welsh. The men below weren't from around here, that was certain, too. Their accents were different. Northern they were, perhaps, or from the western coast.

"That's him!" Dafydd whispered as they rode past the tree and toward the woman. "That's the knight."

Ivor's face was full of fury. "I'd like to take my sword and—" He stopped when the men drew near the mounted woman, whose back stiffened noticeably. "Well, well, well," he whispered. "Not looking pleased to see him, is she?"

Dafydd was puzzled, too.

They listened to the quiet conversation in Norman French. Dafydd knew only a word here and there. He thought Ivor might understand more, but his leader betrayed no particular interest until the woman turned her horse toward the manor and the three people rode in that direction.

"So," Ivor said thoughtfully, "she *is* a Norman. And he's a Norman's lackey, not fit to be called Welsh. I think we should pay them a visit, eh, Dafydd? Us and the men?"

Dafydd was no less disgusted than Ivor that a man who called himself a Welshman would marry a Norman wife and become the servant of a Norman lord, but he was more cautious by nature than his leader. "Think that's wise? Didn't your lover say he's some fighter? And that other fellow looks plenty tough."

"In tournaments, is what she said. They'll be no match for us."

"Maybe."

Ivor waited until Dafydd climbed down, then followed him. Once on the ground, Ivor hesitated. "Maybe you're right. Too hasty we shouldn't be."

Dafydd looked somewhat relieved, but still wary. He had known Ivor for a long time, but he was never able to predict what the man might decide to do.

Except in one regard. Ivor hated Normans and anyone he perceived to be a traitor to Wales. He would show such enemies absolutely no mercy.

Lately, Dafydd had started to fear that Ivor was planning to make an attack on a manor or even a poorly protected castle. Although he had created a web of spies, informers and those who would do what they were paid to, no questions asked, so far Ivor had confined their attacks to armed bands of Norman soldiers, with ambushes and quick retreats to the hills.

Much as Dafydd hated the Normans, and with good cause considering what they had done to his family, he knew that his band did not have the numbers, the weapons or the skills to do much more. If they tried,

Dafydd didn't doubt that many of his friends would never live to see another day.

"I mean, it might be better to remind him that he was born Welsh," Ivor said thoughtfully. "We're not his enemy. The real foe's the Norman dogs who don't belong here. They're his enemy, too, and not to be trusted."

"But his wife—"

"Didn't seem pleased to see him. Maybe the marriage has gone sour already."

"She's beautiful."

"So? She's a Norman—one of the enemy."

"Your own lover is a Norman."

Ivor shrugged. "Who hates her people worse than me."

"What if he doesn't agree?"

Ivor shrugged again, but he was already forming his plan. He was tired of playing cat and mouse in the hills. After all, his family had been rulers here long before the Normans came, and he was certain he would be the one to insure that they—or, more precisely, he—were rulers again, once the Normans were driven out.

It was time for action, although like any good leader he would wait for the best possible circumstances before attacking.

He must choose his target carefully, and make sure that his men were convinced it was the time to move. The cautious ones, like Dafydd, might try to argue against it otherwise.

Ivor glanced at the slender, dark-haired young man walking beside him. Too many of the band were beginning to listen to Dafydd.

Still, it would be a pity if anything were to happen to him. Unless the Normans could be blamed.

"I mean what I say, Liliana," Hu said quietly as they continued to ride toward home. "You can't go out of the gate alone."

Liliana stared straight ahead. "I never left the manor property. I simply cannot stay cooped up in that pigsty all day, every day."

"The folks nearby could see she was all right," Elwy offered helpfully. For his trouble, both Hu and Liliana gave him sour looks.

"I am not a child," Liliana said firmly.

Hu frowned. "No, you're a woman—so you can't go off all by yourself whenever you take a notion to do it. It's not safe."

"Then assign me some men to act as escort."

"That's not possible. I need every man to prepare the buildings for the winter."

"He's right there, my lady. Going to be a long, cold winter, judging by the squirrels, and..." Elwy's voice trailed off as his two companions ignored him.

Elwy took a new tack. "Some surprised we was, meeting the Northrups."

Liliana reined in her horse, a pleased smile lighting her face. "I had no idea they lived so close by! I knew their manor was somewhere near, but nobody told me..."

Hu felt some pleasure at her happy smile, but he would have died rather than admit he was more disappointed that she wouldn't smile like that for him, so he kept his face carefully expressionless.

"Lady Eleanor sends her regards, and asks you to visit her as soon as you want to," Hu said flatly.

Liliana nodded an acknowledgment but did not reply.

Hu nudged his horse forward so that he wouldn't even be tempted to try to decipher Liliana's expressions. He was no closer to understanding her than ever, and the strain of wondering how she felt about things—God's teeth! how she felt about *him*—was driving him nearly mad.

What with that, and being so filled with desire for a woman who didn't want him, he could hardly think of anything else.

For a time, when he had discovered that their nearest neighbors to the south were the Northrups, friends of Lord Trevelyan whom Hu had known since he was a squire, he had managed to forget his problems with Liliana.

Plump, good-natured Lady Eleanor, whose husband had been out hunting when they arrived early after the noon, had greeted them warmly.

Hu had noted the comfortable, if not luxurious, living accommodations of Nevil Hall, Lady Eleanor's pleasant, courteous children and the happy, well-fed servants.

Nevil Hall and its inhabitants provided quite a contrast to the other manor to the north that they had visited first that morning. It had the trappings of luxury, but everything seemed shabby, including the knight and his daughter. Sir William Horton was thin, old and clearly fond of his drink. His daughter, Priscilla, was likewise thin, as well as haughty, rude and

well past the first blush of youth. The few tenants they
had seen looked ill-fed and ill-clothed.

Hu had pointed out to Elwy on the way home that
Priscilla Horton was unmarried, but Elwy had de-
clared that he didn't want a wealthy wife *that* much—
if the Hortons had any money. Which they both
doubted. Sir William had probably used up most of
his money in drink. The wine Lady Priscilla had
grudgingly offered them was the worst they had ever
tasted in their lives.

They had both noticed that Priscilla asked a lot of
questions about the number of fighting men they had.
"Like a madam with a brothel near a camp," Elwy
had said with more accuracy than kindness, declaring
that obviously the woman was looking for a husband. Hu refrained from pointing out that Elwy gave
every indication that he was looking for a wife nearly
as desperately.

More interestingly, Priscilla Horton had wanted to
know their full Welsh names and what part of the
country they were from. They made no secret of their
surprise, since most Normans knew little and cared
less about Wales and its people. She explained that she
had learned much of the Welsh from living so near the
border lands. That made some sense, and whatever
Elwy thought, Hu respected the woman a little more
for it.

As they had talked about their neighbors on the
journey home, Hu had started to enjoy himself, feeling comfortable with Elwy beside him like old times.

The camaraderie lasted until he saw Liliana seated
on her fine horse, her hood thrown back so that her

beautiful face was easily seen—and no one around to protect her.

Now he gave her a sidelong glance and wondered if she would heed his warning. He truly didn't believe the bandits supposedly living in the forest would be much of a threat now that the manor was inhabited again, but he wasn't about to risk his wife to find out.

If she would heed his words. The way things were going between them, she would probably not just ignore his advice, but ride out every day to spite him.

"I would very much like to see Lady Eleanor again," Liliana said wistfully, breaking the silence.

She made it sound as if she was his prisoner. "Never said you couldn't, me," Hu replied brusquely.

Liliana's face didn't reveal her pleasure at the prospect of a visit with the motherly Lady Eleanor. Or her annoyance at Hu's arrogant demand that she remain inside the manor walls.

Or her relief.

Just before Hu and Elwy had appeared, she had suddenly felt afraid, sensing that somewhere in the forest, someone was watching her.

But obviously it must have been her husband and his friend. They had surprised her, coming out of the forest, and she had felt like a child caught hiding from her nursemaid. She didn't know what Hu would say about her riding out alone, but she had been sure he would condemn her for it.

Her concern had been completely justified. He had chastised her as if she were indeed a little child and he the nursemaid. With his friend there, too.

Still, it wasn't unpleasant to think that he was at least concerned for her safety. Maybe she *had* taken something of a foolish risk. Certainly Father Alphonse would say so.

Elwy interrupted her thoughts by starting to sing. The Welsh were always singing, she reflected somewhat sourly. It seemed to be like breathing to them. Even from here, she could hear the men working on the walls singing.

Well, not *all* the Welsh sang. Not her husband.

She looked at him. She had never heard him sing. He must when he was with the others. With a twinge of regret, she wondered if he thought she wouldn't want to hear him.

What would his voice be like? His speaking voice was deep and strong. Maybe he could even play one of those little harps such as some of the other men had. He could sit beside her in the evenings while she made tapestries for the walls, singing soft and low...

"Elwy!" Hu shouted suddenly, kicking his heels into the sides of his horse. "The pigs!"

They galloped toward the manor as Liliana's mare pranced excitedly.

The pigs had escaped their enclosure, and led by one fast-moving sow were running through a broken part of the outer wall.

Several of the workmen came racing out the gate after them, almost getting run over by Hu and Elwy as they pulled their horses to a halt and jumped down.

The men nearly managed to corral the pigs by the riverbank, but the ground was slippery. Elwy sprawled headlong into the mud. The sow, seeing her chance, ran over him and toward the meadow, followed by the rest of the animals.

"Cut them off!" Hu shouted. He dashed ahead and stood with his arms held wide as if he could single-handedly stop the careening pack of pigs. Others joined him, including Elwy, who had scrambled to his feet.

The lead sow slowed to a trot, her head turning from side to side as she sought a way through the growing enclosure of men.

Suddenly the sow stopped and pricked up her ears. Everyone else stood motionless, listening.

Then they heard it. Soft cries of "Su-ee! Su-ee! Here, pig, pig, pig!"

Liliana looked at the gate. Jhone stood there with a basket of apples in her hand. She called again, a little louder. "Su-ee! Su-ee! Pig, pig, pig!"

The sow obediently turned around and trotted toward the serving woman. Jhone tossed an apple to the pig, which she gobbled at once. Meekly the sow followed Jhone through the gate, and led all the other fugitive animals inside.

Hu and Elwy looked at each other, then burst out laughing, as did the rest of the men.

Liliana had to suppress a smile as she rode past them through the gate and toward the stable near the barn. Once there, she called for a lad to take her horse and headed for the hall.

She halted when Hu and Elwy strode into the courtyard. Hu was talking loudly—far too loudly for a nobleman, Liliana thought. It was obvious that he was making fun of his friend's muddy clothes.

Liliana lifted her chin. Hu *should* have been finding out whose fault it was that the pigs had escaped. Really, such familiarity with underlings, even if they were old friends, was not dignified in front of the villeins.

She started walking again, until she heard Hu's voice raised in anger. She turned to see if he was chastising those responsible for the pigs, and saw that Elwy had somehow managed to get hold of him.

Her husband, Sir Hu Morgan, sworn ally of Lord Trevelyan and lord of the manor, was hoisted over his friend's shoulder like a loudly protesting, very vocal side of beef. Elwy carried Hu, who was obviously using every Welsh curse in existence, toward the water trough outside the stable. Then he dumped him in.

Hu sat up. His damp hair was plastered to his forehead and his expression fiercely indignant. He spit water from his mouth and slowly began to climb out of the trough.

Liliana glared at the laughing Elwy. Friend or no friend, that man had no conception of the deference due—

Suddenly, with a great bellow, Hu tackled Elwy. They both rolled around in the mud, pummeling each other. The workmen, who should have been about their tasks, began to shout encouragement, some obviously for Elwy, others for Hu.

Elwy managed to get to his feet and disappeared around the side of the barn. Hu jumped up and rushed after his friend.

Then Liliana saw Elwy. He was inside the barn, hiding on the other side of the open door. He must have crawled in through one of the smaller windows.

She saw Hu coming around the far side. "Watch out—he's in the barn!" she called out.

At that moment, Elwy leaped out of his hiding place, pulling Hu to the ground.

"Get up! Get up!" Liliana cried, rushing to join the small crowd of men who moved toward the combatants.

Elwy tried to crawl away, but the ground was slick from the churning hooves of pigs and horses, and Hu easily grabbed his ankle. He yanked Elwy closer, then got a grip on his friend's belt. Hu struggled to his feet and began pulling Elwy toward the trough.

Liliana held her breath, hoping Hu would succeed in repaying his humiliation. With a cry of triumph, Hu lifted the writhing Elwy and dumped him into the water.

"You did it!" Liliana shouted, jumping up and down with glee.

Hu turned and looked at her, a broad grin on his flushed face.

Liliana clapped her hand over her mouth. What was she doing! She was no better than a peasant girl at the cockfights!

Her face burning, she lifted her skirts and hurried inside the hall. She had to change her gown for the evening meal. She had to make sure Jhone, Dena and Osyth had done everything properly. She had to see if Sarah had all the food in hand...

What she really had to do was calm herself. It had been exciting, though, watching Hu wrestle with his friend. Like a tournament, of sorts.

She hurried around the screen and tugged off her cloak. Then she remembered Hu's startled face as he sat in the trough, arms and legs hanging over the side.

She began to smile, then pressed her hand over her mouth to suppress a gale of laughter.

She didn't succeed. A hearty peel burst from her throat. She laughed so hard she could scarcely undo the knot in the lacing of her gown.

She took a deep breath and tried to control herself. It would never do to have Maude see her like this. After all, she had told Maude to contain herself on numerous occasions... but Hu had looked so shocked and so wet!

Liliana cleared her throat and tried to at least look serious.

She undid the lacing, wondering briefly where Maude was, but decided she could well attend to her own needs for the present.

She selected a finer garment than the one she had worn riding to wear at the meal. No reason, really. She just wanted to. She pulled it on over her shift.

When she heard a sound behind her, she said, "Maude, lace my gown for me, please," and lifted her hair with her hands.

Maude didn't answer. She didn't even giggle. Liliana whirled around and let go of her hair.

Hu stood beside the screen, his wet tunic in one hand. His damp hair curled about his face, and little rivulets of water ran down his bare chest. His muddy breeches clung to his muscular legs. He didn't say a word, although his lips curved in an enticing smile.

He wasn't even sure he *could* speak, not after Liliana had been standing before him holding her hair above her gaping gown, exposing the slender nape of her neck, the smooth white skin of her back and the thin fabric of her shift. He had realized at once how easy it would be to slide his hands inside and . . .

She was staring at him. He cleared his throat. "Got to get some dry clothes, me."

"By all means," she replied, turning away from him again—and again unknowingly offering him that tantalizing view.

He dropped his wet tunic on the floor and came toward her. For a moment, Liliana didn't think she could move. His smile had been devastating. Not mocking or cold this time, but warm and friendly and filled with unmistakable approval. Her heart beat like the thunder of a herd of horses, and breathing became a vague memory.

Until he went past her to the chest under the window and opened it. Well, if he could ignore her presence, she could ignore his. She picked up her hairbrush and began to use it.

Unfortunately, she was acutely aware of her half-naked husband not five feet away, and her own unfastened gown.

Hu tried to act nonchalant as he reached for dry garments, but it seemed every particle of his body realized his beautiful wife was close by. He also remembered the glow of excitement in her eyes out in the courtyard, and the fact that she had cheered for him. He had never seen her look so excited and carefree, and he liked it very much.

He took out a dry tunic and some breeches, then turned. She was brushing her thick golden hair.

"I've got to change my clothes," he said with some hesitation. He felt like a timid youth, ashamed to be naked in front of his own wife.

Despite his best effort, he felt a blush creep up his face. Which was stupid. A lot of women had seen him nude, and he hadn't batted an eye.

She placed her brush on the small table and glanced at him, then quickly away. "I need Maude to lace my gown," she said, and he realized she wouldn't leave with her gown undone.

"I'm soaking wet," he pointed out. He started to shiver.

"I know," she said softly, looking at the floor.

For the first time since he had known her, Liliana seemed shy and uncertain, not haughty and cold. Here, now, she was simply a rather innocent young bride, not a proud Norman noblewoman. Not just lovely, but lovable. "Here, I'll lace your gown," he said softly, his damp clothes forgotten.

"I don't think—"

He tossed his dry garments on the bed and walked toward her with a roguish smile on his face. "Please, my lady. Allow me."

Chapter Seven

Liliana's eyes widened for an instant, but she wordlessly turned so that her back was to him and pulled her luxuriant hair to one side.

Hu came close behind her. He reached for the laces at her waist, his fingers brushing the thin fabric of her shift.

Her silence made him wonder if she sensed the change he felt within himself, and his feelings for her. He noticed she was trembling.

God's wounds, not afraid! Not of him.

He pressed a light kiss to the soft nape of her neck.

"What...what are you doing?" she asked haltingly.

"Helping my wife." He kissed her between her shoulder blades, her thin silk shift the merest of barriers. "Would you like me to stop?"

"No," she murmured, leaning back ever so slightly.

Delighted, he gently tugged on the laces. She had to step back, which brought her body up against his. As he had intended.

"You'll break them!" she chided, but her voice lacked conviction, and he smiled.

"I won't."

Despite his assurance, which he had every intention of abiding by, he was sorely tempted to rip not just the laces, but everything she wore from her body. His fingers slowed at their task as he became more and more conscious of her shapely buttocks pressing against him and the bare flesh at the nape of her neck inches from his lips.

He didn't tie the knot when he finished, but ran his hands slowly down her back.

"Aren't you finished?" she whispered.

"Not yet." His hands traveled leisurely up her arms, and he felt her relax.

"Are...are you sure?" Her voice was rather strained.

He chuckled, unable to contain his pleasure. "Trust me, Liliana. I've done this lots of times."

She stepped away abruptly. "Not with *me*," she snapped.

Hu silently cursed himself for making a blunder any green youth would be ashamed of. "Liliana, I—"

Her eyes flashed indignantly as she knotted her gown with fierce quickness. "You are a lust-filled, lecherous creature!"

He put his hands on his hips and glared at her. "I am a *man*, Liliana," he fired back. "Not some pompous, cold-hearted monk."

"What are you implying? That I should be delighted such a *man* has deigned to bestow his animal desires upon me? That I should be pleased you have apparently behaved no better than a rutting ram?" Her eyes narrowed. "That I should throw myself at your feet and *beg* to be the recipient of your vastly experienced prowess?''

Before he could reply, she marched toward him. ''Please feel free to take your manly prowess elsewhere, my lord. *I* do not want it.''

Then she went around the screen and was gone.

Hu muttered a curse as he reached for his dry clothes and finished dressing.

What had he done marrying a wench like Liliana Trevelyan? She had the tongue of an adder.

And the body of an angel.

He yanked on his tunic. The only thing to do was stay well away from her. Even take a mistress before his unsatisfied cravings drove him mad.

Not that there was another woman in England he wanted as much as his own wife.

He sat down on the edge of the bed with a sigh. Why should he be so surprised she had reacted with anger when he had made such an incredible blunder? Reminding her of his other women had been an incredibly stupid thing to do.

Perhaps he should be pleased she had been angry. At least she had *cared.*

Fine lover he was! Apparently he had forgotten everything he had ever learned about women when it came to wooing his own wife.

On their wedding night, he had gotten drunk, even worse than the first time he had imbibed too much at that long-ago tournament. He had discovered then that he was quick to feel the effects of too much wine or ale, but he had conveniently forgotten that during his wedding feast. Well, not forgotten. Not if he was honest with himself. He had been trying to forget that he didn't feel worthy of such a bride.

Still, how he had ever imagined he could make love in that state was a mystery to him. Naturally a woman with her pride and position could be expected to be annoyed by such loutish behavior.

When they had arrived here, he had stupidly let his passion take control. He had thrown her down on the bed like any ill-mannered oaf in a brothel. No wonder she had been upset.

And then today, to mention other women to her! Oh, God's wounds, was he never going to say the right thing to her? Was there some kind of curse on him, that the very woman he wanted most was the one he managed to upset constantly?

He stood up. He had two choices. He could do as she suggested and take a mistress.

Or he could begin again and woo his wife.

Considering he had wanted Liliana Trevelyan far longer than anyone suspected, he really had no choice at all.

"Liliana?" Hu called softly.

Liliana didn't move under her coverings. Once again, she had taken the feather tick off the bed, pulled it close to the wall and made a bed for herself with her linens. Now she lay snuggled in the covers, pretending to sleep.

"Liliana?" he whispered again.

She felt herself weaken at his deep, gentle voice, just the way she had weakened earlier that afternoon when he had touched her.

She reminded herself that she had to be strong. She couldn't let him know how much she yearned for him to be so close to her again. Not after he had bragged of his many women.

She heard him sigh, but he said nothing more as he moved about the room. After a few moments of silence, she risked opening her eyelids a crack.

He was lying on the floor, wrapped up in his cloak.

He could catch a chill, sleeping there on the cold stones, especially after getting soaking wet that afternoon.

She noticed his dog lying beside him. Well, at least Hu's back would be warm.

She would let him suffer. He deserved it, for upsetting her so.

But the stone floor! He might get sick, very sick, with a fever or something far worse than a chill.

And he *had* been rather subdued at the evening meal, as if he had understood that he had been at fault.

Which he had. Very much. He had treated her the way she supposed most men treated women, bragging about his vast experience. But she was *not* most women.

Not that she expected him to have led a life of chastity. Having many women seemed to be another mark of accomplishment for a knight. To be sure, it was galling to be reminded that he was so accomplished while she knew so little, but she knew she was being naive if she assumed anything different.

And now, in the quiet stillness of the night, she dared to admit to herself that she had enjoyed his caresses and gentle kisses. She even had to admit that, had he not said what he did, she might very well have begged him to continue.

Who was she the more angry with—Hu, for acting like a man, or herself, for weakening in his embrace?

Hu shifted slightly. Again she told herself his comfort was not her concern.

Yet he had not done what she told him to do, at least this night. He had not sought comfort in another woman's arms.

She waited awhile longer, until she was sure he was asleep. Then, moving very slowly and cautiously, she took one of the blankets and covered him with it.

She lay down and turned to face the wall, where she wouldn't see him. Perhaps that way, she wouldn't be so tempted to think about him, either.

Hu, who was wide awake, opened his eyes to look at his wife. Then he smiled.

The Sabbath day dawned bright and sunny. The air was chill, with the crispness of autumn, but the sky was as blue as spring.

Liliana walked slowly from the chapel after Mass. Hu had gone out ahead of her, without saying more than a greeting.

She sighed. For the past few nights, they had both slept on the floor. She kept wondering how long it would be before Hu spoke about it, but apparently the arrangements didn't disturb him much. In fact, she saw little of him except at the evening meal, and then he seemed exhausted and ill disposed to talk.

She was tired, too. She was having a hard time of it, trying to explain to Jhone and the girls just what needed to be done and the proper way to do it. Clearly the people here had no idea how a proper hall was run.

She had also attempted, with Maude's help, to make the area behind the screen a little more comfortable and a little less like a barracks.

Since there was no steward, she had taken on the responsibility of keeping account of the money she spent on food and linens, which was thankfully minimal for the time being. She had learned from her father's stewards that it was a good idea to keep accurate accounts. That way, should anyone—such as Hu—demand to know where her money was going, she could show him.

Once the new floor was put in the hall, she would have to pay for whitewash and paneling for the walls, better furniture and the materials for making tapestries. However, she would worry about that when the time came.

Liliana went out into the bright sunlight and stopped. Hu sat on his horse nearby, with her saddled mare beside him. "I thought we should go to the Northrups' early, so that we can return before dark," he said, smiling at her pleasantly.

"Oh," was all she could say at first. Then, "I'll fetch my cloak."

She hurried to do just that. She had said nothing more about seeing Lady Eleanor, although she very much wanted to do so, and she had believed he had forgotten their invitation.

As she drew on her woolen cloak with its lining of pale blue silky sarcenet, she began to wonder if Hu had some ulterior motive she couldn't discern. But did it really matter? Sir Nevil would be sure to drag Hu off to see his hawks, of which he was inordinately proud, so she would be left alone in Lady Eleanor's pleasant company. For a time, she would not have to worry about what Hu was thinking.

She returned quickly, ignoring the small gathering of curious onlookers while she tried to read her husband's inscrutable face. She noted that he wore his second-best tunic. He had on a cloak against the chill air and carried his sword on his belt. The slight breeze ruffled his curls as his horse danced impatiently.

He looked every inch the nobleman this morning, and she felt giddy at the prospect of riding with him. She put aside what niggling doubt remained of his intentions and decided to simply enjoy a ride on a fine autumn day with the promise of good company at the end.

"Ready?" he asked when she mounted her horse.

"Where is our escort?"

He shook his head, a confident grin on his face. "Not needed. It's not that far." His voice dropped so that only she could hear. "I want to be alone with my wife."

She couldn't have argued with him even if she could have talked. As it was, heat poured through every limb, and she didn't dare trust her voice to remain steady. She nudged her horse to a walk, and with Hu at her side rode out of the gate and down the road.

It was so nice to be away from the manor and the multitude of tasks she had to supervise. She decided it would not be amiss to let Hu know that she appreciated his unexpected gesture. "Thank you," she said sincerely.

"What for?"

"For taking me to see Lady Eleanor."

"You like her?"

"She was very kind to me when my mother died. And afterward."

"I like her, too," he replied briefly, but Liliana could tell that was praise not lightly given. She had to wonder if he could say the same about his wife.

"It was a pity your family didn't come to our wedding. I would have liked to meet your mother," she said after an awkward pause.

"My family are all dead."

"Oh." Liliana felt herself flushing with shame, and justly so. To think she didn't even know that much about the man she had married. "I'm sorry."

He shrugged. "My father died before I was born, and my mother was very ill for a long time, so it was a mercy she died. That was five years ago." He looked at her and grinned. "Wish you could meet my *tadmaeth*, though."

"Your what?"

"Foster father. Baron DeLanyea. A very fine man. He was invited to the wedding, but he couldn't come. He's broken his leg, and his wife—that's Lady Roanna I spoke of before—"

"I recall the name."

He glanced at her and cleared his throat before continuing. "Well, she and his old nurse will be clucking at him like a couple of hens with one chick."

Liliana nodded. She pictured a sickly, elderly man, bedridden and needing constant care. "How unfortunate. Poor old fellow."

Hu gave her an astonished look, then burst out laughing. "Oh, no, Liliana! He's not to be pitied. Not him! My God, he's healthier than me most of the time. Why, left for dead in the Holy Land he was, and he still walked all the way home." He sobered a little at her peeved expression. "Not laughing at you, Liliana. Just the idea you had."

She had to smile at his sincerity. "I would like to meet him." And find out more about *you*, she thought.

She saw his gaze stray to the sheep grazing in the meadow nearby, together with some of the cattle. "Hu," she said. She felt a little awkward using his name, especially when he turned and looked at her. "Why did you get so many sheep? My father says most manors keep cattle in this part of the country."

"The sheep were a wedding present," he replied. "From Baron DeLanyea."

"Oh."

"And as for keeping sheep—them I know. Cattle I don't."

"But surely it can't be difficult to raise cattle."

"I like sheep."

"Oh."

"I was a shepherd until I was eight years old. My grandfather taught me all there was to know about sheep, and dogs, too."

A *shepherd*? She was wed to a man who had been a shepherd? She had known he wasn't nobly born, but...

But he had journeyed even farther than she had suspected, from northern Wales to her father's castle, and from such humble beginnings to knighthood and an estate.

She had to respect a man of such skill and ambition—and who spoke of his grandfather with such protective pride and love. "He sounds like a wonderful man," she said softly.

"He was."

"How did you come to stop being a shepherd?"

For a moment she thought he wasn't going to answer.

"When my grandfather died," he said, "Baron DeLanyea became my foster father. He made me a squire, and later a knight."

"And Elwy—was he a shepherd, too?"

"No." Hu smiled broadly, and she was relieved at the return of his good cheer.

"Was he sent to your lord to be fostered, too?"

"No, Elwy's a bastard."

Hu gave her a sidelong glance. Somewhat to his relief, Liliana didn't look disgusted when she heard Elwy's lack of parentage. Normans often had peculiar ideas about illegitimate children, whereas the Welsh tended to accept them simply as children.

"Is he Baron DeLanyea's son?"

"God's wounds, no," he answered with a deep chuckle. "He just turned up one day near Craig Fawr, the baron's castle. Soon after, Jacques, the cook and a tremendously fat fellow, found Elwy in the pantry, his tunic full of bread.

"Elwy ran out past him, and ten men had to chase him all around the courtyard before they finally got him cornered. He was a lot lighter on his feet then, was Elwy. Half-starved he was, mind you, and dirty! Worse than the other day in the mud.

"By this time, Emryss—Baron DeLanyea—and his wife come out to see what was going on. Emryss looks at him—" Hu squinted one eye shut "—he's only got the one eye," he explained. "Emryss just looks at him. Elwy shrugs his shoulders and smiles at them as charming as you please."

"He wasn't punished?"

Hu shook his head. "Lady Roanna, she asks what the baron's going to do with the boy. 'What do you think I should do?' Emryss says. 'Why, make him a squire, of course,' says she, as if it was as plain as the castle wall. 'Anyone that can get past Jacques and nearly get away from so many fine soldiers is too clever to send away. I think it would be better to make an honest squire of him.' So Emryss did."

He caught sight of her expression and frowned. "Elwy never stole another thing after that. He's the most honest man I know."

"I didn't mean to imply that he was dishonest."

"Good." Hu pressed his lips together. He was trying very hard to be congenial. So far this morning, things had been going better between them than he had hoped.

But the only thing worse than insulting him and his country was insulting his friend.

He decided it would be wise to change the topic of conversation. "Lady Eleanor—I suppose she has been a help to you?" he asked.

Hu knew, from his younger days at tournaments, that Sir Nevil was a great friend of Lord Trevelyan. It would make sense that his warmhearted wife would be only too happy to assist Liliana with her many responsibilities.

"Yes. But I soon understood what to do, and what was expected of me."

"Were you very old when your mother died?"

"I was ten. There was some talk of sending me to be fostered, too, but . . ."

"But?"

"I refused to go."

That was an easy scene to imagine. He could see why Lord Trevelyan would give in rather than face a stubborn, determined, young and motherless Liliana.

"My father was glad he didn't," she said with more than a hint of defensiveness. "I soon took over all of my mother's duties."

Yes, Hu could see that, too. He had seen how she managed her father's castle with the skill and diplomacy of a woman many years older.

At once Hu felt as if he had been struck by an arrow between the eyes. Of course! She had had to take her mother's place at such an early age, so her childhood had been cut very short. That would explain so many things! Why she was always so serious. Why she took such pride in manners and deportment and clothes. Why he found it so difficult to know what she was thinking. Why he thought he saw, more than once, a loneliness in the depths of her green eyes.

She hadn't been free to enjoy life without a myriad of responsibilities for a very long time.

He wanted to shout with triumph. And yet, at the same time, he felt a little pity for her, too. He understood why she held herself aloof and apart, seeming to have no need for any friend or confidant.

He pointed to a stream spilling down the rocky side of a small gorge and pulled his horse to a stop. "I'm thirsty," he announced, dismounting. "Would you care to drink?"

"Yes, that would be very refreshing."

Without warning, he reached up and put his strong, lean hands around her waist to pull her down. When her feet touched the ground, she was very aware of the nearness of his body and disappointed when he let go.

Hu strode toward the stream. By now they were deep in the forest, and Liliana couldn't help feeling a bit apprehensive as she hurried after him.

"You don't think we need to be worried about outlaws here?" she asked, trying to keep her voice calm.

Hu shook his head and rose to his feet. "No. I've had some of the men looking about, and they think they've gone. At least there's been no sign of them for days."

She cocked her head and gave him a shrewd look. "Then why were you so worried about me riding out alone?"

Hu's neck flushed as he cleared his throat. "No one can be absolutely sure they've *all* gone. If there's a few left, they probably wouldn't attack an armed man. But a lone woman? A very beautiful lone woman?"

Liliana's heart started to pound at his deep, melodious words. She suddenly felt awkward and foolish for not knowing how to respond to him. To avoid talking, she bent down to drink.

Hu watched her as she leaned forward to lift the sparkling water in her delicate hand and put it to her ruddy mouth. It was all he could do to keep from taking her in his arms and pressing fervent kisses on those damp lips.

But he wouldn't. He would wait until he was sure she wanted him to. He didn't want to make any more mistakes by letting his desire get the better of him.

There was a sudden movement in the bushes on the other side of the bank.

Hu's hand went to the hilt of his sword. Liliana stepped quickly toward him, one hand clutching his arm. "What's that?" she whispered.

As if in answer to her question, a deer's head appeared over the top of the bushes. Apparently catching their scent, it turned and ran off.

Liliana let go of him and stepped away. "Perhaps we should be on our way," she suggested, turning and heading to their waiting horses.

Hu didn't move. "Perhaps."

Chapter Eight

Liliana scanned the surrounding trees and clasped her hands together nervously while she waited for Hu to catch up to her.

"We don't want to be late arriving at the North-rups'," Hu agreed lightly. He took her hand, placed it on his arm and led her to their waiting horses. Liliana was anxious and apprehensive, so he decided this was no time to press his attentions on her, tempting though that might be.

He tried not to notice the desire that grew from even that slight touch as they walked.

They mounted and rode on. It was shortly before noon when they reached the prosperous manor of the Northrups. Both Sir Nevil and Lady Eleanor were evidently pleased to have their company, and greeted them warmly.

They shared a very pleasant meal, and afterward Sir Nevil took Hu to see his hawks, while Lady Eleanor and Liliana stayed behind.

Liliana wasn't sorry to see the men leave. Sir Nevil was a kind and generous man, but all he ever seemed to think about was his hawks and his fine wines. She had spent much of the meal wondering how Lady Eleanor put up with his endless, boring chatter.

When the tables were cleared and taken down, Liliana sat beside Lady Eleanor, who was settled in a heavy oak chair beside the hearth. She was sewing on a garment she had taken from a basket nearby. It looked to be a child's shift.

She was very calm, considering she had ten children, the youngest of whom was two. The three oldest were daughters, each married to a respected, if minor, lord. The oldest boy was being trained as a squire by Lord Gervais, another of Sir Nevil's friends. The youngest children had been taken for a nap by their nurse, and the older ones had scattered to unknown destinations outside.

Liliana looked around the comfortable though not luxurious hall and couldn't help wondering if her home would ever be as nice as this.

Lady Eleanor looked at her companion with a warm smile. "Tired, my dear? Is there a *special* reason?"

Liliana blushed and stared at the floor. "I don't think I'm with child," she said quietly. She had had some vague half hope of talking to Lady Eleanor about intimate relations between a husband and wife, but now that the subject was broached, she wasn't sure she was ready to.

"It's early days yet," Lady Eleanor said kindly. When Liliana remained silent, Lady Eleanor looked at her shrewdly. "Is everything quite all right, my dear? Are you ill?"

Liliana twisted her skirt in her hands, took a deep breath and, after an awkward pause, said, "Hu and I ... that is ... I'm not sure...."

Lady Eleanor put down her sewing. "Liliana, what is it? What's wrong?"

Suddenly Liliana had the distinct idea that if she didn't say something to kindhearted Lady Eleanor now, she never would—and her marriage would turn out to be a disaster. She leaned closer. "Hu and I...I'm not sure if we've—"

"What?"

"Consummated the marriage."

Whatever Lady Eleanor had been expecting in the way of confidences, it obviously had not been that. She fell back against her chair and stared, dumbfounded. "I never thought the wife of Hu Morgan—" she began, then ceased when she saw Liliana looking at her, distress on her lovely face. "I mean, my dear, I know Hu is a fine young man. I'm sure there's a very good reason for this. Your woman's time...?"

Liliana shook her head. She swallowed hard, and Lady Eleanor knew her proud young friend was not finding it easy to confide in her. In all the time she had known Liliana, she had rarely asked for advice of any kind, and indeed, had not seemed to require much. Lady Eleanor pitied her in a way, for she knew that Liliana had not had an easy life after her mother's death, despite appearances to the contrary.

Now, however, she was very careful not to let that pity show on her face, or she knew Liliana would never say a word more.

"On our wedding night, Hu got drunk."

Lady Eleanor nodded. "I know. I was there."

"Well, that made me angry—and justly so."

Lady Eleanor nodded, but said nothing.

"He staggered into our room and then he..."

"Yes?"

"He fell asleep."

"Disappointing, I'm sure," Lady Eleanor said placidly, picking up her sewing again. "But many men get drunk at their weddings. Poor Nevil never even got up from the table."

Liliana smiled wanly. "I know they do. So I forgave him."

"That was generous of you."

Liliana glanced at her companion sharply, but Lady Eleanor continued to sew, her head bent over her work.

"Then he took me to our new home." There was more than a touch of bitterness in her voice as she recalled that day. "It's a ruin, Lady Eleanor. How could anyone be expected to live in such a drafty, dilapidated hall?" She leaned forward again. "There's not even a proper floor—or a proper bedchamber."

"Dear me."

Lady Eleanor didn't seem to understand just what kind of a hovel she was expected to live in, Liliana thought. "It's a disgrace!"

Lady Eleanor sighed softly. "When Nevil and I were married, we had to live with his parents for a year while this hall was being built. You don't remember Nevil's mother, do you?"

"No," Liliana said warily.

"It's not just to speak ill of the dead, so I won't. I will only say that I would have preferred living with Nevil in the poorest cotter's hut after one day under that woman's roof. In fact—" Lady Eleanor flushed a little "—I suggested to Nevil that we come here before the hall was finished. I had borne Alice by then, and was well along with Luginia, but even with the workmen hammering around me all day, it was a vast..." She sighed and glanced at Liliana. "Sometimes we must be prepared to compromise."

"But the men sleep in the hall, too," she protested.

"Naturally."

"I am not used to such accommodation."

"Obviously—and perfectly understandable."

"Is some privacy too much to ask?" Liliana demanded. This conversation was not going the way she had envisioned.

"Let us just say that you are not pleased with your new home," Lady Eleanor said calmly. "Did you refuse Hu his rights as your husband?"

Liliana knew she was blushing, and that made her even more frustrated. "I asked him to take me home."

"Meaning to your father's?"

"Yes," Liliana replied defiantly. "But before he agreed—"

Finally Lady Eleanor looked shocked. "He agreed?" she interrupted.

"Yes, he did. But first, he—he..." Liliana couldn't go on.

Lady Eleanor reached out and sympathetically patted her hand. Obviously the poor girl was having a difficult time talking about this. She could well believe that Lord Trevelyan's spoiled daughter had had some fanciful notions about married life. No doubt she had listened to too many minstrels with their love songs, and with a betrothed as handsome as Hu Morgan, who could blame her for expecting life to be like something out of a minstrel's ballad?

Lady Eleanor could also easily believe that Lord Trevelyan would not have discussed the more mundane aspects of wedded life, such as patience and compromise. Obviously he had not realized that two young people as proud and stubborn as Liliana and Hu should be warned about such necessities.

So Hu had exercised his prerogative in the nuptial bed, but—surprisingly—Liliana had apparently not enjoyed it. The young bride had surely been nervous and frightened, but Lady Eleanor was still rather taken aback to think that Hu Morgan's wife would have any cause to complain. Her own husband found the tales of that particular knight's amorous exploits highly entertaining, and told her everything he knew. "He was rather rough, I take it?" she asked gently when Liliana did not continue.

Liliana grew even redder.

"It's all right, Liliana. I have borne ten children, and three of my daughters are married. I doubt you could tell me anything so very shocking. Did he cause you pain when he made love to you?"

Liliana glanced at her. "No, not at all."

Lady Eleanor's eyes narrowed slightly. "It didn't hurt?"

"No. I was more surprised than hurt, I think."

"By the blood, or by what he did?"

"Oh, there wasn't any blood," Liliana said quickly, her eyes widening. "Is there supposed to be?"

"Sometimes." Lady Eleanor cleared her throat delicately. This was going to require a great deal of careful diplomacy. She might have guessed that Lord Trevelyan wouldn't have told his daughter about the physical nature of the marital relationship, either.

"My dear, I want you to tell me *exactly* what happened."

"Exactly?"

"Exactly. I promise no other soul shall know."

Liliana took a deep breath and twisted her gown even more. "Well, we argued, as I said. Then he picked me up and threw me on the bed. When Maude, my maid, brought some of my things, he was very rude to her and ordered her to sleep in the kitchen."

"Yes," Lady Eleanor prompted gently.

"I told him not to touch me. I told him…I told him he smelled like a peasant."

It was all Lady Eleanor could do to keep from rolling her eyes in dismay. No man alive would want to hear something like that from his bride.

Liliana's mouth hardened a little. "He pushed me back on the bed. He kissed me, and then I felt—" her voice dropped to a whisper "—his tongue inside my mouth."

"Yes?"

"Then I hit him."

Lady Eleanor's surprise got the better of her tact. "You *what*?"

"I slapped him, to make him stop."

"Did he?"

"Yes."

"He did?"

"Yes."

"Then what happened?"

"I suppose, since he had done all that needed to be done, he had no reason to stay. He left. The next day he told me I could go back home if I wanted to," she continued, her voice defiant. "But I couldn't. I

couldn't let him shame me, not after that." Her voice
grew less confident. "Could I?"

It took Lady Eleanor a few moments to think of
what to say. "Liliana, he was allowing you to return
to your father not because he wanted to shame you.
He said it because the marriage was not consummated."

Liliana sat perfectly still.

"What he did was just a different kind of a kiss."

Liliana had never felt so completely stupid in her
entire life.

"Your mistake is perfectly understandable, my
dear." Lady Eleanor smiled softly. "What did Hu say
when you didn't leave?"

"He . . . he didn't say much of anything," she replied in a subdued voice. "He's hardly spoken to me
since, except for today when we were riding here."

"He hasn't tried to be with you since?"

"No—yes—I'm not sure."

"Haven't you been sleeping together?"

"No."

Lady Eleanor frowned slightly. "Well, I must say,
my dear, that Hu has been very patient with you."

Liliana looked at her sharply. "Patient?"

"Well, he could have forced himself on you, you
know. He would have been within his rights."

"He did force himself."

Lady Eleanor shook her head. "He was a little
rough, perhaps, but he *did* stop."

Liliana considered her companion's words and her
thoughtful expression, then she leaned forward and
spoke in a conspiratorial whisper. "What was *supposed* to happen on our wedding night?"

Before Lady Eleanor could reply, they heard Sir Nevil's booming voice and Hu's answering tones as the men entered the hall.

"I think your husband feels it's time for you to be heading home," Lady Eleanor said reluctantly. Then she smiled as if inspired. "I believe it would be best, my dear, if you were to ask your husband to explain it to you."

Hu would have given much to satisfy his curiosity as he rode home beside Liliana.

She had been very quiet during the noon meal with the Northrups. Too quiet. Surely Lady Eleanor would have realized something wasn't quite right between the bride and her new husband. He was certain the warm, friendly Lady Eleanor would persuade Liliana to tell her what was troubling her the moment the men were out of hearing.

He glanced at Liliana, who was even quieter now. He suspected she rarely confided in anyone, but he was sure if anyone stood in the place of a sympathetic mother, Lady Eleanor would be it. Nonetheless, he knew full well what he was feeling.

Jealousy. He was jealous that she might have confided her feelings to someone other than her own husband. Other than him.

Unfortunately, Sir Nevil had been intent on detailing all the care and special qualities of each of his hawks, keeping them at the mews for what seemed an interminable time.

"I told Sir Nevil we will send our men to help with the slaughter at *nos galan gaeaf,*" he said when he couldn't stand the continuing silence any longer.

"Nos galan gaeaf?"

"Winter's Eve—or All Hallows' Eve, you probably call it."

"Oh, yes."

"In return, Nevil says he'll give us enough fodder to last the winter. That will save us having to spend money to buy food for the animals."

The only sound to disturb the quiet was the soft thud of the horses' hooves on the forest path.

"I've invited him to our *galan gaeaf* feast. He says he'll bring some wine. We're invited to their feast, of course. Very nice of them, too..."

He fell silent. What was he doing, rattling on like some besotted youth so delighted to be with his lady love that he would say anything?

She was always going on about courtesy. Wouldn't it be a *courteous* thing for her to respond? Hu reached out and grabbed the bridle of her horse, halting the animal. Liliana looked at him with a startled expression on her face.

"What is the matter?" he demanded. "Have I offended you—again?"

She frowned. "No. You haven't. I was just... thinking."

He dropped the bridle and kicked the side of his horse with his heels. Clearly she was in no mood to talk to him. Why had he even bothered?

"Hu?"

"What?"

"I had a pleasant talk with Lady Eleanor."

No doubt. And no doubt the Northrups were talking about their private business even now.

"I...that is, she..." Liliana paused uncertainly.

On their way to the Northrups and even a few moments ago when he spoke of All Hallows' Eve, Hu had seemed kind and gentle and exactly like the kind of suitor she had always dreamed of. She had been wondering if this would be the appropriate time to confess her woeful ignorance of what exactly was expected of her in their bed when Hu had changed. Clearly he was annoyed that she hadn't been paying much attention to his talk.

She opened her mouth, deciding he deserved an apology for her inattentiveness, although she still wasn't sure if she was ready to discuss anything else, when suddenly a man dropped out of a nearby tree onto the road. He swaggered boldly to the middle of the way and stopped, staring at them.

Liliana halted her horse. She heard Hu draw his sword. More men appeared at the side of the road, slipping out of the forest as silently as shadows. They were unkempt and ragged, but very well armed.

She glanced at Hu, who was sitting calmly in his saddle, his sword across his lap.

"Good day," Hu said coolly. He did not take his gaze from the man in the middle of the road. Liliana nudged her horse a little closer to her husband, mindful of the bold stares of the men surrounding them.

The man replied in what Liliana recognized as Welsh. Hu responded cheerfully, but he didn't sheath his sword.

Ivor bowed low and looked around at his fellows, a serious expression on his face. "Did you hear him, this traitor?"

"Hu ap Morgan ap Ianto, from Craig Fawr, he is."
Ivor spat on the ground directly in front of Morgan's
horse. "*I* am Ivor ap Rhodri ap Cadog Fawr ap Ma-
doc ap Cai Bach ap Rhodri y Mawr."

Ivor saw the Norman lackey's eyes flash with rec-
ognition, and pride flew through him. The Welsh
cared little for wealth or deeds of valor. What mattered was *cenedl*—a man's kindred. And he had already learned that Hu Morgan's kin were nothing
compared to the family of Ivor Rhodri.

"Greetings, then, Ivor ap Rhodri ap all the rest,"
Morgan replied in Welsh, still as cool as melting snow.
"Have you business with me?"

Ivor scowled. This man knew to whom he was
speaking, and yet he was treating Ivor as if he was no
more than a peasant. "Wanted to be sure it was true,
what people are saying. That a traitor has come to rule
our people."

"I am not a traitor."

"You belong to a Norman lord."

"I *belong* to no man. I owe my allegiance to Lord
Trevelyan."

"And you got a Norman wife." Ivor came closer.
His mouth turned up in a leering smile. "Not that I
can blame you for that, when she's as lovely and ripe
as—"

That was as far as Ivor got. In the next instant
Morgan was off his horse and had his sword tip at the
base of Ivor's throat.

"You and your men get off my land," Morgan ordered through clenched teeth.

Ivor barked a few words at his band, who dis-
persed into the trees. He glanced at the sword, but he

didn't move. "No. Our land first it was, not the Normans'."

Morgan lowered his sword a little.

"You could be one of us, Hu ap Morgan. With men like you, we could drive the Normans from here in a year."

Morgan gestured toward the trees with his weapon. "Go. Before I kill you for frightening my wife."

Ivor took one look into Hu Morgan's eyes and went off into the trees.

Liliana watched Hu mount his horse, his expression cold and hard to read.

"I thought you said the outlaws had gone," she said, trying not to sound afraid.

"I was wrong."

"Obviously."

"There's nothing to fear from them."

"Nothing?"

"That's what I said."

"We're ambushed by a band of ruffians in the forest, and you hold your sword to the throat of that man, who apparently isn't impressed, and you expect me to believe we have nothing to fear?"

"That's what I said."

"Who was he?"

"He won't trouble us again."

"You know who he was, don't you?"

"He told me. It doesn't matter."

"Hu Morgan, I want to know what happened. I'm not a child to be patted on the head and told not to worry."

"He made a request, which I refused. I put my sword to his throat because I didn't like the way he looked at you."

"There's more."

Hu glared at her. "You wouldn't understand."

Liliana glared back. "How can I, when I don't speak your language and you won't tell me? Perhaps I shall have to consult a seer when I want to know what's happening on my own estate."

"They'll leave the forest now."

"How can you be so sure?"

"Because I am!"

Liliana spurred her mare into a gallop.

With a curse, Hu kicked his horse and followed. He raced after Liliana, but her mare was light and very swift. He was also discovering his wife was an excellent rider, and she seemed especially keen to get away from him.

He didn't know why he was so bent on catching her, or what he would say to her if he did. He pulled on the reins, slowing his horse to a walk.

It had been bad enough discovering that the outlaws were bolder than he had given them credit for, but now he couldn't even be sure, despite what he had said, that they had any intention of leaving.

To think their leader had the audacity to tempt him to join them! He had never considered himself a traitor for swearing allegiance to a Norman. Nor for marrying a Norman wife.

Nonetheless he knew how men like Ivor viewed the coming of the Normans. A plague would have been preferable, for it wouldn't have harmed the governing of the land or the church they were familiar with.

The Normans had changed much, there was no denying that. Lord Trevelyan was fair and just, but men like him were all too rare. Most Norman lords ruled their lands like petty kings, demanding, arrogant and determined to destroy any vestige of the native ways. So back there in the forest, he had sympathized.

But it had only been for a moment. He had given his word to Lord Trevelyan that he would be loyal to him, and he had given his loyalty to Lord Trevelyan's daughter, his wife. He owed everything he had to the Normans. If the Welsh still ruled, he would be nothing more than a shepherd, a landless peasant from an inferior family, worth less than a ram.

Lord Trevelyan had said that he was free to run his estate as he wished, and if he wanted to do it in the Welsh way, that was acceptable. That was exactly what Hu intended to do—take the best of the Welsh way and the Norman way and marry them together.

Of course, he thought bitterly, if that type of marriage went the way his own was tending, it did not bode well.

He could see well down the road now, and watched as Liliana rode swiftly through the manor gate. It had not been wise or kind to take his anger at Ivor Rhodri out on her, but she had chosen a bad time to pester him with questions.

He reached the gate and rode through. There was no sign of Liliana.

Elwy stood in the courtyard, a small group of the local farmers with him. Their faces were anxious and worried.

"What's happened?" Hu asked, dismounting quickly.

Elwy nodded at a hen nearby. The bird moved like a man who had had too much wine, dragging a wing along the ground. Then Hu noticed that each of the men held a dead hen in their hands. He looked at Elwy with dismay.

Elwy nodded slowly. "They've got it, alright," he said mournfully. "And those others, the same."

Hu cursed softly, knowing there was nothing that could be done. The malady, which paralyzed chickens, would go through the flock, with no telling what birds might be carrying the sickness until they showed the symptoms. First their wings would droop, then their legs would become crippled as they lingered before dying.

And not only would his birds be affected. If these villeins also had sick chickens, there was no saying how many would live or die on the estate.

They would have to start anew, with new chickens, a new coop and new ground, lest the old ground be tainted.

Elwy came closer. "There's more," he said quietly.

Hu looked at him.

"There's a messenger from your father-in-law in the hall."

Chapter Nine

As she rode into the courtyard, Liliana seethed with anger and frustration at Hu's attempts to hide the truth. All she had wanted was an explanation for what had transpired in the forest. She had been frightened by the unexpectedness of the ambush, by the number of men in the outlaw band and by the lustful expression in the leader's eyes when he had looked at her.

Instead, her husband had treated her dismissively, as if what had happened could not matter in the slightest to her. As if her interest was mere idle curiosity.

Beneath her anger, she was aware of something much worse. She was hurt and disappointed that her husband would not confide in her. That she was, after all, merely a wife.

She dismounted quickly, handing her reins to one of the lads who hurried out of the stable, and strode across the courtyard. Out of the corner of her eye she saw Elwy talking to two or three villeins, but she paid them no heed.

She was trying to think of another reason Hu might not want her to know exactly what had passed between him and that outlaw, a reason that did not pertain to her.

Her steps slowed. Could it be that Hu *knew* the man? After all, they were both Welsh, apparently.

Everyone knew that several tribes of rebellious Welshmen harried the border lords, who were given rather a free hand from King John to suppress any uprisings. Surely Hu had nothing but contempt for such rebels, especially now that he had sworn loyalty to her father, a Norman lord.

The angry tone of his final words to the outlaw, whatever they actually meant, made her believe that if Hu did indeed know the man, they were neither friends nor allies.

As she entered the hall, she reflected that it would be a terrible thing to live with a traitor.

Derrick, one of her father's oldest and most trusted soldiers, stood in the hall. She made no effort to mask her surprise, but kept a frown from her face when she saw his incredulous expression as he looked at the barren walls and floorless beams over their heads.

"Derrick," she said calmly, "what a joy it is to see you."

Startled, he turned to her, his wrinkled face breaking into a pleased smile. "And I you, my lady."

"To what do we owe the honor of your visit?" She indicated a bench against the wall.

We should have a chair, she thought as she joined him.

"I've brought this, my lady," Derrick said. He reached into a leather pouch tied to his belt and retrieved a parchment.

She held out her hand for the document, but Derrick hesitated. "I'm sorry, my lady," he said awkwardly. "It's supposed to be given to your husband."

"Of course," Liliana said with a thin smile. It wasn't surprising that in most men's eyes she had become merely a minor appendage to her husband, but she hadn't expected such treatment from her own father. "How is my father?"

"Very well, my lady."

"Have the wedding guests departed?"

Derrick gave her a knowing grin. "All but the Beaumares."

This time Liliana's smile was a little more genuine. She might have known Averil and her husband would be the last to leave her father's castle—and his generous hospitality.

"And your journey? You had no trouble, I trust."

"No, not at all. I started out at first light, and the weather was good for riding."

She wondered if the outlaws who had accosted them in the forest had seen Derrick and wisely left him alone. He was an excellent fighter, despite being past middle age. Of course, they might also have decided he wasn't wealthy enough to bother with, if robbery was their motive.

The door to the hall banged open and Hu strode in. Liliana and Derrick rose quickly. Hu nodded an acknowledgment as he marched toward them.

"Greetings, sir," Derrick said respectfully. "Lord Trevelyan has asked me to give you this." He handed Hu the parchment.

"Thank you. Is it urgent?" Hu asked bluntly, ignoring Liliana.

"I don't believe so, sir."

Hu glanced sharply at Liliana. "Have you offered our guest some wine?"

"I was about to," Liliana lied sweetly. In truth, she had been so curious about the contents of the message and to find out if Derrick had encountered any outlaws that she had completely forgotten even basic courtesy. To think Hu had to remind her!

"I will find Jhone, and tell Sarah we have a guest for the evening meal, as well."

She went to the corridor that led to the kitchen. It took a mighty effort not to turn around and see if Hu opened the message, but she managed it.

When she returned a few minutes later, Hu and Derrick were nowhere to be seen.

"Oh, isn't that just like a man?" Liliana muttered, putting her hands on her hips. But she had no time to go searching for Hu and Derrick now. It was nearly time for the evening meal, and she wanted—needed— to make sure that whatever Derrick thought of the hall, he would have no reservations about the quality of the food.

A short time later, a disgruntled Hu sat at the high table. Liliana sat on his left and Derrick on his right.

Elwy had told him the number of hens they knew were sick, which for now was small. All the infected birds had been killed and the rest moved to different ground. He hoped that would keep more from falling ill, but only time would tell.

Afterward, he had told Elwy about Ivor Rhodri. Elwy's response was an elegant curse. A bastard himself, he had little use for the highborn, be they Welsh

or Norman, so Rhodri's parentage did not impress
him. Like Hu, Elwy saw such men, who tried to ef-
fect change with swords and fear and with no thought
to whom they might be hurting, as outlaws, not patri-
ots.

He had agreed with Hu that they should mount
more patrols of the forest and try to drive the rebels
farther into the border lands. Or better yet, to the far
remote areas.

Neither man had any wish to spill Welsh blood, so
they hoped the rebels would see that it would be wiser
for them to leave than to fight when they realized Hu
had little sympathy for their cause.

Hu settled back in his chair. He might as well have
been made of wood for all the part he was taking in the
conversation. Liliana seemed determined to ask in-
numerable questions about her father, his guests, his
household and even his livestock. Derrick answered
every one down to the minutest detail.

Hu stopped listening after a while. The message
from Lord Trevelyan was still tucked inside his belt,
where he had put it when he took Derrick to show him
the sheep. He felt as if it was a coal burning his skin,
and he was desperately trying to figure out how he
could discover its contents without having to ask Liliana. He couldn't ignore any message from Lord
Trevelyan, even if it was not urgent, but he certainly
did not want Liliana to know the extent of his ignorance.

Elwy laughed loudly. He was seated at the far end
of the table, and Hu had a sudden urge to join him,
although he knew that wouldn't be seemly. Not that he

should care, since this was his hall, but Derrick's presence made a difference.

Liliana leaned closer to Hu. He knew she was trying to get nearer to Derrick, who was recounting some kind of story about the Beaumares' latest squabble, but he couldn't help being distracted when her shoulder touched his. Indeed, he felt like that part of his body was on fire.

Apparently, however, such contact meant nothing to Liliana. She was too intent on listening to some old soldier spilling gossip.

Hu tipped back his chair so that she wouldn't touch him. Liliana darted an inscrutable glance his way, but he didn't care what she thought.

He fingered the parchment at his waist and felt the seal give way. He let go and reached for his goblet. Tomorrow he would find out what the message was somehow.

Now he was going to forget about Liliana, her father, Normans and Welshmen and everything else, and enjoy himself.

Elwy laughed again, the sound booming out over the hall. Hu got up, ignoring Liliana's icy look, and went toward his friend, who had pulled Liliana's pretty little maid on his lap. Elwy whispered something in the girl's ear, and she began to giggle.

"Seducing my servants?" Hu asked in Welsh with a grin.

"Who, me, do something like that?" Elwy replied, his hand wandering toward the girl's knee. "Never!" He whispered something else to the girl. Maude giggled again, looking shocked at whatever it was that

Elwy was telling her. With Elwy, it might be almost anything.

Hu smiled at her. She *was* a pretty little thing. And it was obvious that she liked men's company. No doubt *she* would never complain that he smelled like a peasant. She wouldn't push him away and tell him to leave.

She coyly whispered something to Elwy, darted a glance at Hu, then stood up and went out of the room. Hu raised one eyebrow as he looked at Elwy.

Elwy frowned with mock displeasure. "Saving herself, she tells me. Pity is that!"

"Shows she has some sense. Not going to be fooled by your charm," Hu replied.

"Thinking she's after you, boy. No taste, poor thing."

"She's just anxious to please."

Elwy chuckled. "Your wife is looking murder at her."

Hu smiled, but he didn't doubt Liliana would fight any woman who tried to take her husband, even if she didn't particularly like him. He would be *hers*—and that would be enough.

Elwy gave him a shrewd look. "I think that maidservant wouldn't care you were married, though, Hu," he said quietly.

"I would."

Elwy grinned with obvious relief.

Hu laughed. "Give us a song."

When Elwy began to sing, Liliana shot them a look that was cold even for her, but Hu was determined not to worry about Liliana and what she might be thinking. For once.

Nonetheless, Hu sighed when Elwy started to sing a particularly bawdy battle song about saving the women of a town based on their talents in bed. He let his thoughts wander to memories of the various women he had known, and their talents. Then his gaze moved slowly over the women in the hall.

Maude was pretty, but Liliana was beautiful. Maude would surely be accommodating, but she would probably accommodate any man who wooed her. Liliana, now... Liliana had to be won.

He heard Maude giggle again. That maid would no doubt giggle the whole time she was with a man.

Liliana never giggled. In fact, he had only heard her laugh that once, when he wrestled Elwy into the trough.

Baron DeLanyea's wife, Lady Roanna, was a quiet, serious woman who didn't laugh overmuch, but whenever she did laugh, the baron's face seemed to light up with joy, as if she was bestowing a rare gift. Wasn't it Lady Roanna who once said a woman should marry a man who could make her laugh? At the time, he had been rather shocked. He hadn't thought it a very fine idea to marry a woman who would laugh at you.

But now, as he glanced at Liliana, he began to understand what Lady Roanna might have meant. It had pleased him a great deal when Liliana had laughed. She had seemed more relaxed, gentler, somehow.

She always seemed so anxious when they were alone. Perhaps, if he could make her smile, she wouldn't be.

Liliana would never giggle in bed. He looked at her slender back as she reached for an apple from the platter. What *would* she do? Would she moan? Or would she pant? Would she murmur gentle endearments? Tell him how to please her?

He felt a stirring in his loins. God's wounds, he wanted to find out.

At that very moment, Liliana turned to him with an expression of distaste on her lovely face and rose to her feet. "I am going to bed," she announced.

Bed? That was a good jest. He would surely find her sleeping on the feather tick shoved as far into the corner as possible.

She came toward him. "No doubt you'll stay up half the night with your friends. Could you at least be a *little* quiet?"

"I shall do my best not to disturb your slumber," he answered with his most charming smile.

A brief look of confusion crossed her face, which pleased him. She turned toward Derrick. "I bid you good night, Derrick."

"Sleep well, my lady," Derrick replied.

"Good night, my love," Hu said lightly.

Liliana darted him a scathing look as she turned to go. He called out to Elwy to sing something else, then for more wine.

The next morning, Liliana awoke with her head aching again. It was no wonder, since Hu and his cronies, and even Derrick, had talked and laughed and sung—loudly—for most of the night. Didn't they realize they were keeping the rest of the household awake?

She looked across the floor. Hu was not there.

She could see sunlight pouring in through the small window above. It must be late in the morning. Perhaps she had already missed Mass.

Where was Maude? It was bad enough that the girl had made a fool of herself last night, although all the men and even Hu seemed to find her obvious ploys for attention amusing.

Where *was* Hu? She sat up abruptly, the ache in her head replaced by a sick feeling in her stomach. She had seen the way Maude looked at Hu, but she had put it down to the girl's naturally flirtatious nature. Surely she wouldn't dare... Surely he wouldn't, either.

She got to her feet swiftly and tugged the linens into place on the bed. She took no time to smooth them but struggled into her gown, yanking on the laces. She tied them quickly, not caring if they were tight enough or not.

Then she went around the screen.

The hall looked as if a battle had been fought there. The tables were still in place, but men were sleeping on top of them. Linens were on the floor, trampled and dirty. Half-full goblets were scattered everywhere.

Derrick, snoring loudly, sat slumped at the high table, his hand still around a chalice.

Hu was not there, either. Liliana grimly stared at the mess. Then, on the high table next to Derrick's elbow, she saw a parchment and recognized her father's seal.

Cautiously she reached for the message. The seal was already broken! She opened the letter and read the message as quickly as she could.

Aghast, Liliana stared at the parchment.

Then she heard the murmur of voices, one of which she thought was Hu's, coming from the kitchen corridor, followed by a woman's giggle. With a determined stride she went that way.

When she reached the kitchen, Liliana stopped dead. Hu knelt on the floor in front of Maude, his face inches from her breasts. "What is *this?*" Liliana demanded.

Hu blinked groggily. "I hit my head."

Maude stared at her irate mistress, her face growing bright red. "It's true what he says, my lady," she sputtered. "He hit his head. I was washing the blood. See?" She held out a bloody rag.

Liliana came forward, noting that Sarah, her mouth wide open, was watching. "Get to work," she snapped at both women. Maude nodded rapidly and went past her into the hall. Sarah began banging some pots around.

Liliana walked toward Hu, looking intently at his forehead. Yes, there was a cut in his scalp. She could see blood on his hair. "What happened?"

Hu climbed unsteadily to his feet, then sat down heavily on a bench. "I fell."

"That's to be expected when a man gets drunk," Liliana observed coldly. She held up the parchment. "Why didn't you tell me about this?"

He gave her a disgruntled look as he stood up and grabbed hold of her arm. "Outside. No need to let everyone know our business, is there?"

He propelled her into the courtyard. Elwy, snoring as loudly as Derrick, was lying on the ground, unmindful of the risk of breathing in the damp night air. Liliana's nose wrinkled with disgust.

"He likes to sleep outside," Hu said between clenched teeth. "Now, what's the matter this time?"

"Why didn't you tell me?"

Hu glanced at the parchment, trying to think clearly although his head felt as if it had been kicked by a horse. "Suppose *you* tell *me* what's so worrisome?"

"It's barely enough time to get things ready, that's what." She tapped her foot impatiently on the ground.

"What things?"

"The hall, for one. I can't have my father sleeping with the rest of the men. And what about Lord and Lady Beaumare? They'll have to have separate sleeping quarters."

So that was what the message from Lord Trevelyan said. He was coming for a visit, and apparently not alone. But when? "I think a month's plenty of time—"

"If they were coming in a month, I might agree. Obviously you didn't give his message your full attention. They are coming in a fortnight."

Hu stifled a groan. A fortnight—and then his protective father-in-law would arrive, no doubt to see just how his spoiled daughter was being treated by her husband.

"I'll need every man working on that floor," she said determinedly. "And the walls have to be whitewashed, and we'll need more tables and benches, not to mention beds—"

"No." Much as he wanted to impress Lord Trevelyan, there were other more important tasks. "I've promised the men to Sir Nevil. He wants to slaughter his animals this week."

"My father cannot sleep in the hall." Liliana crossed her arms and glared at him. "And furthermore, you and your men cannot stay up half the night singing your outlandish songs, or I'll—"

Hu came so close his nose was inches from hers. "You'll what?"

Suddenly Elwy groaned loudly as he sat up. *"O'r annwyl!* Not had such a fine time since that tournament over near London," he said loudly in Welsh. He belched and scratched himself, then, with a broad grin slashing his homely face, looked at the couple staring at him. "Fine hospitality, Hu. You're a credit to Wales." He lay down again. "Just needing a little more rest, me, then I'll be ready for anything." His eyes closed.

Hu grabbed Liliana by the shoulders and steered her away from his friend. Through clenched teeth he said, "I'm the lord and master here. *I'll* say where my men go and what they do. If you and your father think my hall is not good enough, then you can all sleep in the barn. Or the fields. I don't much care. Now, I've got a manor to run, dear wife. In my own way."

As Liliana watched Hu march away, she surreptitiously blinked back tears. Who did he think he was, talking to her like that? And about her father, who was responsible for him being the lord of this manor!

And just what had he been doing with Maude?

"My lady?" Jhone stood in the doorway of the hall.

"What is it?"

"Am I to be getting the morning meal? There's men—"

"Sleeping everywhere like pigs. I know." Liliana frowned. "I am going to Mass. I want them up and gone by the time I return."

Liliana felt for her veil, then realized she had forgotten it. She turned and marched into the hall to fetch one before she went to the chapel.

As she grabbed the filmy fabric, she vowed that while Hu Morgan may be the lord, she was the lady. She knew her duty. Acceptable accommodations must be provided for her guests, and she would make sure they were, with or without his help.

Chapter Ten

Later that morning Liliana bade farewell to Derrick, giving him a message that said she would be delighted to have a visit from her father and the Beaumares. Then she went looking for Elwy.

Apparently none the worse for drinking or sleeping outside, he was surveying the work on the walls. Hu was, fortunately, nowhere to be seen. She had decided what needed to be done, and she wanted no interference.

"Bailiff, I require some assistance," Liliana said when Elwy turned to her quizzically.

"Your husband's at the mill, my lady," Elwy said respectfully. "Helping put the grindstone in place."

She noted that when he spoke to her there was no sign of the easy familiarity that he had with everyone else about the manor. Naturally she was pleased by that.

"Wanting me to fetch him, maybe?"

"No, thank you. The floor of the hall must be built at once. Send some men to do it."

"Well, my lady, the boys and I got to finish repairing this part of the wall today. Hu's orders, my lady, and—"

"I need the floor finished by Sunday."

Elwy scratched his head. "Apologies, my lady, but we can't help you today."

"You mean you *won't*."

"I mean," Elwy said with a hint of defiance, "we *can't*."

"Oh, very well." Liliana spun around and nearly collided with Jhone.

"What is it?" Liliana demanded as Elwy moved off.

"I can build the floor, my lady," Jhone said quietly.

"What are you talking about?"

"I can build a floor," Jhone insisted. "My father was a carpenter. I used to help him before he died."

"You're not strong enough to carry the planks."

For the first time since Liliana had known her, Jhone smiled broadly. "Yes, I am," she said softly, but her eyes had an undeniably determined gleam. "And I know of someone who can make the planks. There's nothing to lose if you let me try."

Liliana surveyed the young woman, noting the muscles on her upper arms. Maybe she was strong enough. And if her father had been a carpenter, perhaps Jhone did know enough to build the floor. How difficult could such a task be?

Besides, it would be humiliating to have her father and the Beaumares arrive to find the hall in its present state.

"Very well. You may try," Liliana said.

Maude stared at the piles of cloth lying on her mistress's bed.

"What are you doing, my lady?" she asked when Liliana's head emerged from the bottom of a chest, her hands filled with yet more linen.

"I might have known my father would do this," Liliana said triumphantly. "He told me how much linen he was giving me, but I should have guessed I would find nearly twice that."

"There does seem to be quite a bit."

Liliana looked at Maude. "Most of it is plain and unhemmed, however, no doubt because there was only a month to prepare for my wedding. We shall have to work very hard to get it ready."

"Ready for what, my lady?"

"Our visitors."

"Visitors?"

"My father and the Beaumares will be arriving in a fortnight. We must have plenty of linens."

Maude giggled. "Especially for the table, the way Lord Beaumare spills his wine."

Liliana frowned. "Yes. And we'll need tapestries, too, for the upper hall."

"I don't think there's time—"

"Of course there is. Provided we think about our work and not about men."

Maude flushed hotly. "Really, my lady, it was just that he cut himself and I thought it should be washed—"

"Naturally, Maude," Liliana said, sorting out the linen by size. "I know I have an unreasonable temper. I tend to get very angry very quickly. Even violent, sometimes. It's a great flaw I've been trying to correct without much success, I'm afraid."

Maude shifted uncomfortably.

"Here, take this cloth for the table and start hemming. We *must* be ready in time."

"Yes, my lady," Maude said meekly, silently vowing to stay as far away as possible from her lady's husband.

"Damned stone!" Hu cursed loudly as he tried to push the grindstone into its proper space. Around him, others muttered oaths in Welsh, Saxon and Norman while they, too, helped to move the heavy grindstone.

"Got it!" Jack, the miller, cried from his perch in the rafters above when the stone fit into place. "It's in!"

"God's teeth, about time, too," Hu mumbled. He picked up his old, torn tunic and wiped the sweat from his brow and naked chest. Although the day was cool, all the men inside the mill had stripped off their tunics while they worked to repair the machinery and then move the grindstone back into place.

"We'll have it going in no time now," the miller said, a beaming smile on his face. "Thank you all."

"Just better not hear of any cheating," Hu said with a frown.

The miller looked shocked. "That's a base lie," he protested, aghast, until he saw Hu grin.

"All deserving some ale, I think," Hu said as he pulled on his tunic. "Come, you, to the hall."

The men smiled their thanks and followed him to the manor. Hu noticed with pleasure that the repairs on the outer wall were coming along well, due to Elwy's competent supervision. He wondered where the reeve was, but there were women and children in the orchard picking the apples, so Ralf must be there.

He shouted a greeting to Elwy and the masons and mortar makers as he entered the gate, then saw a huge pile of logs near the door to the hall. "What's all this?" he called to Elwy.

Elwy hurried over. "None of my doing. Your lady sent that ugly serving wench to the village this morning. I thought she was going to the market, but this afternoon a wagon come with all this. The driver was an old fellow I never seen before. When I asked him what he was doing, he said Jhone told him the lady of the manor needed planks. She said he could cut the trees from the forest if he would make the planks. Look you, here he comes now."

They both watched in disbelief as a mumbling, wizened little man, who looked as if a gust of wind would blow him away, lifted a large log from his wagon and tossed it to the ground. He jumped nimbly down, then proceeded to drag it a short distance away. Scattered about the ground were wedges and a hammer, and it was obvious he was in the process of splitting logs for planking.

"Get me Ralf," Hu ordered.

Elwy nodded and hurried off. Hu watched the old man work for a while, marveling at the competent way the fellow handled his tools and trying to make out what it was he was saying, until Ralf ran up to him.

"I'm sorry, my lord. No one told me—"

"Where have you been?"

"In the village, and the orchard, of course," Ralf gasped as he tried to catch his breath. His eyes narrowed when he saw the old man. "What's Wynn doing here?"

"I would like to know why he wasn't working here before," Hu demanded. "I've never seen a man split logs so straight. Why isn't this fellow working on the mill, or the scaffolding, or the barn?"

"Well, my lord, he's gone childish, as you can see, so I thought—"

"He's doing as good a job as any carpenter I've ever seen."

"Where should I put him to work?" Ralf asked meekly.

"Let him keep on doing what he's doing," Hu answered, his tone not noticeably warmer, "until I tell you otherwise."

"Very well, if that is what you want."

"I do."

"Any other orders, my lord?"

"You can tell the villagers the mill should be working after tomorrow. The fee stays the same."

"The same? But my lord, all the extra expense of repairing it—"

"I said the fee will be the same."

Ralf nodded as Hu marched toward the hall.

If Hu noticed the scaffolding that Jhone had worked all day to build, he said nothing about it to Liliana. Nor did he mention the work being done on the inside of the hall.

Not that day, or the day after, or the day after that. It was as if he was blind to what was going on around him.

Liliana tried to convince herself that she was pleased he didn't trouble her about anything else, either, but she realized she watched him whenever he was near, particularly if he talked to a woman. Once or twice he caught her gaze, and to her dismay she always felt embarrassed—as if she was the one who might be taking a lover.

She was also inordinately short-tempered and anxious, but that had to be because of her father's imminent arrival as much as her husband's activities.

Unfortunately, her anxiety only seemed to make people avoid her. Not that it mattered. What mattered was that no one find fault with the hall.

On the fourth day, Liliana went outside to find out if Wynn needed to fetch more logs for the floor. She saw Hu's horse, saddled and ready, standing in the courtyard. There was a small group of men, also mounted, gathered near the gate.

She wondered where he was going and if anybody was going to tell her.

"Fox hunting, we are," Hu said casually from behind her.

Startled, she turned around. His dark curls ruffled in the slight breeze, and his cheeks were ruddy from the chill autumn air.

"Gareth thinks there's too many up in the hills."

The breeze blew a strand of her hair that had escaped from beneath her veil and chin band. He reached out and tucked it inside, his fingers gently touching her cheek. "You're shivering."

"I am cold," she lied as the blood rushed hotly through her veins. "When will you return?"

"Late." He pulled her cloak around her, his lips curving into a devastating smile. "Better?"

"Yes," she whispered. She wondered if he was going to say anything more or come any closer. But he didn't. He joined his men, mounted his horse and headed for the gate.

With a sigh, she went inside the hall. Was there any other man in all the country who could make a maiden blush and tremble simply by tucking in a strand of hair?

She must not think about such things. She should confine her thoughts to more practical matters, such as food. If Hu and the men were going to be gone all day, there would be no need to prepare so much food for the meals. She had best tell Sarah.

She should also insure that Osyth and Dena learned how to cut the bread better. She had chided them that morning, for the slices had been thicker than planks.

She paused outside the kitchen and took a deep breath to restore her usual dignified calm. She was still trembling like a leaf, though, and try as she might to deny it, she knew the cold draft in the passage had nothing to do with it.

"Is this better?" she heard Dena say inside the kitchen. "I don't want her to be cross again."

Liliana waited in the shadow of the door.

"Better," Sarah said approvingly. "Well, I suppose she doesn't want to waste anything."

"If I was as rich as she was, I would eat a whole loaf at every meal," Dena replied.

"And you'd soon be so fat, no man would look at you twice," Osyth chided from somewhere farther inside.

"I don't care about that," Dena snapped, showing a flash of temper that Liliana had never suspected she possessed.

"Not yet, but when you're older, you will."

"You're only a year older than me."

"But twice as wise."

Sarah's delighted cackle interrupted them. "Listen to you two! Osyth, you've got time yet to worry about the men. Best make sure you turn that meat properly."

"I don't see why we can't have a boy to do this."

"Because," Sarah answered patiently, "his lordship has all the boys working on the buildings."

"Isn't he handsome?" Dena said with a sigh.

Liliana frowned darkly and leaned a little closer to the door.

"I know I'd swoon if he ever looked at me twice," Dena remarked.

"He has," Osyth said dryly.

"You know what I mean—the way he looks at his wife sometimes."

Liliana moved even closer.

Osyth emitted a throaty chuckle. "If I was her, I'd never be letting him out of bed."

"Watch that meat!" Sarah admonished.

"Maude spends as much time away from them both as she can now," Dena observed more quietly. "I don't know what happened, but I think Maude's afraid of her."

"Maybe she thought Maude was making eyes at her husband," Sarah said.

Osyth sniffed derisively. "Even I can tell that Maude would make eyes at any man that moved. She doesn't mean any harm by it. Besides, we all know whose breeches Maude really wants to climb into."

The girls and Sarah shared a laugh. Outside, Liliana sighed with relief, and something more—a sudden burst of happiness that Hu apparently looked at her with... But that didn't matter, she reminded herself.

Besides, it wasn't proper for her to listen to gossip, even if she did feel relieved that Maude had every intention of staying away from Hu.

Nor was she envious. She couldn't be envious of serving wenches. Could she? She was used to maintaining her own counsel, to having no one she could chat companionably with. There was Lady Eleanor, but Lady Eleanor was more like a mother than a friend.

"I said watch that meat!" Sarah said sharply. "She'll be cross again."

"She's always cross," Osyth grumbled. "We're doing all the work, and all she does is give orders like a queen."

"Well, she *is* the lady," Dena said quietly. "I suppose all ladies are useless like that."

"Look at all Jhone's doing, with never a thank-you."

"It would be nice if she was a little more like her husband. The men can't say enough good things about him."

"Because he doesn't just sit in a chair and give orders," Sarah said. "Look how he helped at the mill."

"Almost finished with that?" Osyth asked. "No doubt she's got a lot more for us to do, while she sits by the fire and sews. Do you know, I've just realized what she's like."

"What?" Sarah asked.

"A boar with teats—foul-tempered and useless!"

There was a gasp from Sarah and a shocked giggle from Dena that ended in a choking sound when Liliana marched into the kitchen.

"Sarah," Liliana said calmly, not looking at the two young girls, "my husband and some of his men will be away for the day. Remember that when you are preparing the meals."

Then she turned a cold gaze on the two young girls. "I trust you have improved in your tasks, that you can spend so much time in idle gossip."

With that, she turned and went to the hall.

The moon had risen and was high in the sky when Hu and the others returned from their successful hunt.

Gareth had been right, for they had killed several young foxes that would have destroyed many of their valuable sheep. Afterward they had shared celebratory ale up in the hills with Gareth, and then ridden home.

Hu was tired and ready to sleep, although the prospect of sleeping on a hard stone floor, with the most beautiful wife a man could imagine sleeping on a soft feather tick not two yards away, seemed the height of absurdity.

For the past few days he had been sorely tempted to try to reconcile the differences between Liliana and himself. Many times he, Hu ap Morgan ap Ianto, had come perilously close not only to apologizing, but to begging for Liliana's forgiveness.

Which was rank foolishness. She was the haughty and proud one, always making demands.

Unfortunately, he still desired her so much he could only sleep when he had worked himself to exhaustion. He knew she wasn't as happy in her self-imposed prison of rank and manners as she pretended, but he had no idea how to proceed. Rather than make a fool of himself, he had tried to maintain a respectful distance until he felt confident enough of her feelings to try wooing her as if she were merely a lovely, lonely woman instead of his wife.

The men bade him good-night and went to their quarters in a barracks that was finally completed. They had been sharing close quarters until the roof was thatched.

Hu headed for the hall, wondering what he would find this time. Every time he entered it, he marveled at what Jhone had accomplished. She was a better worker than most carpenters, and he knew Baron DeLanyea's workmen were more impressed than they cared to admit. The other two young girls, whose names he could never remember, seemed to be doing a fine job with the everyday tasks of washing the tables and helping prepare the food. He saw very little of Maude, but he knew from Elwy and the others that she was sewing on linens nearly every minute.

His brow furrowed. Maude, who had been rather too friendly, now ran from him like a startled deer. Either she had clearly understood that he had no interest in her and was ashamed, or Liliana had scolded her for washing her husband's head.

He smiled. He hoped that was the case, for it meant that Liliana was jealous. Jealousy was always a fine quality in a woman.

He pushed open the heavy door and looked around. The floor was nearly half finished. Liliana was right. The upper walls would look better with some whitewash. Perhaps he could spare one or two men to help complete the work.

As his eyes adjusted to the dimness, he made out a shape kneeling at the edge of the completed area and heard the sound of a hammer tapping. He peered at the person working in the moonlight. It was obviously a woman, from the long hair and plain gown, but he didn't think it was Jhone, who knew how to wield a hammer. This woman did not.

The hammer rose and fell, and a most unladylike curse reached his ears—in a voice he recognized immediately.

Liliana! Liliana was kneeling on the floor, hammering nails. He wouldn't have believed it if he wasn't seeing it for himself. He grinned and leaned against the wall, hiding in the shadows. Was she really that desperate for the hall to be completed?

Perhaps he could spare three or four workmen.

The hammer rose and fell again, and this time Liliana gasped and grabbed her thumb.

Hu rushed toward her. "What did you do?"

She looked at him, horrified, as he knelt beside her. "What are you doing back so soon?" she demanded.

"Soon? It's after midnight. Let me see your thumb."

She moved away. "It's nothing. I missed, that's all."

"Let me see it."

Reluctantly Liliana held out her hand, and he took her slender palm in his. "It's not swelling, so I don't think it's broken," he said.

"I knew that."

He sat beside her on the floor. "Why are you doing this?" He gestured at the planks.

She shrugged and seemed to be trying to hide behind the veil of her unbound hair. "It has to be done."

"But not by you."

She shrugged again and didn't look at him.

"Liliana, what's the matter?"

"Nothing. My thumb hurts, that's all."

He moved closer. "No, that isn't all."

"Yes, it is."

"No, it isn't."

Liliana bit her oh-so-kissable lip. "I can't get them in straight," she said reluctantly, gesturing at the plank.

Hu looked at the nails sticking crookedly out of the wood. It looked as if a blind man had tried his hand at carpentry.

Liliana waited for Hu to laugh at her. She knew she—and her botched attempts—must look completely ridiculous.

She should have realized how late it was and gotten to bed, if not to sleep, before Hu returned.

She should have paid no heed to the maids' gossip, for surely she had been doing everything a lady could reasonably be expected to do, and just because those girls had no notion of a proper lady's duties . . .

Hu picked up the hammer and an iron nail. "You're not holding the hammer right," he said quietly, with no hint of teasing, or worse, patronizing her. "Hold it more at the bottom, and let the weight of the head do all the work. See?'' He proceeded to demonstrate, making it look very easy to hit the nail and drive it in straight and true.

''Is there anything you *can't* do?'' she asked, trying to sound nonchalant.

''Ask Elwy. He'll tell you plenty.''

She might have known he would make jokes. He never took anything seriously, except when she needed something. Then he was very serious indeed, as if she was asking him to cut off one of his limbs.

Nothing was going right in her life. Not one thing. Her marriage was a mockery, her hall a ruin, and the servants hated her. She turned away, took a deep breath and blinked her eyes rapidly, but it didn't work. Her shoulders began to shake as a sob escaped her throat.

''Liliana, what is it?'' he asked gently. ''What's the matter?''

''Go away,'' she sobbed, wiping at her cheeks. ''Just go away.''

''I'm not going anywhere until you tell me what's wrong.''

It would have been easier to ignore him if he was arrogant or rude. But there was such genuine concern in his voice that she could not control her tears.

He put his hands on her shoulders and turned her gently toward him, pulling her close.

For a moment she simply enjoyed the feeling of his strong arms around her, her cheek against his shoulder.

For a while he said nothing, just began to stroke her back. When her sobs quieted, he spoke softly. "What is it? Please, tell me."

The instinct to hide the vulnerability that had kept her isolated for so long urged her to move away, to say nothing, to ignore his concern. But her heart told her she might lose a chance for true happiness if she did.

"Nothing I do is right," she whispered against his strong shoulder.

"That's not true," he answered, stroking her hair. "You've got everyone working well here."

She pulled away from the comfort of his arms. "Oh, yes, I can give orders well enough, but..."

"But what?" he prompted softly.

She shrugged her shoulders and looked at the floor. "Nobody likes me," she confessed.

Hu sat back on his heels. It had never occurred to him that Liliana might care what other people thought of her. She always seemed so self-reliant.

At the same time he recognized and appreciated that she was confiding in him. Here, now, something had changed between them, and he was vastly pleased.

"Nobody hates you," he said hopefully.

"Nobody likes me, either."

He heard the overwhelming sadness in her voice and reached out to pull her close again. "*I* like you."

She gave him a look that was half skeptical and half hopeful, but made no attempt to pull away.

"I've always liked you," he said truthfully. "I've liked you for years."

"Years? What are you talking about? We didn't meet until my father's tournament two months ago."

"Not properly introduced till then, I grant you. But I knew you nonetheless."

He felt some of the tension leave her body as she nestled against him. A tender warmth suffused him while they sat thus in the moonlight.

"It was years ago," he began, settling himself to tell the story, "when Lord Gervais had a tournament. I was a squire and you were, I believe, about ten years old. It was the day of the squire's tournament. I had picked out my prey, a big fellow who looked plenty rich for fine ransom, but he wasn't such an easy person to defeat as I had thought. He gave me quite a struggle, and I was getting winded. Then I saw something move in a tree nearby. It was a girl."

Liliana gasped slightly, but he kept on talking. "Everybody knew women and girls were not supposed to watch, but a girl had climbed up a tree and there she was, watching me. Imagine, this girl who would defy a man like Lord Trevelyan! This beautiful creature in a blue gown with such golden hair like I had never seen.

"The other squire knocked me down. But I knew the girl with the golden hair was there, so I got up and fought back to impress her. I thought I must have, because when I defeated the squire, I looked at her. Some proud I was, I confess. Then she winked at me. Not a coy little smile, such as another girl might make. But a wink—like a companion who really understands things. Well, I liked her for that. I still do," he finished in a soft voice.

Liliana smiled at him with charming shyness. "Why didn't you tell me? I didn't know who that boy was— you had your helmet on. And I wasn't allowed at the feast, or any of the meals with the visiting knights. My father thought their ways too rough."

"So that's why you don't remember Baron De-Lanyea. He's the kind of man you don't forget."

"Why didn't you mention this when you met me at my father's?"

He grinned ruefully. "Too shy."

"You?"

"Me."

"But you always seem so... so sure of yourself."

"Just like you, eh?"

She looked at him with some surprise. "Yes," she replied thoughtfully, "just like me." After a moment, she said wryly, "You're very good at making people think you are anything but shy."

"Takes practice, that's all."

"I see. So there are some things you are *not* good at?"

He frowned, and for an instant she feared she had angered him. But then he smiled with delightful sheepishness. "Shame it is for a Welshman to confess, but I have no voice for singing."

"Really?"

"No need to sound so happy. It's a serious failing, I assure you."

She eyed him skeptically. "Your friends don't seem to hold it against you."

"That's true."

"At least you *have* friends," she added wistfully.

Hu held her a little tighter. "I would be your friend, Liliana," he said softly.

Her breath caught in her throat as he kissed her gently. It was a kiss not of passion, but of soft warmth and understanding.

She looked at him in the pale moonlight, feeling closer to him in her heart than she ever had to another person. "Hu, I don't know how to make friends."

"Perhaps if you would let them see that you are not sure of yourself. Let Jhone teach you to help her. Admit that you don't know everything."

"Is that what you do?"

Hu hesitated for a moment. "I try."

"It doesn't seem quite right..."

"It will. Trust me."

Liliana nodded. "I will try." Her voice dropped to a whisper. "Hu, I'm glad you saw me that day."

"Not half so glad as I am." He kissed her, this time with some of the passion she aroused in him.

To his delight and excitement, he felt her return that passion, her lips moving slowly against his, her hands gripping him tightly.

He stood up and pulled her into his embrace, kissing her with all the desire he had been trying to suppress.

The feel of his hard, strong body against hers and his tongue gently pushing against her mouth filled her with need and a craving so strong she could not deny it. Instinctively she opened her eyes, half frightened by the intensity of her own response—and then the yearning in Hu's black eyes.

He was her husband, she his wife. She wanted him now, in every way—and she would fight her needs and desires no more.

"Are you afraid of me, Liliana?" he asked softly, his lips traveling slowly down her cheek to her neck.

"Yes. No. I don't know." With a low moan, she arched against him and let herself enjoy the sensations of his body and hers, his lips against her flesh.

He pulled back. "I don't want you to be afraid of me."

She looked at the floor and took a deep breath. "It's only that I don't..."

"Don't what?"

"I don't know about..."

"About?"

Liliana took another deep breath and tried to smile, but she felt that it was time to admit her ignorance. "I don't know anything about what happens when a man and a woman..."

"What?"

"In bed, when they're together."

"God's wounds!" Hu exclaimed. "Is that why—" He started to chuckle.

Liliana pushed him away. "You see why I don't want people to know of my ignorance! They'll laugh—just like you are now! I wish I had never said anything!"

"I'm sorry," he said, putting his arms around her. "I'm happy, that's all. I thought you were angry with me!"

"Well, I *was*. You were so rough and mean."

"I humbly apologize. If I had known that you were completely...unenlightened, I would have acted differently. And then, you *did* tell me I stank."

"You did—but I'm sorry I said so."

Hu smiled. "So I admit my faults and ask for forgiveness."

"Accepted. And I likewise."

"Accepted with delight." Hu drew her close and she lifted her face for his kiss, but instead he picked her up in his arms. "I am ready, dearest wife, to teach you everything I know—or at least as much as I can in one night."

Chapter Eleven

"Hu?" Liliana asked in a small voice. She looked at him uncertainly while he carried her down the scaffold leading to their hall and their bed.

"Yes?"

"Promise me you won't laugh."

"Not before," he said lightly, "and not during. I make no promises for after. Not a serious event, you know."

"Now you're teasing me."

"Liliana," he said as he went around the screen, "I confess, I am. It's just my way. You'll have to get used to it, I'm afraid."

She didn't answer as he set her down, his strong hands lingering on her arms.

"There's nothing to fear. Truly."

"I...I can't help it. Lady Eleanor said..."

He gazed at her, his face concerned and serious. "What did Lady Eleanor say?"

"Something might hurt."

He frowned. "So that's what you and Lady Eleanor were discussing?"

Liliana bit her lip. "Not really," she said truthfully. "She said I should ask you about it."

Hu smiled. "Glad I am for that."

He drew her into his embrace and kissed her gently.

It was as if she had never been touched before. All her senses reeled with the taste of his lips on hers, the scent of his skin, the texture of his hard muscles. She wanted to feel more of him. Moaning softly, she pressed her body hungrily against his.

When she moved against him, it was all he could do to keep from ripping the clothes from her willing body.

He wanted to go slowly with her, to be gentle and tender as he had been with other virgins. As he fought to control his burning desire, his kiss deepened and his arms tightened around her.

She was his, here in his arms. Her green eyes shone with passionate desire. Her body molded itself to his, her hips moving instinctively and so seductively.

He lost the battle.

In his eagerness, his hands tore at the lacings of her gown until at last he could feel the silky flesh of her naked back beneath his palms. Then he realized she was trembling.

With great effort and once more fighting to control his hunger, he stepped away. He cleared his throat. "The Welsh have a custom. *Caru yn y gwely,*" he said softly.

She gave him a look that was at once quizzical and shy.

"It means 'courting on the bed.'"

"Oh?"

"Yes. So we should, uh, get in the bed."

"Without our clothes?"

He cleared his throat and nodded as he turned away. God's teeth, who was the one acting like they didn't have the first notion what was going on? He hadn't been this tentative even his first time, with Efa in the barn. Of course, Efa was somewhat famous for her willingness, and he had been anything but shy.

He rid himself of his garments quickly, and without looking at Liliana got into the bed. Only then did he glance at his wife—at the moment her shift fell to the floor and she stepped free, as naked as Eve in Paradise. His breath caught in his throat. Hu ap Morgan ap Ianto was completely, utterly overwhelmed. "You are the most beautiful woman in the world," he whispered, tearing his gaze from her perfect figure and the half shy, half wanton expression in her eyes. "I do not deserve you."

Liliana smiled as she got into the bed. "I have never wanted any other man in my whole life," she whispered. It was the complete truth. And she was ready now to let Hu know it, too.

He returned her smile. "I am so happy, Liliana. And so proud."

This time it was Liliana who bent to press a fervent kiss on his lips, Liliana who moved her mouth upon his, desire flaring in her throbbing veins.

It had been a very long time since she had felt free to do as she pleased, but here, now, she felt primitive and intoxicating freedom as he caressed her. Desire and passion tore through her body, and she sought to return the pleasure he was giving her with his lips and his touch.

When his hand cupped her breast, she gasped with surprise, then moaned softly as his lips took the place of his hand, creating such unexpected bliss that she could scarcely breathe.

She barely noticed another part of his body, hard and hot against her stomach, when his knee moved gently between her legs.

"Liliana," Hu whispered, his lips against her ear. "Liliana, I'm going to touch you—"

"Oh, please, yes!" Her hands roved over his back and his chest. She lifted herself to press a kiss to his chest.

She gasped when she felt his fingers moving below her navel.

"Don't be afraid, Liliana, my dearest," he muttered as his lips trailed down her neck to capture her nipple. His tongue teased the peak, making her writhe with pleasure.

"What...what are you doing?" she gasped as his fingers continued their exploration.

"Making you ready for me."

She didn't understand. But she didn't care. She trusted him, and what he was doing felt so very, very good...

His mouth found hers. This time she opened her lips willingly and let her tongue join with his, moving slowly and sinuously. His fingers continued to stroke her and an unbearable, wonderful tension began to build inside her.

He pulled away for a moment, raising himself—and in the next instant she felt him enter her. *There!* Her eyes flew open at a brief, sharp pain.

Hu, his hips undulating slowly, kissed her gently. "That is the pain. Does it still hurt?"

"No," she murmured truthfully as his movements increased in speed—and in pleasure. Her hands reached for him, pulling him closer. She needed to feel his whole body pressed against hers, to have even more of him.

His movements quickened, sweeping her along in a wave of pleasure and desire. Sensation built upon sensation, until her body felt as taut as a bowstring.

Then Hu groaned, and release flooded through her, too.

After a long, blissful moment of stillness, he moved off her and lay beside her, smiling. "Thinking it was worth the wait," he said softly, reaching out to touch her hair.

"Oh?" Liliana blinked, and tried to think clearly. Not that it mattered. She didn't care if she never thought coherently again, as long as they could do this together.

"Not in pain, are you?" he asked solicitously.

"Oh, no." Liliana turned toward him and winced. "Well, perhaps a little."

Hu frowned.

Liliana smiled and reached out to brush a curl into place. "It's all right."

He kissed her. "And it's only the first time anyway."

"Really? How wonderful."

"*You're* wonderful."

"No, you are."

"Very well. We're both wonderful—and so is making love."

"Hu?"

"What?"

"How often can we do this?"

He began to chuckle. "As often as we like."

"At night?"

He gave her a devilish grin. "Any time."

She looked shocked. Then she grinned just as devilishly.

He gathered her into his arms. "I am the happiest, luckiest man in the world!"

She sighed contentedly. "I was so afraid you had married me only for my father's land and money."

"I did."

Glaring at him, she wrenched herself away. "What?"

He smiled warmly. "Your father offered me the land and the money—and then you. I didn't think I could refuse any of it."

"You're teasing me, aren't you?"

Hu nodded. "You're learning, my dearest wife. I would have married that bold girl in the tree if she had been as poor as a pauper."

"What if I was as ugly as . . . as a leper?"

"Definitely not," he answered solemnly.

"I *hope* you're teasing me."

"Well, not a fair question, was it? You're not ugly and you know it." He kissed the tip of her nose. "You're as lovely as an angel." He gave her a sidelong glance. "Would you have married me if *I* was as ugly as a leper?"

"No, I don't believe I would."

"That makes us even—and honest. I think you only married me for my looks, anyway."

"To be honest, partly."

He rolled over on his back and looked at the beams above them. "Liliana?"

"Yes?"

"Why *did* you marry me?"

"I told you, because you're handsome." She tried to laugh, but was all too aware of his naked body beside her. She began to caress him. "Now it's very late, my lord, and we both should get some rest."

He took hold of her hand and gazed steadily into her eyes. "Liliana, why did you marry me?"

Liliana saw his need to know the truth. "I think I've been in love with you since the day you got your head stuck in your helmet," she answered sincerely. She lay beside him and snuggled against his hard, warm chest. "I've known many handsome men, and bold fighters like you, but when you couldn't get your helmet off, I heard you laughing about it to your friend. You were so jovial—not arrogant like most of the men I had ever met. I followed you to the smith's. I couldn't resist going closer, and I knew you were only pretending not to hear me. Well, that was so...sweet, I suppose I couldn't help loving you."

"Liliana..." Hu drew her to him and kissed her softly, the knowledge that she truly cared for him tempering his desire with gentleness. Her arms went around him, and this time she pulled *him* closer.

She had to smile. "I do have a temper, I know. And sometimes I sound angry when I'm..."

"What?"

"Frightened. Like the day that outlaw stopped us. I was afraid, but you wouldn't talk to me."

"There was nothing to say."

"Who *was* he?"

"A Welshman who thinks the Normans don't belong here. He knows now that I've sworn my allegiance to Lord Trevelyan."

She looked at him steadily. "Don't you think you should be sure they've gone away, Hu? He has so many men—"

"Boys, mostly, with poor weapons. He seemed an intelligent fellow. I'm sure he's realized it would be hopeless to attack us here."

"But the walls—"

"Will be finished soon." He kissed the tip of her nose. "You worry too much about your lord's concerns. I just want you to think about this—" he kissed her lips softly "—and this—" he caressed her breasts "—and making babies..."

She wanted to protest that his concerns were hers, too, but his actions distracted her and were infinitely more pleasant than discussing thieves and troublemakers.

"Hu?"

He struggled to open his eyes. "Is it morning already? It can't be."

Liliana laughed softly and kissed his cheek. "It *is* morning, and if we don't hurry, we'll miss Mass."

Hu closed his eyes and pulled her close. "So we miss it," he muttered before kissing her.

She pulled away. "That wouldn't be right," she chided gently. "Besides, I think a prayer of thanks would be in order."

"Oh?"

"Oh, yes..."

It was a few minutes later when Liliana finally and reluctantly extricated herself from Hu's embrace and their bed. She put on her shift and reached for a gown. "We must go. People will talk."

"Let them. I don't care."

"*I* do." She drew on a plain green garment that Hu hated at once. Now that he had seen Liliana naked, he hated any garment she wore.

"I know." Hu threw back the coverings, exposing his entire body to Liliana's lustful gaze. When he saw her face, he quickly covered his lower body. "*O'r annwyl*, I have created a wanton wench!"

She sauntered close to him, cupping his face in her soft palms. "Don't you like it when I look at you like that?"

Hu groaned and glanced down at the sheets, which did nothing to hide his arousal. "God, woman, how am I supposed to go to Mass *now?*"

"We have some time yet."

"Huh!" He got to his feet and went to a basin, where he splashed cold water over his face. He shook himself like a dog, which made his hair curl even more. "That's better," he mumbled.

"Yes, it is. After all, Maude will be here any moment, and I certainly don't want her to see you like that."

"She'd run to the hills anyway." He pulled on the breeches he had so hastily discarded last night. "She barely looks at me these days."

"Oh?" Liliana asked innocently.

"What did you say to her?"

"I only told her that I had a terrible temper."

"That's all?"

"Well, perhaps I said a violent temper. I suppose she might have taken it to mean I might do her harm if she paid too much attention to my husband."

"I knew it!"

"Such arrogance!"

Hu tugged on a tunic. Out of deference to Liliana's notions of propriety, he chose one of his better ones. "I am not arrogant."

"You are, too."

"I am not."

"Then tell me, my humble husband, something else that you *cannot* do."

"What do you mean?"

"Last night you said there were lots of things you couldn't do, like singing. Tell me something else you are not good at."

He regarded her thoughtfully. "My manners aren't good."

Liliana sat on the bed. "I knew that already."

Hu scowled.

"Ah! You see!" Liliana cried triumphantly. "You expect me to confess my ignorance to all and sundry, but you spare yourself."

"Very well." He looked at her, his face suddenly serious.

She wondered what he had to say that would make that troubled look appear.

"I cannot read."

She rose quickly and took his hand in hers, lifting it gently to her lips to kiss it. She knew his confession signaled a new trust in her, and happiness filled her heart. "I would never have suspected it." She smiled. "I will teach you, if you like."

"No," he said, shaking his head ruefully. "I'm too old for that."

"I can teach you to read and write, and you can teach me Welsh."

He grinned. "Interesting idea, that. But teaching me to read will be as difficult as teaching Welsh. Given our tempers, the lessons might not last for long."

Liliana returned his rueful grin. "That's probably true."

"We'll have to wait until the work on the manor is completed."

"That might be years."

"I know."

"You're terrible!"

"Are you so keen, then, to learn Welsh?"

"Yes, I am."

"After your father's visit, perhaps." He glanced up at the floor beams. "Speaking of that, I'll have Elwy send some men to finish."

"No, you won't."

Hu saw the stubborn look on Liliana's face. "Why not?"

"Jhone and I will finish it." She came toward him and put her arms around his waist. "But I would accept some help with the whitewashing and paneling."

"I knew this was going to happen," Hu said sadly as he encircled her with his arms.

"What? My father's visit?"

"No. I knew you would be able to make me do whatever you wanted."

"You have been able to resist me quite well so far," she noted dryly.

"So far. But—" his hands began to wander over her body "—that was before we were truly husband and wife."

"I shall have to remember my power, my lord," Liliana said gravely as his hand slipped into her gown at the back. "Hu?"

"Um?" His hand crept slowly toward her breasts.

She pressed her arms down, effectively halting his progress. "Hu, that...other night. Our first night here..."

"I remember it well." He kissed the lobe of her ear.

"You said you made a vow. About women. What was it?"

Hu drew back and she saw a frown crease his brow. "It doesn't matter now," he said.

"But I want to know," Liliana said, hoping he wasn't going to shut her out again.

He shrugged and pulled his hands from inside her gown.

"It was after that tournament where I first saw you," he said, gazing at her steadily. "Another squire and I got drunk. There was a girl, younger than us, with yellow hair. We..." He paused and took a deep breath. "You really want to know about this?"

"I really want to know."

"We weren't trying to hurt her or frighten her, but we were too drunk to think clearly. She didn't seem very friendly, we thought. All we wanted to do was kiss her. I mean that, Liliana."

"I believe you."

"Urien Fitzroy found us and he was some angry. You know Fitzroy, the fellow who trained Lord Gervais's squires."

"I've met him. I would not like to have Fitzroy angry with me. What did he do to you?"

"He hit us and shoved our heads in a water trough. Then he made us promise never to do anything like that again. And I haven't. Nor would I."

"So you wouldn't have forced me?"

He shook his head. "No, Liliana." He smiled slightly. "No matter how angry you made me."

"Or how I hurt you with my harsh words?"

"No matter what."

Liliana took his hands in hers and gazed into his deep, dark eyes.

At that moment they heard a familiar giggle.

"God's blood!" Hu muttered, dismayed at the interruption. He saw Liliana's equally disappointed expression as he went toward the screen, he said, "Ah, Maude," he said, "What a pleasure to see you on this beautiful morning!"

"It's raining, my lord," came Maude's surprised and subdued reply.

Liliana quickly covered her mouth to stifle her giggles. If this kept up, one day she might be tittering as much as her maid.

But she suddenly realized she was too happy to care.

A week later, Lady Eleanor sat happily beside her husband at their feast celebrating the end of the autumn butchering. The hall was filled with tenants and neighbors. Of all those present, Lady Eleanor's gaze strayed most often to the young couple on her left.

She nudged her husband gently. "It seems," she whispered when he turned to her, "that Hu and Liliana are getting along these days."

"Eh? What? Of course they are. Why shouldn't they?" Nevil asked.

Lady Eleanor smiled. Her husband could never be praised for his discernment, but it was obvious to *her* that whatever difficulties the Morgans had been having, they were in the past. Indeed, Hu could hardly stop looking at his lovely wife, and she smiled at him so much, Lady Eleanor didn't think the young woman had touched any of the food in front of her at all.

"Sir Nevil!" Hu called out. "Next week, you and your wife must come for *nos galan gaeaf!* We'll show you how the Welsh hold a feast!"

"My pleasure, my pleasure," Nevil, who never refused an invitation to a feast, replied.

Lady Eleanor nodded her approval, then surveyed her assembled guests. Things were going so well these days, with those outlaws seemingly gone and Hu and Liliana so clearly in love....

Her gaze focused on Priscilla Horton, at the far end of the high table. The grim woman gobbled her food as if she was a starving mongrel tossed a shank of roasted meat.

Poor thing, Lady Eleanor thought with sympathy. She might very well be starving. Her bones showed clearly beneath her old, worn gown.

"My dear," she said quietly to Nevil, nodding toward Priscilla when she got his attention, "perhaps we could try to help Priscilla Horton."

"She won't take money," he reminded her.

"I know. I was thinking of something else. Maybe we could find a husband—"

"For that carrion crow?"

"The girl can't help how she looks."

"She's no girl. Hasn't been for years."

"Well, you know what I mean. Perhaps there's some fellow among our acquaintance in need of a wife."

"Nobody's that needy."

"Nevil! Be kind! I think she's miserably unhappy. Her father's a drunken miser—" she glanced at the man who had already passed out from too much wine "—so it's no wonder she's the way she is. A husband might make all the difference in the world."

"Or a miracle."

"Nevil, I'm serious."

"So am I. But I'll keep my eyes open for some poor fellow who desperately needs an ugly harpy for a wife."

"She *is* a noblewoman."

"Pity that's the only thing in her favor."

"At least it's something. Perhaps that friend of Hu's..."

"Elwy? He's got his eye on some widow, I hear, just rode into their town." He raised his voice and turned to the other end of the table. "Isn't that right, Elwy?"

"What's that, Sir Nevil?" Elwy replied, looking up from the platter of meat before him.

"Aren't you interested in that widow?"

"Yes, but she's not very clever," he said mournfully.

"Oh?"

"No. Not taking any notice of me, is she."

The guests laughed at Elwy's comically sorrowful expression.

Except for Priscilla Horton. She had seen the pitying looks Lady Eleanor cast her way. She had also noticed the sickening display of affection the Morgans were putting on for the benefit of everyone in the hall.

It was disgusting, the way they looked at each other as if they could scarcely wait to get into bed. They were even holding hands under the table like besotted children.

Liliana Trevelyan had always been as vain as it was possible to be, with her fine blond hair and lovely clothes.

Priscilla glanced with envy at Liliana's beautiful dress of fine silk damask, and the silky veil that floated about her shoulders. Even the woman's crown, a wide, stiff band adorned with golden threads, probably cost as much as had ever been spent on *her* clothes for her entire life.

What would Lady Liliana be like if she had had a miserable, miserly wretch of a father instead of a doting one? Would she be so fine and pretty if she had been beaten and half-starved all her life? If *her* father had come to her in the night and forced her to—

No. She wouldn't. Nor would Liliana have her bold, handsome husband who could barely bring himself to look at a woman like Priscilla Horton, even though he was just some Welsh peasant who had the luck to win a few tournaments.

She reached for her wine goblet, unceremoniously pushing her father out of the way. Well, let these fine, happy people pity her all they liked. No doubt it made them feel superior to see her. To offer her money. To pretend to care.

They had never really tried to help her. She had needed them years ago, when she was young and innocent. Surely they must have known what her father was like. Surely they should have guessed the kind of brute he was.

Priscilla smiled. She had found a way to control her father, and a way to have her revenge on all these fine Norman nobles.

It had taken her some time, but she had found out how to contact the rebel leader. She had chanced to see Ralf, the Morgan's reeve, at a fair, talking in a hushed voice to a man she knew to be a Welshman from the next valley. She had confronted Ralf shortly afterward, claiming that she knew for a certainty that he was in league with the Welsh rebels.

The fool had tried to deny it, but his face told her plainly that she had guessed the truth. Priscilla said she had no wish to betray him to Lord Trevelyan or any other Norman. Instead, she thought they could both benefit from helping the Welsh.

He revealed that he gave—or, more accurately, sold—information about the comings and goings of his lord. Priscilla knew that her information was better than that, since she was invited to the gatherings of the Normans. She had persuaded Ralf to arrange a meeting with the leader of the Welsh rebels.

At first Ivor had not been willing to believe she would give him information, but she soon convinced him otherwise. Especially when it became obvious to her that he didn't just appreciate the information she was able to provide him. He appreciated *her*, as no man ever had.

Her gaze met Liliana Trevelyan's and she stared boldly back. Maybe she wasn't as beautiful as Liliana, but she had a lover, one whose family had been highborn for several generations. No doubt she could teach Liliana a thing or two about pleasing men, too.

The spoiled wench looked away, and Priscilla smiled grimly.

No, she wasn't as unfortunate and homely as they all wanted to believe. One day soon, she would pay them all back for ignoring a helpless child, when her lover was the rightful ruler of this land. And her husband.

Chapter Twelve

Liliana stepped back to survey her work, a satisfied smile lighting her whitewash-spattered face. "Well, Jhone, what do you think?"

"I think you missed a spot, my lady," Jhone said softly, gesturing near the floor with her brush.

Liliana cursed softly and touched the spot. "There."

"Looks lovely."

Liliana stepped back again. "Yes, it does, if I do say so myself. It should be dry by the morning, and we can start hanging tapestries right after Mass."

"I would wait another day to be sure, my lady."

"Really? My father's visit is only two days away. It's difficult to be patient."

"You've worked so hard, it would be a pity to ruin the tapestries with wash."

Liliana grinned ruefully at Jhone, whose clothes, she noted, were nearly spotless. She glanced at her own gown of plain brown wool, which was splattered with white drops. "I suppose I'm anxious to see the hall completed."

"The men are going to panel tomorrow after-noon?"

"Yes, the part we finished yesterday, where the high table will be. We won't be able to do more before our guests arrive."

"It will be grand enough," Jhone assured her.

Liliana nodded. The hall was coming along better than she had dared to hope.

Jhone knew as much as any carpenter and worked both swiftly and silently. Liliana helped, getting more proficient as time went on, although she was still more enthusiastic than skilled.

Maude sensed that things between her master and mistress had changed, and was much more her jovial self. She had gladly worked long into the night sewing linen and then a plain but huge tapestry for behind the high table. Liliana had had visions of all the walls being covered with tapestries, but had realistically given up that impossible notion for the present.

Sarah, Osyth and Dena had outdone themselves by trying out a variety of dishes to astound the visitors—with some failures—and also by sewing linen, cutting rushes, sanding the floors and tables and even building two beds.

Liliana had helped with everything. At first she had found admitting her ignorance difficult, but the women had been surprisingly matter-of-fact about it. If anything, they seemed to respect her for her confession, just as Hu had predicted. They had all taken the time to show her things, and listened carefully when she explained what she knew, especially about the food.

"My lady?"

Liliana turned from her work to see Jhone's concerned face. "What is it?" she asked, fearing they had forgotten some necessary preparation.

"I have heard some disturbing...rumors."

Since Jhone did not engage in village gossip, Liliana put down her brush to listen with all her attention. "What rumors?"

"It is said that someone has been helping the Welsh rebels, someone who lives around here."

"Who would be stupid enough to assist outlaws?"

"There are several Welsh families, both in our village and the valley, but some say it's a Norman."

Liliana eyed the servant shrewdly. "Why do you tell me this now?"

"Because I hoped the rumors might go away when your husband came. But the rumors persist, my lady, so I think it would be wise for your husband to maintain the extra patrols."

"I will tell him," Liliana said. "He is quite certain that the rebels have gone away."

Jhone did not seem at all relieved. "I hope so, my lady."

"So do I," she replied. She told herself that surely Hu's opinion was more important than Jhone's.

She reached for the bucket. "That's all for today, Jhone. I have to put on a less...decorated gown before the evening meal."

Jhone gave her a rare smile. "Maude's got a surprise for you, my lady."

"She's moved my things upstairs?" Liliana asked hopefully.

Hu had insisted that the men close off a part of the upper hall for a bedchamber, to her delight, but they were not due to move into the separate accommodation until the night before her father's arrival.

"No, my lady."

"She's decided to enter a convent?"

Jhone's laugh was a fine reward for Liliana's jest, and she hoped proof that some of Jhone's worry had been alleviated.

"What is it, then?"

"Go and see," Jhone ordered, then flushed. "I'll take the buckets, my lady," she added respectfully.

Liliana hurried down the stairs and around the screen.

There was a wooden tub half-filled with steaming water that gave off the pleasant aroma of herbs. Beside it stood a glistening ewer of what had to be cold water, another steaming bucket of hot water and fresh thick linens.

With a happy smile, Liliana tore off her scarf, undid her gown and stepped out of her clothes. She stuck her toe into the hot water.

It was a trifle too hot, so she added some cool water, then got in. She sat down with a luxurious sigh and closed her eyes.

This was indeed a wonderful surprise. Whitewashing was hot and messy work, especially when one was as inexperienced as she. However, she thought as she slid a little lower, it was rather satisfying. She had improved the more she did, and felt proud of her efforts.

She heard a giggle and opened her eyes. "Maude, thank you for thinking of this."

"I've brought more water, in case you should be wanting to wash your hair," Maude answered with a smile, holding up another bucket. "This water's warm."

"Wonderful. I'll do that. How long until the meal?"

"A while yet, my lady."

"Good."

"I'll just be going along, then, my lady, to see if the girls need any help."

"Mmm..." Liliana answered contentedly. She bent over and wet her hair, then proceeded to lather it with some of the soap, singing to herself. She put her hand out for the bucket, but she couldn't find it. She hesitated to open her eyes, fearing that she would get soap in them.

"Let me help."

"Hu?"

"I should hope you're not expecting any other man, in your present state."

Liliana smiled. "Rinse my hair, would you? There's a bucket—"

A cascade of cold water descended upon her and made her squeal.

"That's freezing!" she spluttered, wiping her eyes and tasting the soap.

"Sorry for that. Here's the warm."

Another deluge assaulted her. Before she could chastise him for nearly drowning her, she realized he was climbing into the tub, too.

"Hu!"

"Hot, dirty work it is, slaughtering cows. Disgusting, really, but I suppose it's got to be done."

By now Liliana could see, although she had already felt enough to know that her husband was naked and had squeezed in across from her. "There isn't enough room," she said, trying to sound annoyed.

"Pity, but I don't mind," he replied with a wicked grin.

She had to smile, although the sight—and touch— of his nude, muscular body was difficult to ignore. "At least I certainly won't be able to say you stink, although I'm not sure how the men will react to the scent of the herbs."

Hu grimaced. "Forgot about that."

"In your eagerness to join me?"

"Aye." He leaned toward her, the water sloshing precariously near the top of the tub. "You look wonderful when you're naked."

"You're going to tip us over."

"I don't care."

"I do."

Hu moved away with a disgruntled look. "Very well."

Liliana pushed back her hair. "Did you finish?"

"All done, thank the Lord, although next year we'll have more to do, I hope."

"Yes. Have any more of the chickens gotten sick?"

"Not so far, but we can't breathe easy yet."

I'm not breathing easily now, Liliana thought ruefully. "We finished the whitewashing."

"Good." Hu rested his head against the side of the tub.

"Tired?"

He opened his eyes and sat up. "Depends," he said slyly.

"It's nearly time for the meal."

"O'r annwyl!"

"What does *that* mean?"

"Not exactly time for a lesson, is it?"

"Why not?"

Hu smiled slowly. "Right. Why not? Well, that means, 'dear me.'"

"That's all?"

"As close as I can figure."

"Oh."

"Next word." He reached out and touched her lips with his finger. *"Ceg."*

"Ceg."

His finger trailed down her neck. *"Gwddf."*

She sighed softly and closed her eyes. "What?"

"Neck."

"Oh."

"Bron. Breast."

Her breathing began to quicken as she pressed against the hard wooden side of the tub.

"Teth," he whispered, bending closer. "Nipple." His tongue flicked across that part of her body, and she moaned with pleasure.

"How do I say make love with me?"

He shifted forward between her legs. "Your body's already said it."

He put his hands on her hips, guiding her so that her willing body was over his, her legs wrapped around his lean torso, his legs around hers.

"There isn't room," she protested halfheartedly, then gasped when he entered her. She gave no more thought to the confines of the tub or even the time of day. All she knew was the delight she felt in his arms and the fulfillment their bodies gave each to the other as Hu began to thrust inside her. Her hands tightened their grasp on his shoulders. A low moan escaped her lips when his tongue danced over her breasts.

Her whole body seemed an instrument of pleasure as tension built to an excruciating peak. He groaned softly, and she felt him stiffen and throb even more within her.

She cried out at the burst of release. He kissed her deeply, a low chuckle rumbling through his chest. "Shh," he cautioned. "What will the servants think?"

"I don't care," she murmured, leaning her damp cheek against his shoulder.

He let go of her naked body, releasing her gently although he remained inside her. "*O'r annwyl*, woman. Impatient you make me."

She raised her face and smiled at him. "Time was short. Besides, we had best get out before Maude returns."

He kissed her forehead. "She would know better than to interrupt."

"I would not gamble on her discretion."

"She keeps secrets pretty well."

"How do you know?" Liliana gingerly stepped out of the tub and wrapped a cloth around herself.

Hu grinned slyly and tried to grab a stray end of her covering. "Know you, then, which man she wants?"

Liliana playfully slapped at his hand. "As long as it isn't my husband, it doesn't matter."

"You never forget, do you?"

Liliana sat down and began to brush her wet hair. "Not something like that."

"There's nothing to forget."

"That's good."

"It's Gareth Maude wants."

"The shepherd?"

"Aye."

Hu climbed out of the tub, unabashedly naked. "Let me do that," he said, taking the brush from her hand. "Wanting to do this for a long time, me."

Liliana sighed as he began to run the brush through her hair. "I must say it's something new in my experience to have a naked male attendant. I feel like an infidel with a eunuch for a servant."

"Wounding my pride, that is, to compare me to a eunuch."

Liliana laughed softly. "I certainly know you are not."

"That's one thing I don't want you to forget."

She twisted around to look at him with a roguish smile. "Oh, I won't." She ran her gaze over his body. "We didn't finish our lesson."

"Enough, I think."

"I do not agree, my lord. What is this called?"

Now it was Hu's turn to gasp when she grabbed him. It was all he could do to respond, between his surprise and delight.

"I like that," she remarked, bending to kiss it softly. "And these?" Her fingers caressed him slowly.

He moaned softly.

She let go and he opened his eyes. "What are you trying to do, Liliana?"

Her look was wide-eyed innocence. "I want to learn. You said you would teach me."

At that moment they heard a loud crash in the hall.

"See? I told you you would drop it!" Osyth chided from somewhere close by.

"Well, you went the wrong way," Dena complained.

Liliana felt a blush heat her face as Hu stepped away. Nor was she the only one embarrassed to think they might have been overheard. Hu began to tug on his chausses as quickly as he could.

"You're blushing," she pointed out needlessly, but she was too delighted to find evidence of his confessed shyness to remain silent.

"From bending over, my face is red," he replied. He tried to look serious when he straightened, but his eyes were filled with laughter. "Much as I hate to suggest it, you should be getting some clothes on or—" he came close and brushed her shoulder with his fingertips in a way that made her tingle with desire "—I may not concern myself with anything but *you*."

Liliana stood up and gave the tub a rather wistful glance. "It will be better when we have our own bedchamber."

Hu's grin was as devilish as only his could be. "A mistake that was, I'm beginning to think. I don't believe I'll ever get out of that room."

Liliana nodded in agreement and smiled her happiness.

Priscilla's lip curled in disgust as she lifted her father's head and let it fall back onto the scarred, soiled table with a thud. He let out a low groan but didn't stir in his drunken stupor.

"Sleep well," she muttered scornfully, shaking the jug. It wasn't totally empty, but near enough.

Money well spent, she thought grimly.

After enduring years of misery caused by her father's debauchery, Priscilla had discovered that the easiest thing to do was keep him permanently intoxicated. To that end she starved herself and denied all but the most basic of necessities. Now he left her alone, and that was worth the sacrifice.

As the moon rose, she went to fetch her cloak. The air was chill and damp, but she had business—and pleasure—to attend to.

The few remaining servants who were too old or too stupid to move on were in the kitchen arguing about food, as usual. Priscilla paid them no heed, but hurried outside to meet her lover in the nearby woods, her blood already burning with the thought of his fiery passion.

Priscilla tugged at her lover's clothes, pulling him down to the ground while she kissed him feverishly.

He was used to her ways and responded with fierce eagerness, not bothering to do more than lift her skirt before thrusting inside her. As for the rest, it was quickly over.

Then Ivor stood up to pull his breeches into place. "I've missed you," he said, infusing something like sincerity in his words.

"Say it so that I can understand."

He sighed and used the awkward Norman words she had taught him. "I have missed you. My love," he added as an afterthought.

Content, Priscilla sat up and gestured for him to sit beside her. "Where have you been?"

He sat down, but not so close that his body would touch hers. "It is too dangerous for me to stay here."

"It hasn't been before."

"Morgan makes it different."

"Bastard!"

Ivor didn't understand the word, but he heard the searing contempt in her voice.

She saw his look and touched his leg. "How long can you stay with me?"

Ivor smiled slowly. She was not a very attractive woman, but useful and so willing to try anything he suggested that he often wondered just how much she would do to please him.

"Not long," he said with a hint of true regret. "Do you know for certain now if Lord Trevelyan is coming here?"

"Yes, he is. They're having a feast. As if I want to go, to watch them fawn over each other. It's disgusting."

"A feast?" He knew that word.

"I suppose it makes them happy to patronize me. Like giving alms to a beggar. Well, I won't go!"

Ivor glanced at her while she continued her unintelligible ranting. She was skinnier than a starving hen, homely, old and bitter. Compared to Morgan's Norman wife . . . Well, there was no comparison.

His manhood stirred at the thoughts of the yellow-haired beauty with her ripe lips and ruddy cheeks. "Does your father go to this feast?"

As always when her father was mentioned, her expression grew murderous. "Yes," she hissed.

"You will not?"

"I told you, no."

"But you might find out something important for me. I need to know when they will finish the rebuilding on Morgan's estate, and if he's getting more men from Lord Trevelyan."

"I don't want to go there," she replied peevishly. "Morgan and his precious, spoiled little wife."

He decided not to compel her. She had taught him her language, provided his men with food and told him many things about the Normans who ruled this area. The information she had given already was invaluable, and she could still be useful, although one day soon a bitter and jealous woman like her would surely be tempted to brag about her lover. Perhaps it would be better if she did not go. "You know his wife?"

Priscilla gave him a shrewd look. "Why?"

Ivor shrugged.

"Stupid, undeserving wench."

Again, Ivor could only comprehend the feeling, not the exact words. He didn't doubt that Priscilla was jealous of the wealth, if not the husband.

"Then do not go," he said after a moment.

Priscilla smiled and ran her hand up his thigh. "Please come to me soon, my love. Nothing would please me more."

"When is the feast?"

"In two days."

Ivor frowned. "It will be dangerous for me to come again so soon, and alone."

"You and your men have nothing to fear from me."

"I know." Ivor moved closer and slipped the cloak from her shoulders.

"I need you," he whispered, pressing his lips to hers. He untied the lacing of her gown. When he pushed it down over her nearly nonexistent breasts, she moaned hungrily.

He paused. "Perhaps I shouldn't bring my men. They might want you, too."

"You would protect me, wouldn't you?"

"Protect?"

"Save me."

"If you wanted me to. But you would like my men, and I expect my woman to be..."

"Accommodating?" There was a touch of displeasure in her voice.

"What does that mean?"

"You would like to watch me, with your men?"

Ivor's nod was genuine and his lustful gaze the nearest thing to love that Priscilla had ever known. "Ah, Priscilla, you want so much to please me, I should make you my wife."

She lay on the ground and pulled him on top of her. "How many would you bring?" she whispered.

Chapter Thirteen

Liliana sighed contentedly as she surveyed the nearly completed upper hall. The walls had dried with only a few streaks—all where she had worked, she had to admit—but the tapestries did much to cover the less satisfactory areas. The men Hu had sent had done a fine job on the oak paneling, which Osyth and Dena had polished to a fine, pale gleam.

By far the most important improvement was the separate sleeping area. In view of the imminent arrival of their guests, they had decided to divide the space into two, with a wall in between. Hu had insisted that the wall be of thick oak, which few sounds short of screams would penetrate. Given the wild abandon she felt when they made love, this was a comforting notion.

She went to one of the tables and straightened the linen. She wanted everything to be ready when her father and the Beaumares arrived. Fortunately, Hu and the men had finished the fall slaughter, no more hens had become sick, the apples had all been harvested and Sir Nevil had not only sent the promised fodder, but also some wine.

"Fine it looks, so stop fussing."

Liliana smiled as Hu came up behind her, his arms encircling her waist. He kissed her ear.

"It does look nice, doesn't it?"

"Should, since you made me take my men from more important tasks to finish it."

She tried to ignore the pleasant sensations his lips were causing when he nibbled on her earlobe. "You know Jhone is just as much to thank as the men."

"You're right."

She twisted so that she faced him, then gently pushed him back to survey him critically.

"No, this is not good," she mused. "You are simply much too handsome for your own good."

He pulled her into his arms. "A mistake it was to teach you teasing. Now you never stop."

"I will, if you really want me to."

"No," he muttered as he bent to kiss her deeply.

"You're a good teacher," she sighed, stepping away. "Too good, I think. And definitely much too distracting."

"What's troubling you now?"

"I've been thinking about Priscilla Horton." The messenger had returned to say Lady Priscilla would not attend their feast, with no explanation offered.

Hu gave her an incredulous stare. "Why? I, for one, am glad she's not coming. She would spoil things worse than the Beaumares."

Liliana could not help recalling the naked hatred she had seen in Priscilla's eyes at the Northrups' feast. It was a bitter, burning hate that was frightening to see, as if she hated the whole world.

She could well believe that Priscilla would blame the whole world for her misfortunes, and not without some cause. What did the world have to offer a poor, ugly spinster well past her youth? That would surely make any woman bitter and angry, perhaps enough to turn on her own people.

"She frightens me."

"Frightens you? Priscilla Horton? She's only a woman."

Liliana frowned even more deeply. "Only a woman, maybe, but she's still capable of doing harm if she chose to. Jhone says that there are rumors someone is helping the rebels. Some even believe it's a Norman."

"Believe me, Liliana, there is no traitor in our midst, or I would know of it by now."

Liliana wanted to feel as confident of that as Hu, but she couldn't help feeling a nagging dread that if the rumors of a traitor were so persistent, there might be something to them.

She opened her mouth to speak but Hu said, "I hear them coming."

"Really? You do?" All thoughts of Priscilla Horton and rebels flew from Liliana's mind and her eyes widened with barely disguised panic. "How do I look? Is my veil straight?" she demanded, her hands flying to her head.

"You look wonderful. The hall looks wonderful. I look wonderful. Stop fussing!"

Liliana gave him a brief, uncertain smile as she hurried to greet her father, hoping that he wouldn't be disappointed with their efforts.

In fact, Lord Trevelyan was anything but disappointed. He had been uncertain what might happen when Liliana saw the state of the hall, and had more than half expected to see her riding through his castle gates the day after she arrived at her new home. He had been most pleasantly surprised when she did not.

Now, as he surveyed the nearly completed, vastly stronger outer wall, the tidy, well-repaired outbuildings and his daughter's glowing face, he was happy and relieved.

His pleasure almost compensated for having to put up with the Beaumares for the entire journey.

"Welcome, Father!" Liliana cried as he dismounted and she hurried toward him.

He smiled warmly at her, and at Hu standing behind her. "A great improvement, I must say," he remarked, surveying the courtyard.

"Welcome, Lord and Lady Beaumare," Liliana said. Her tone lacked much of the warmth of her previous greeting.

Averil's lips curved slightly in acknowledgment. Barris struggled down from his horse, huffing and puffing from even that slight effort. "I'm parched," he announced loudly.

Averil coughed a summons, and Barris turned to help her from her horse.

"Come inside. I have some refreshments prepared," Liliana said graciously. She led the way to the hall, followed by her father. Hu dutifully escorted the sharp-eyed Averil, leaving Barris to come last.

When they each had a goblet of wine, Averil looked around the hall. "It is so unfortunate," she said consolingly, "that laborers today don't seem to be very skilled at their tasks."

Averil, so good at noticing anything out of place, was too busy staring at a streak on the wall to notice Liliana's stiffening back or Hu's slight frown. "I mean, my dear, you must have had a terrible time with the fellows who did this. If only I had known, I would have sent you some fine workers I know."

"How kind," Liliana replied sweetly. "Not from your estate, surely. You spend so little time there, it must be difficult to know what your tenants are capable of."

Averil's look made it clear that she wasn't sure if Liliana was being critical or not, and Liliana's face certainly gave no clue. "Yes, well, as a matter of fact, the men I'm thinking of usually work for Lord Gervais."

"It does happen that an apprentice did do that part of the wall," Hu said with a serious expression, "but I'm certain there will be an improvement as time goes on."

"I hope so," Averil said.

"Good wine," Barris muttered.

"It's from Sir Nevil," Liliana remarked.

Lord Trevelyan smiled warmly. "I knew he would be a good neighbor to you. How is he?"

For a time the talk turned to the Northrups, whom Liliana had invited for the feast the next day.

Averil, who had been forced to be quiet for a few minutes, interrupted to complain about her journey. "The trees grow so close to the road," she said loudly, "that a bird dropping nearly landed on my best cloak!"

"In Wales, that would be considered a sign of good fortune," Hu said, his tone and his expression grave.

Liliana wondered if that was true, until she happened to catch Hu's eye. Trying not to smile, she said, "After your *difficult* journey, I am sure you must want to rest before the evening meal."

As Liliana rose to her feet, Averil looked taken aback. She had several more complaints to make about her journey. Now they would have to wait.

Hu stood near the hearth with Elwy. He had been dressed and ready for the evening meal since before his father-in-law's arrival.

"Right pleased he looked," Elwy commented.

"Some relieved I was, I can tell you," Hu answered. "God's teeth, felt like I was nothing but a squire again, waiting for a good word."

"I'd say you got it."

"Thank God."

Elwy gave him a sidelong glance. "Probably helped that your wife looks like she's living in heaven."

Hu chuckled. "She's not the only one feels that way."

"As long as the mill don't get struck by lightning again, or more hens get sick, or the sheep get the murrain..."

"Cheerful fellow, aren't you?"

"Reminding you life is a vale of tears, boy."

Hu gave his ever-optimistic friend a skeptical look. "Remind yourself. How's that widow?"

"Talk of a vale of tears! Say anything and the flood starts. Her late husband was a saint, I take it."

"Hopeless, is it?"

"Yes. But there's a wool merchant come in yesterday. Three daughters he has, all pretty and all unmarried—"

Elwy stopped talking when Lord Trevelyan entered the hall. Both young men bowed.

"You've done a fine job on the hall," Lord Trevelyan remarked as he approached. "I never would have guessed you could have accomplished so much in such a short time."

"You can thank your daughter for that, my lord."

"Oh?"

"She organized it all, and helped with it, too, although Lady Beaumare would say her work needs improvement," Hu said with a grin.

"What?" Lord Trevelyan looked rather shocked. "You mean Liliana..."

"She'll never make a carpenter, but as a whitewasher, there's cause for hope."

"I knew my daughter was skilled in many things, but this comes as something of a surprise."

They shared a friendly chuckle, then Lord Trevelyan grew serious. "I saw a number of bonfires being prepared. I have heard, as you know, that there are outlaws in the forest. I didn't realize the problem was serious enough to warrant signal fires."

"I've had my men patrolling, but they haven't seen any sign of rebels. I think they must have moved off. The fires are to celebrate Winter's Eve, tomorrow night."

"Ah. That is a relief, I must confess." Lord Trevelyan smiled at his daughter's husband.

This marriage was turning out to be even better than he had dared to hope. He knew that Hu Morgan was a fine young knight, but he had feared that Liliana would balk when she saw the state of the manor. In a way, he realized, it had been a test he had given his daughter, and only now, when it appeared to be a success, did he dare to recognize how disappointed he would have been had she failed.

"What are you worried about?" Hu asked the next evening as he lay on the bed and watched Liliana dress for the feast. She wore a lovely gown of deep scarlet brocade, with a silk veil and chin band over her hair. "Everything's ready and your father's pleased with what's been done." He grinned. "Not heard any more rumors, have you?"

"No." Liliana suppressed a disgruntled frown at his mocking tone while she adjusted her veil. "I just want everything to be perfect for the feast."

"Not a saint, any of us, so nobody expects perfection."

Liliana put on a supple leather girdle over her gown. She surveyed her husband critically. He wore his best tunic, and his hair had been brushed, although that did little to tame his unruly curls. Nonetheless, he was so handsome, she knew it didn't really matter. "If only Averil Beaumare weren't here! She's always seeking fault!"

"With her husband, that's all the poor woman probably has to do. Gives her pleasure, surely, to poke holes in other people's clothes."

"I suppose you're right."

"Forget her, then, and enjoy yourself."

"I'll try."

* * *

"Wonderful feast, eh?" Sir Nevil said loudly to anyone within earshot. "Amazing what some people can do with a pig."

Liliana smiled happily. The meal had been as good as she had ever dared to hope. She must be sure to thank Sarah, as well as Osyth and Dena. Jhone had organized the order of service so that the courses came and went with military precision. Even Averil Beaumare hadn't been able to find fault with anything so far.

She glanced past Hu and her father to where Averil was seated beside Barris.

Averil was staring critically at a red stain in front of her husband, obviously conveniently forgetting that it was Barris who had spilled most of a goblet of wine on Liliana's finest cloth, the only one large enough to cover this table.

Would nothing ever suit that woman? Liliana thought peevishly. Then Barris belched loudly, and Liliana saw Averil's face turn scarlet with embarrassment.

Liliana looked at her own husband, so handsome and charming, relating some story about sheep to her father. Well, perhaps Hu was right and Averil could only feel happy by finding fault with others.

Hu stood and raised his voice. "Time for dancing—and other things."

With a speed that impressed Liliana, the men moved to take down the tables. Gareth, who had been silent and almost invisible at the far end of the hall, picked up his small harp and began to play. Hu took Liliana's hand and led her forward for the *estampie*, a dance wherein the first couple danced alone, followed by other couples each taking a turn.

Hu was no dancer, as Liliana knew from her wedding, but he made a valiant effort and seemed so at ease despite his lack of skill that Liliana couldn't help enjoying herself. It was more than enough to be close to him.

The Northrups followed, then the Beaumares, then Lord Trevelyan and Liliana. By this time, all in the hall were clapping their hands in time to the music, and some were singing to Gareth's tune. A *carole* came next. All those who wished to dance joined hands in a large circle, moving in time to the music.

Osyth and Dena rushed about serving wine and ale to the thirsty participants, until they, too, were drawn into the widening circle.

Liliana was about to remark that they were neglecting their duties when Jhone appeared before the high table carrying an intricately carved jug. It had three small, round knobs around the rim, each with a small hole in it, and a handle that reached to the bottom. Hu took the jug and offered it to Lord Trevelyan.

"It's a Welsh tradition that all the guests drink from this vessel on Winter's Eve," he said solemnly.

With a smile, Lord Trevelyan took the jug and drank.

Averil, who was seated beside Liliana, said, "That's the ugliest thing I have ever seen in my life. How is one supposed to get anything through such a tiny hole? I have heard that the Welsh are not generous, but I had no idea..."

Liliana tried not to listen as Averil continued to make snide remarks about the Welsh and their traditions while Sir Nevil and Lady Eleanor sipped from the jug. Liliana noticed that they each held the container the same particular way, with their fingers covering two of the knobs. They all drank out of the same hole nearest the handle, too.

As Hu presented the jug to Averil, who seemed somewhat mollified by the gesture, Liliana became aware of muffled snickers and chortles from the people watching the guests. She gave Hu a sidelong glance, but he had assumed a virtuous, noble expression, which made her instantly suspicious.

Averil lifted the jug to her lips and applied her mouth to the hole farthest from the handle. Ale poured out of the other two holes, over her face and down her dress.

Liliana clapped her hand to her mouth and tried to stifle a laugh at Averil's indignant, shocked expression. It didn't help that everyone else was in paroxysms of laughter, including the lady's husband.

Hu hurried forward, a very picture of solicitousness. He grabbed the veil off Averil's head—unfortunately revealing Averil's rather scanty hair—and began dabbing at her face. "Oh, Lady Beaumare, how unfortunate. I thought you knew about the puzzle jug."

"I...no one told me...it's abominable!" Averil spluttered as she snatched the veil away. "My dress and my veil are ruined, utterly ruined!"

"Never liked 'em anyway," Barris bellowed good-naturedly. "I'll buy you new ones. It's worth the gown to see your face!"

Averil snorted indignantly and marched away toward her sleeping quarters.

"That wasn't very nice," Liliana whispered to Hu as he stood beside her.

"No," he whispered back, "but now we can have some fun without her to spoil it, eh?"

"It's a good thing my father did it correctly or I hate to think—"

"I told him the secret. And the Northrups, too."

Liliana giggled. "You *are* wicked, Hu Morgan."

"I know. Wonderful, isn't it?"

Then Hu called for quiet and nodded at Elwy, who dashed out the kitchen corridor. Before Liliana could ask what was happening next, Elwy returned with a basket filled with apples and candles.

The Welshmen gathered around as Elwy dragged a bench under one of the beams. For the first time Liliana noticed that a hook had been fastened there.

"Who did that?" she asked Hu, who turned to her with a grin.

"I did."

"Why? What's he doing?"

"It's for a game. You'll see."

She watched as Elwy hung up a string. On one end an apple dangled, on the other a candle, both suspended at shoulder height.

"Hu, you have the honor!" Elwy called, pulling the bench away and moving to the hearth, where he lighted another candle.

Hu bowed low and went toward Gareth, who had a short length of rope and a piece of cloth in his hands. Gareth tied Hu's hands behind his back, then covered Hu's eyes with the cloth for a blindfold, while Elwy lit the suspended candle.

Suddenly Liliana knew what this game was. It was like bobbing for apples, except that Hu had to try and bite the apple and not the lighted candle! "Hu, I don't think—"

"This is for the men. The ladies can try to get the apples in the water."

Liliana didn't know whether she should be indignant at Hu's condescending tone or relieved that no one was suggesting she try to avoid catching a lighted candle with her teeth. She decided to keep quiet and silently prayed that Hu didn't burn his marvelous lips.

Elwy and Gareth turned Hu around several times, rather roughly, too, judging by Hu's cries of protest. Everyone gathered round in a circle. They were fairly silent as Hu inched his way toward the dangling apple, only calling out words of what sounded like encouragement. Liliana suspected that it would be considered unsporting to call out actual assistance, but when Hu came dangerously close to the candle, she had to bite her lip to keep from shouting a warning.

Hu stood still for what seemed an interminable length of time as the apple and candle continued to swing slowly around him. Then, like a frog after a fly, he suddenly lunged and got the apple in his teeth.

Everyone applauded but Elwy, who muttered about luck and predestination and an unnatural sense of smell while he untied Hu's hands and removed the blindfold. Now it was Elwy's turn.

The unlucky Elwy proceeded to eat beeswax, and Liliana discovered that her father had come to stand beside her. She smiled gaily at him, even though her gaze strayed to Hu, standing in the circle shouting.

Elwy admitted defeat. Gareth, showing remarkable determination, attempted to locate either the apple or the candle with his chin.

"I hoped he would make you happy," Lord Trevelyan said to the daughter he loved above all things. "It's been a long time since I've heard you laugh like this."

"You chose a good husband for me."

"I did, didn't I?"

The games, including several intended to prophesy one's future, lasted for several hours longer. There was also more singing and dancing, until finally Barris Beaumare drank himself into a stupor, Maude and Gareth disappeared together, Jhone began tidying up around the men who were still drinking, and Osyth and Dena fell asleep.

"Now I know how it ends, but I've got to start it right," Elwy said for the tenth time, reaching for more wine and trying to recall a story he claimed was the funniest he had ever heard. "There was an old miller...or was it a priest?"

Hu grinned at Liliana, who was attempting to stay awake.

"Well, I'm afraid I shall have to wait to hear that story another day," Lord Trevelyan said as he rose to his feet and smiled at Liliana. "I fear I will sleep far too late tomorrow, but I have had a most enjoyable time, my dear. Good night."

"Good night," Liliana said, watching him go toward his sleeping quarters.

"I've got it!" Elwy said. "There was an old friar who decided to go to Canterbury...or was it Rome?"

Hu shook his head with a rueful grin and stood up. "Good night, Elwy."

"Not leaving me here?"

"Tell me your story in the morning."

"Spoil-fun."

Hu held out his hand and helped Liliana to her feet. "Good night, Elwy," she said, stifling a yawn.

Hu knew Liliana was exhausted, but instead of leading her to their chamber, he started toward the door to the courtyard.

"Where are we going?" Liliana asked sleepily.

"There's something I want to do before I go to sleep."

"Oh?" Liliana sounded more alert.

"You're a wicked, wanton woman—and you're too tired, anyway. It's another tradition, that's all," he said, going out into the chilly night. The sky was clear, and the bright stars twinkled in the heavens.

"Oh."

"If you're that disappointed—" He paused in the courtyard and pulled her to him, kissing her deeply. She pressed against him, moving her lips in such a way that he almost forgot what it was he wanted to do.

She stepped back. "It's too cold. I need my cloak."

"You won't soon." He started for the gate, and she ran to catch up to him. He paused and bent down to pick up a stone. "Get one," he said, pointing at the pebbles from the mason's cutting.

Liliana hurried to comply, by now shivering and wanting nothing more than to get into bed. With Hu.

"Come on." He led her through the village to where some of the Welsh tenants had kindled a huge bonfire. There was no one near it now.

"Where is everyone?" she asked, going as close as she could for warmth.

"They've gone inside." He opened his eyes wide and spoke in a low voice. "The spirits are abroad this night."

Liliana glanced over her shoulder nervously. "Then let's go home, too."

"Not just yet. First throw your stone into the fire."

"Why?"

"We come back in the morning and search for it. If we find it, that means good luck for the coming year."

"And if we don't?"

"Bad luck, of course."

Liliana looked at the stone in her hand by the light of the fire, wondering if she would be able to recognize it again. With a shrug, she tossed it into the leaping flames. Hu did likewise, then he grabbed her hand and started running.

"I'm out of breath!" Liliana panted.

"Don't want to get caught by the spirits."

Liliana didn't ask what might happen if they did, nor did she really want to know as long as they were returning to the hall.

"Now can we go to bed?" she demanded as they hurried inside.

"There's another Welsh tradition that has to do with making love on Winter's Eve," Hu said in a tone that made her legs turn to water and her heart start to pound with anticipation.

"Really?"

"No." He grinned mischievously. "But thinking we should start one. Something about bringing luck."

"I think I'm the luckiest woman in all of England anyway," Liliana said softly as she led him into their new bedchamber.

"Hu, stop," Liliana said the next morning beside the mound of ashes. "It doesn't matter. I found my stone."

"I have to find mine," he replied firmly, crouching down and sifting through the powdery ash with his fingers. "I know I threw it right over here."

"It's merely a superstition, you know."

He rose slowly and frowned. "It is a tradition, and for luck."

"It's going to rain again soon. You can look for it when the water's washed away most of the ashes."

"Go, then," he said stubbornly, "but I'll keep looking a little while yet."

Liliana kissed his cheek and walked to the manor while Hu bent down to sift through the ashes again.

A man stepped out of the shadows of the nearby trees. "Greetings, Hu ap Morgan," he called softly in Welsh.

Hu straightened slowly, very aware that he had no weapon. The man came closer. "Greetings, Ivor ap Rhodri," he replied in his native tongue.

"Happy I am to see that you have not forgotten Winter's Eve."

"I told you to leave my land, Ivor." There was more movement in the trees, and not from the wind.

"And I told you, Hu ap Morgan, who I am. No Norman's pawn can order me from the land of my fathers." Ivor smiled slowly. "Right I am, and you know it. This land doesn't belong to Norman lords, but to

Welshmen. We were the rulers here long before the Normans came." Ivor came closer still. "They've taken away our land, our kings, our churches. Coming in here with their castles and orders and laws and arrogance. Treating us like slaves to do their bidding. Marrying their daughters to us, to make us soft. To trick us into believing we are their equals."

Hu clenched his fists. "What do you want?"

"I can understand how tempting it would be, Morgan. Even I might have agreed, if someone offered me a woman like that."

"Get off my land, Ivor."

"Fighting me with your bare hands, is it, Hu?" Ivor smiled and shook his head. "A brave man you are, but I did not come to fight with you."

"Why, then? To celebrate *nos galan gaeaf* with me?"

"To ask you to join us, to help us to overthrow the Norman invaders. You could be a great leader."

"Even though my family is nothing?" Hu replied skeptically.

Ivor stood there, unmoving. "Your children—speaking Welsh or Norman?"

"What is it to you what they speak?"

"A Welshman, that is what I am. That is what you *used* to be. Take away the land, the religion, the language and the poetry, and what are we left with?"

Hu looked at Ivor's scornful face. "Think you the Welsh so weak we can't survive the Normans? That our language and our poetry can be taken away? We're tougher than you believe, Ivor."

"The Normans are leeches, taking our life's blood."

"Raised by a man both Welsh and Norman, me. I *know* we can all live in peace." He took a step toward the rebel. "Nor were the old ways always best, as many a man would tell you. I'm for judging each man on his own merits, not his kin or his language."

Ivor sniffed. "Because you've known one good Norman?"

"More than one."

"You've sold out your heritage for a beautiful woman and some dirt."

"I will not justify my decisions and loyalties to you, Ivor. If I find you on my land again, you will find me armed. Now take your men and go."

"If you will not join with us, Morgan, you are an enemy of the Welsh."

"If you fight against me, you are *my* enemy."

Ivor shrugged and prepared to join his men. "Then we are enemies, Hu ap Morgan."

As he walked away, Ivor realized his heart was pounding and the sweat was pouring from his body. There had been no doubt in his mind that Morgan would have fought him then if he had a weapon in his hand.

Still, he was vastly relieved that Hu Morgan had no wish to join with them. If he had, Ivor wouldn't have been leader for another hour, despite his family's prestige. Not with a soldier like Hu Morgan to take command.

"What does he say?" Dafydd asked when Ivor rejoined the rest of his men.

"He is no Welshman now."

Chapter Fourteen

Hu never did find his stone.

And despite Liliana's wish to make light of "mere superstition," it seemed as if his luck had disappeared with it.

They lost nearly the whole flock of hens. The weather turned cold early, and it rained six days out of seven, slowing the work on the buildings and the walls. Some of the sheep also fell ill, and although Gareth claimed it was merely those animals least able to withstand the rigors of the journey from the north, Hu knew Gareth was worried. He rarely appeared in the hall now, spending most of his days with the sheep.

At least Ivor and his men did not return, and Elwy, steadfast, loyal, ever-jovial Elwy, retained his good cheer.

There had even been one day of glorious happiness, when Liliana told him she thought she was with child, but it had been a premature hope. Her woman's time was merely late.

One December day, Hu stood near the outer walls. The day was cold, and dark clouds loomed on the horizon. For now, it was not raining, but he didn't like the look of the sky.

"Hu!"

He turned and smiled to see his wife approach him, stepping delicately around the piles of building material that awaited use. "Hu, when are you going to have the walls finished?"

"When we can, we will. It's too wet."

"Couldn't you at least build a wooden palisade around the top?"

Hu's smile faded slightly, even as he reached out to take her hand. "My responsibility, the walls, Liliana. Yours, the hall."

She sighed softly, noting the lines of worry on his brow. Well, he was right, she supposed, so she pursued another subject. "I must ask you to talk to Gareth."

"Gareth? Why?"

"He's upsetting Maude."

Hu gave her a puzzled look. "That's none of my business."

"He's so concerned with the sheep, he's ignoring her, and she's been out of sorts for days."

She was relieved when he gave her the ghost of his old grin. "What do you expect me to do? The sheep are important. And I thought you'd be happy Maude wasn't giggling all the time."

"Well, for that I *am* thankful, but she's neglecting her duties. Don't you think Gareth could come to the hall for a little while?"

"I will consider it."

Liliana smiled happily and reached up to kiss his cheek. "Thank you."

He didn't respond to her kiss, or even look at her. His gaze was fastened on the horizon. "Where is Elwy?"

"In the hall."

"Tell him to come to me."

She bristled slightly at the commanding tone, but said nothing as she walked away. Hu hadn't really been himself since the feast, with all the troubles that had come.

She had been so happy when she thought she was bearing his child. How like his old self he had been that day, smiling and joking and trying to think of names.

Of course, some of his suggestions had been completely outlandish Welsh ones, totally unpronounceable. And he had asked her, with the strangest expression on his face, what language their children would speak. She had replied that obviously the children would speak what their mother and their nursemaids did.

She recalled the disappointment on his face when she had to tell him she had been mistaken. She had told him about the child too soon in her urge to give him joy.

It did seem to be taking rather long for her to get with child, considering that they made love nearly every night, and with great vigor.

She entered the hall. Elwy stood near the hearth, complaining as usual about his inability to find a wife. He continued to face disappointment as women spurned his offers of marriage, which he made to different choices, on average, once a week.

"Not understanding these females," he muttered loudly. "To be sure I'm not as handsome as some, but I'm not that ugly."

"Perhaps it's your reputation," Liliana said lightly as she drew near.

"What's wrong with it, my lady? A fine fighter, aren't I?"

"That's not the one I mean," she replied, trying to maintain a seriously thoughtful demeanor. "Maybe if you didn't flit from woman to woman—"

"*Flit*? I don't *flit*. What am I supposed to do if a woman says she's not of a mind to marry me? Sit around and mope all day?"

"Maybe it's a test they're giving you, to see if you really want them. If so, you're failing every time."

Elwy looked nonplussed. "Think it could be so?"

She shrugged, but couldn't keep a grin from her face. "Hu wants to see you. He's at the wall, near the gate."

"Maybe I'll ask that widow again," Elwy said pensively as he picked up his cloak and went out.

By the time Elwy reached Hu at the wall, all thoughts of the widow or women in general had fled from his mind. Flakes of snow were falling, getting thicker every moment, and the wind was beginning to whip them around the courtyard.

Hu nodded a brief greeting as Elwy climbed toward him. "Looks like a blizzard, this."

"God help us!"

Hu nodded. "If it gets any worse, we'll have to get the sheep in."

Hu knew, as did Elwy, that in a heavy snowfall the sheep would find themselves as sheltered a spot as they could. Even if they were eventually covered by drifts of snow, a sort of cave would form. Enough air could pass through the snow so that they would be able to breathe. The great danger was that the sheep would starve to death, for once they had eaten the grass around their feet, they would begin to consume their own wool.

And then they would die.

"Where's Gareth?"

"In the barn, with the last sheep that took sick."

"Get him, and have Ralf muster as many men as he can find from the village."

"Aye."

Hu and Elwy made their way to the manor, panting with exhaustion. All day they had searched for sheep stranded in the snow. Gareth had taken several men on the other hills. Ralf had gone to the village, to find more men who could help search.

The snow had been falling steadily for two days now. Hu and Elwy, who knew just how much was at stake, and Gareth, who treasured each animal, had been out in the blizzard almost continuously, walking through the hills, poking each drift with a long staff to see if an animal was hidden there. Mott proved invaluable, finding sheep by their scent.

They had found several sheep huddled in the woods, sheltered by some bushes, including one of the rams, but there were many more unaccounted for.

Liliana hurried to the men when they came inside, their heads and cloaks covered with snow. "Come to the fire," she urged. "And rest."

She looked at Hu carefully. He walked heavily, grimacing with pain sometimes. His face was pale except for his flushed cheeks, and he could scarcely catch his breath. "What's the matter? Are you ill?"

"I fell into a gully. It's only my ankle twisted. I'll be all right."

She glanced at his feet. "You're bleeding!" she cried, pulling him to a seat on the bench.

"Cut it on a branch. Just get me some food and a drink and bandage it up. Gareth come back yet?"

"No," Maude answered, coming to him with a bowl of steaming broth.

Liliana pulled away his leggings. An ugly wound appeared. "If it wasn't so cold, you could have bled to death," she murmured. "You must be weak from the loss—"

"Wrap it up again, tight, so it doesn't bleed."

She looked up at his pale, careworn face. For an instant she wondered what had happened to the boy she had married. The face looking at her, so cold, so determined, was a man's face. A warrior's face, engaged in battle.

But she did not want him to become a casualty. Not for some sheep. "You can't go out there again, Hu," she said firmly.

He reached for the bowl of broth. "Some food and some drink is all I need." He gave her a strange look. "Are you forgetting I was a shepherd, Liliana? I have done this before. I know where and how to look better than the villagers."

She rose slowly. "You are hurt badly. You *cannot* go out. It's only some sheep."

He stared at her, his eyes hard and shining. "You don't command me, Liliana. The sheep are important. They must be found."

"Let others do it, then. *You* don't have to."

"That may be the Norman way, but it is not mine." He bent down and with swift tugs wrapped his leg. "Mott, come."

He rose and went to the door. Elwy, with a shrug at Liliana, also got to his feet. "He'll be all right, once the sheep are in," he said softly. He joined his friend and went out into the blizzard once more.

By nightfall, Elwy, Hu and Gareth met at the gate of the manor. Although exhausted and cold, they exchanged pleased smiles, for they were fairly certain that they had recovered most of the flock.

They entered the gate. It was after Gareth had closed it that he turned to find Hu lying face down in the snow.

"He refuses to drink the medicine I have prepared," the long-faced monk said with a touch of irritation. "Unless he takes it, there is nothing more I can do."

Liliana sniffed the noxious brew the learned priest held before her and prayed that this medicine would be effective. They had tried everything they could think of after Gareth had carried Hu into the hall, feverish and delirious, but so far, nothing anyone had prepared seemed to help.

Her father had sent Derrick with an invitation for them to spend Christmas and Epiphany at his castle. Derrick had quickly returned with the news of Hu's illness, so Lord Trevelyan had sent Father Peter, who was reputed to work near miracles with his medicines, along with word that he would be happy to provide anything they might need to make Hu well.

At times they believed the fever had broken, but it would return by nightfall. Father Peter had muttered that he had never encountered anything quite like it. Liliana had never been so frightened in her entire life, and rarely left Hu's bedside after that.

Elwy, thankfully, was taking care of the manor business. He had also taken her advice and begun to build a palisade as a temporary wall. It was obvious that they wouldn't be able to finish the masonry wall before the spring.

If only Hu had listened to her, Liliana thought as she looked at him. There had been no need for him to risk his life in the blizzard. They had plenty of other men who could have found the sheep.

"My love, please drink this!" she urged softly, holding the medicine to his lips.

He muttered something in Welsh, then clamped his dry, cracked lips together. She managed to pour sips of the liquid into his mouth.

Elwy, who had left supervising the walls to see how Hu fared, hovered anxiously near the door. He whispered something to Maude while Father Peter frowned morosely.

"What is it?" Liliana asked nervously, wondering if Elwy was telling Maude the meaning of Hu's words. "What did he say?"

"Hu's been sick like this before, my lady," Elwy said gently.

"How long did it take for him to recover then?"

Elwy shrugged his shoulders. "A few days."

"He's already been sick a few days."

"It might have been the medicine Mamaeth gave him."

"Medicine? What medicine?" Father Peter demanded.

Liliana shot the priest a look. "Who is Mamaeth?"

"An old woman on the baron's estate."

Liliana bit her lip. The baron's estate, where Hu had grown up, was a long way to the north. "How far is it to the baron's castle?"

Elwy shook his head sorrowfully. "In winter, it will take many days to get there and back."

"Father Peter!"

"Yes, my lady?"

"How long will my husband live?"

Father Peter stroked his chin. "My lady, your noble husband might recover quickly if he takes the medicine. Or he might linger for some days. Or he might...expire...at any time."

"In other words, Father, you do not know."

The priest flushed a little. "Far be it from me to correct a lady."

Liliana looked at Elwy. "Will you go and get this Mamaeth?"

He shook his head. "I cannot."

"Why not?" Liliana demanded.

"Hu left me in command here. I can't desert my duty."

"I will be here."

Elwy looked away. "Hu's orders are my lord's orders. While he lives, I will not disobey."

Liliana could have screamed with frustration. "*Someone* has to go. I will not simply allow my husband to die."

Her gaze went around the room and fastened on Maude. "Gareth," she announced, ignoring Maude's gasp. "Gareth must go."

"But my lady, the snow!" Maude started to protest.

Liliana had been giving orders too long to listen to a maid's protests, not when her husband's life was at stake. "Elwy, find Gareth and tell him what he must do. At once."

Elwy hesitated, but at that moment, Hu moaned softly. "Aye, my lady."

Maude turned and followed him out the door as Liliana again bent over Hu and tried to coax him to drink.

Ralf stood shivering in the Hortons' barren hall. The fire in the hearth was so meager, he doubted it would warm a mouse, of which he was certain there were many in this dilapidated place.

Lady Priscilla, wearing nothing more than her usual threadbare gown, was apparently immune to the cold, or perhaps better used to it. Grudgingly she pointed to a chair beside the fire. "So? What is it you have to tell me?"

Ralf glanced at Sir William, slumped over a filthy, scarred trestle table, a goblet clutched in his fingers.

"He's asleep," Priscilla said, her voice as cold as the walls around them. "He won't hear anything."

"Hu Morgan is very sick."

"What of it? Is he like to die?"

"I don't know."

"So why come to me?"

"Because his wife has ordered the workers to build the wall."

"I'm not a fool, Ralf. It's too cold to do masonry work."

"Elwy and his men are to build a temporary one of wood. They're working quickly, too, so if Ivor had any plans to attack—"

"I know nothing of Ivor's plans."

"Well, if he was going to, he shouldn't leave it much longer. And that shepherd, he's gone for help."

Priscilla leaned forward expectantly. "More men?"

"I'm not sure. He's gone, that's all I know. Left this morning at daybreak, on a good horse, too."

Priscilla leaned back in her chair and regarded her visitor steadily. "Is that all?"

He rose. "That's worth plenty."

"If Ivor says so. I will pass on what you've said."

"Tell him I don't know how much longer I can stay here. People are beginning to suspect."

"People? What people?"

"Jhone, for one."

"She's a servant."

"Lady Liliana listens to her, I think. I'm not going to stay and be found out. I want my money for this, and soon."

"Are you giving Ivor ap Rhodri orders, Ralf? He won't like it."

Ralf looked at the floor, away from Priscilla Horton's dark, piercing eyes. "No."

"Good. Now go back home. I'll see that you get your money."

Ralf glanced up at her. A cringing smile crossed his thin face. "I'm only asking for what's right. I'm risking a lot, doing this. If Morgan finds out—"

"You are a dead man. Yes, I know. Good day, Ralf."

The man turned and hurried out of the hall, nearly stumbling in his haste.

Ivor stepped out of the shadows. "That man's going to bolt."

Priscilla nodded. "I suggest you stop him, my dear."

Ivor came toward her, watching the lust flare in the woman's face. "Not today, my love. Soon, but not today."

Chapter Fifteen

"Liliana?" Hu struggled to sit up and peered at the woman sitting beside him in the dimness. He had been ill, he knew, but for how long?

"No, my lord. It is Jhone. Please, drink this."

Hu slumped against the pillows. Why was Jhone helping him, and not Liliana? "Where is my wife?"

"In the yard, talking to Elwy about the wall. Now you must—"

"Wall? What wall? No one can work on the wall in the winter." His wife should have been here, tending to her husband.

"She gave orders for the men to build a temporary one of wood."

"*What?*" Hu sat up abruptly. The room started spinning, and he had to lie down. That sort of temporary structure might damage what had already been built. He hadn't bothered to explain that to Liliana, because the walls were not her responsibility. On the other hand, he thought angrily, he might have guessed. . . .

"Drink this now, please, and then I will fetch Lady Liliana."

"What is it?"

"Medicine."

Hu managed to down some of the noxious brew Jhone offered him. He wiped his lips with the back of his hand. "How long have I been ill?"

"You have been sick for some days, my lord. She thought it best—"

"Go and get my wife. And Elwy, too."

"Father Peter will be here shortly. He's come every day at this time—"

"God's teeth, I don't give a—" He took a deep breath and fought to keep his voice calm. After all, it was not Jhone's fault his wife had taken to acting the lord's part. "Just get me Liliana and Elwy."

He lay back against the pillows. He had plenty of questions, and he didn't think he was going to like the answers.

"Do you think that will be high enough?" Liliana asked pensively as she looked at the wooden wall.

Elwy nodded. "Aye, I think so. Anything more would need more supports, and that might damage the stone."

"I understand."

"My lady!"

Liliana turned to see Jhone hurrying toward her across the frozen courtyard. For a moment she was afraid that Hu's illness had worsened, until she saw Jhone's smile. "Is he awake?"

"And seemingly quite well. He wants to see you."

Liliana hurried off at once. Jhone watched her disappear inside the hall, then turned to Elwy. "He wants to see you, too."

"*O'r annwyl,* woman!" he said, tossing down the stick he had been using to make measurements. "Why didn't you say so?"

"Because I thought Lady Liliana might want a few moments alone with him, that's why."

Elwy grinned. "Oh, right you are there, I suppose."

"But I wouldn't wait here too long. He did not seem pleased to hear that you were doing this." She nodded at the wooden wall.

Elwy cursed softly. "I knew it was a mistake to obey her." He gave Jhone a look like a lost puppy. "What could I do, with her ordering and him sick?"

Jhone gestured toward the gate. "Here comes Father Peter. You had better let him in."

Elwy sighed. "Aye, and then I'd best go see Hu. Though I'd rather face a wild boar."

"I'll go with you."

Elwy looked at Jhone and smiled warmly. "Nothing like facing trouble with a friend, I always say."

Jhone's face betrayed nothing, but her heart leapt with joy at his smile. True, her mind told her, he called her "friend," but perhaps in time that could change.

Liliana rushed into the bedchamber. "Hu!" she cried, holding him tight in her embrace.

Hu, somewhat mollified by the delight in her eyes and the warmth of her greeting, put his arms around her.

She pulled back, sat on the bed and eyed him carefully. "The fever is gone, but you still don't look well."

"Fine thing to say to your husband," he muttered somewhat grumpily. "Is that why you weren't here?"

She looked very charming in her dismay. "I was talking with Elwy—"

"About the wall. Jhone told me. I don't think that was a good idea, Liliana."

"But we were too vulnerable—"

"That is *my* responsibility." He reached out and tugged her gently toward him. "Yours is to look after your husband and see that he is well, and—" he kissed her lightly on the lips "—happy."

She frowned a little. "I still think—"

"I beg your pardon, my lady."

Hu let go of Liliana and surveyed the long, lean, corpselike man standing in the doorway. "Who in the name of the saints is he?" he whispered.

Liliana stood up quickly. "Come in, Father Peter. As you can see, he is much better today."

"As I can see, my lady." The man came inside the room. "Obviously there is little need for me, or to send for that . . . other person."

Hu looked from the disgruntled priest to his wife. Elwy and Jhone appeared in the door. Jhone saw how crowded the chamber was and slipped away.

"What other person?" Hu asked.

"She sent Gareth to bring Mamaeth," Elwy explained.

Hu stared at them. "Mamaeth? Sent Gareth all that way to bring her back here? That was a stupid thing to do."

Father Peter looked as if he quite agreed, Elwy coughed and Liliana crossed her arms. "We thought you were dying," she said through tight lips. "We thought the woman might be able to help you."

"Well, you were wrong."

"Guess I'll go see to the livestock," Elwy said after an awkward moment of silence.

"Any more hens get sick?" Hu asked. "And the sheep? All well?"

Liliana bit her lip in frustration. She had been horribly worried for days, fearing the worst, and now she was apparently dismissed. Because she hadn't sat beside his bed every single minute?

She *had,* for hours when he was his sickest. Then, when Father Peter told her he thought the worst was past, she had begun to concern herself with the estate. She didn't want everything to fall into ruin while her husband lay ill, not when she knew more than he probably did about the management of a manor.

How was she supposed to know when he would wake up?

Why wasn't he grateful she had taken care of things?

Why wasn't he telling Elwy and the others to leave, so they could be alone again?

"Since you are better, my lord," she said, interrupting talk about the cows, "I will see to dinner."

With that, she turned and left the room. Father Peter followed wordlessly behind.

Elwy watched her go, then turned to Hu. "What's wrong with you, man? Did your sickness addle your wits?"

"What the hell are you talking about?"

"She's been worried sick about you—and you treat her like that?"

"She's been giving orders she had no right to give. She could have waited for me to get better."

"You fool! We didn't know when—or *if*—you were ever going to get better. Not until recently, anyway."

"She might have stayed by my bedside."

Elwy gave Hu a shrewd look. "That's it, isn't it, boy? You're angry because she wasn't weeping by the bed."

Hu looked away. "There wasn't any need to send for Mamaeth. You should have told her that."

"I'm no learned priest, Hu. I didn't know what was wrong with you."

"I shouldn't be angry, I suppose, but it's a dangerous journey. He didn't go alone, did he?"

"Sent three of the men with him. And not me you should be apologizing to, anyway, but your wife."

Hu ignored the last part of Elwy's speech. "Any sign of the rebels?"

"No."

"I want that wooden wall torn down."

Elwy stared at him, dumbfounded. "You *have* gone mad. You haven't even seen it."

"It will ruin the mortar on the top."

"Do you think we're all dolts? The masons told us how to do it right."

"Oh." Hu shifted under the bedclothes. "Is it finished?"

"Not yet."

"I suppose it might as well be completed—as long as the masons say it's all right."

Elwy went to the door. "I think you need more rest, Hu."

"Will you . . . ask Liliana to come here?"

Elwy sighed with relief. "God, Hu, between you and your wife and your foolishness, you're going to send me to an early grave."

Hu looked at Liliana standing in the doorway. Her carriage gave little hint that she was apologetic or anything but haughty, but he saw the uncertainty in her eyes. He *had* been rather harsh with her.

"I should not have been so angry," he said softly.

She smiled gloriously and came toward the bed, closing the door behind her. "I only did what I thought best."

"I know. Always foul-tempered when I've been sick, me, so pay me no mind next time."

Liliana shuddered. "Don't even think there will be a next time." She sat down on the bed, the bed she had not slept in for so long, and looked at her husband.

Hu's hair was tousled and matted, and his chin rough with whiskers, but he looked wonderful to her. "How is Maude, since Gareth is gone?"

"Not happy, but she will feel better when he returns."

"I feel better, Liliana."

She leaned closer to kiss him. "Do you?"

He pulled her toward him. "Much."

A few days later, Hu looked at the wooden barriers erected around the manor. Some were uncompleted, but it wouldn't take long to finish the work. Mott sat patiently at his side.

"Looks fine," Hu said matter-of-factly, ignoring Elwy's I-told-you-so expression.

"Where's Ralf?"

Elwy shrugged. "Haven't seen him. Not since yesterday. Looked a bit out of sorts then. Maybe he's sick."

"Should we summon Father Peter for him, or should we spare him?" Hu asked with a grave face but laughing eyes.

Elwy grinned.

"We can look for him later. How about going hunting? Right sick of staying around here, me."

"That sounds good," Elwy said. "Thought you might be thinking of it, since you've got your bow with you."

"And me thinking I was a sly fox."

"What will your lady wife say?"

Hu frowned, and this time his eyes were not laughing. "I want to go hunting. There is nothing else to be said."

Elwy nodded. "Aye, my lord."

Suddenly Mott stiffened and sniffed the air.

"Smell that?" Hu asked, scanning the horizon. "It's smoke."

He pointed to a billowing plume of heavy black smoke arising from the north. There could only be one explanation for smoke like that—a large building was on fire, either by accident or by attack.

"It's the Hortons'. Call the men!" Hu shouted as he ran to the stable.

Elwy began to summon the men working on the various tasks around the manor. "Leave the work and come with me," he ordered.

Liliana hurried out of the hall, clearly worried by the men mustering at the gate.

Hu appeared on his horse and looked down at her. "We'll see what's the matter at the Hortons'. The old sot probably set his own hall on fire. We should stay until the fire's out."

"You don't think it's an attack?"

"Doubt it. There's been no sign of the outlaws for weeks."

"Must you go, then? You're just getting better—"

"It's my duty. They're loyal to your father, too. Besides, I'm not planning to have to fight."

"The Hortons would be an easy target."

"True enough." Hu twisted in his saddle, now uneasy. He had no liking for either of the Hortons, but he would not want harm to come to them. "All you that have weapons, bring them."

Liliana grew even more worried as the workmen rushed back to their quarters. "Must you *all* go, then?"

"As you said, the Hortons are an easy target."

"If all the men go, so are we."

By now the workmen were again ready to depart, this time armed with swords and bows.

"Elwy!" Hu called out, scanning the courtyard for him.

"Here."

"I'm leaving you to protect the manor," he said, ignoring Elwy's disappointed face. "Pick ten men to stay with you."

Elwy glanced at Liliana, then at Hu. "Very well," he said grudgingly.

Liliana's tentative smile made Elwy's discomfort rather less important to Hu, and he bent down to give his wife a farewell kiss. "I'm sure you'll be quite safe," he said lightly. "We'll be back as soon as we can."

"Be careful. I fear it could be a trap," she said.

Hu grinned self-confidently. "Not likely. We'll be back before the evening meal. You'll see."

He signaled for his men to move off, and waved as they went out the gate.

Ivor turned to Dafydd with a triumphant smile as the band of mounted men rode past them through the forest. Hidden in a ditch a short distance from the road, they could easily see that most of the fighting men from Morgan's manor were in that swiftly moving group.

Dafydd did not return the pleased expression. "Did you have to kill her, too, Ivor?" he asked quietly, his words full of shame and reprimand.

"She was a traitor, and traitors should die," Ivor said with disdain. He believed it with all that remained of his heart.

"To set the place afire to draw Morgan away, I understand. But cold-blooded murder—"

"What does one more dead Norman matter?"

"Priscilla Horton was your lover."

"She was all my men's lover, except yours," Ivor answered, grabbing Dafydd by the tunic and drawing him close to his snarling face. "She was useful, and that was all. But if it's justice you're after, then I was only repaying an eye for an eye. It was *her* killed her father."

"And who was it put her up to it?" Dafydd demanded, knocking away Ivor's hand. "Who was it said he'd wed her if she did what he wanted?"

"The important thing was to draw Morgan and his men away from his manor. We've done that, so shut your mouth and let's go."

Dafydd's mouth became a hard, determined line. "If you touch Morgan's wife, Ivor, I'll kill you myself."

"What's it to you what happens to her? She's a Norman, isn't she?"

"She's a woman first, and I won't see a woman hurt, or worse, Norman or no."

"Wasn't it you told me how the Normans used your sister before they killed her, with you looking on?"

"That is why I would stop you."

Ivor smiled coldly. "Then don't come with us. Stay home, like an old woman. All these other men are brave enough."

Dafydd rose to his feet, staring at a man for whom he had lost all respect. "It's not about bravery, Ivor. It's about honor. I will not let you do this."

Suddenly Ivor's foot lashed out and sent Dafydd tumbling backward. Around them, men who had not heard the gist of their argument stared in surprise.

"He's a traitor," Ivor said. All his hatred for people who would betray their own rose in him like a poison. He drew out his sword. "Am I going to have to kill you, Dafydd, or will you go running like a pet to that Morgan?"

Ivor didn't wait for an answer. He attacked his fallen companion.

Dafydd twisted away, but not before the sword struck. He cried out in pain, clutching his shoulder as blood stained his tunic. The other men stood quickly, their faces filled with confusion and fear. Then Ivor stabbed Dafydd and struck him below his ribs.

Ivor frowned as he wiped his bloody weapon on his breeches. He sheathed it and kicked Dafydd under a bush. "Leave him here. We've got other work to do."

With that he signaled to his dumbfounded men and headed for the manor of Hu Morgan.

Chapter Sixteen

"My lady!"

Liliana put down her sewing at the sound of Jhone's agitated voice. Hu and his men had not been gone for very long, but it seemed like a whole day already, and she hoped Jhone would say they were returning.

"What is it?" she asked as Jhone rushed inside. One look at her servant's face, and Liliana began to tremble. *"What is it?"*

"There's men coming!"

"What men?" Even as she asked, Liliana forced herself to move toward the door.

"I don't know, but they're armed."

"Close the gate!" Liliana called as she stepped out into the cold air. If the men were friends, the gate could be opened, but she was not willing to take any chances with Hu and most of the men gone.

Two of the mortar makers moved to obey. "Where's Elwy?" she demanded of them.

"The barn."

Liliana was about to go to him when she heard a cry of alarm.

The laborers had not been fast enough. Just as one of them started to shut the heavy oak door, the leader of a group of heavily armed men rode swiftly into the courtyard. She recognized the leader at once as the outlaw in the forest.

He called out an order. Two of his men dismounted.

Then *they* closed the gates, shoving the mortar makers away with harsh Welsh words, effectively sealing everyone inside.

As Elwy emerged from the barn, his sword drawn, Liliana moved into the hall and stood just out of sight inside the door. She could see the courtyard clearly.

"Who are they, my lady?" Jhone whispered behind her.

Liliana glanced over her shoulder at her servant. "Maude and the others—are they in the kitchen?" she whispered urgently, her gaze returning to the leader of the strangers and Elwy.

"Yes, my lady."

"Go to them and hide there. Do not come out unless they set fire to the hall."

"But, my lady—"

"Now, Jhone," she whispered in a tone that brooked no protest.

She watched Elwy approach the leader. "Who are you and what do you want?" Elwy demanded in French.

The leader answered scornfully in Welsh. The rest of his men dismounted and began pushing and shoving the Welsh workmen into a small group.

Elwy spoke again, his words fierce and angry.

Suddenly, several of the armed men rushed Elwy. Before he could strike, they knocked the sword from his hand. Others pushed him to the ground.

Their leader laughed coldly and raised his sword, ready to strike.

"Stop!"

Not so very many generations ago, Liliana Trevelyan's ancestors had been Northmen, ferocious, savage warriors who swarmed out of their cold, rocky land to terrorize the coasts of Europe. Now, as she went into the courtyard to face the men who would dare to threaten her people, her manor and her husband's friend, all that savage warrior intensity of her forebears surged through her body, giving her a courage she didn't know she possessed.

But when the leader saw who had shouted, he began to smile with a strange mixture of hatred, impertinence and lust.

Liliana straightened her shoulders. "What do you want?" she demanded.

The black-haired man's eyes widened for a moment before he answered quickly, his tone arrogant. He sauntered toward her and continued to rake her body with his gaze.

Her courage began to falter, but she kept her face impassive and her hands clasped in front of her to still their trembling. She told herself to show nothing. After all, she was used to being stared at, whether with respect or interest, and this man was a coward, for only a coward would attack Elwy thus. She had no respect for or fear of cowards.

And surely Hu would be back soon.

She looked questioningly at Elwy when the man stopped talking, unsure of the meaning of his rapid speech.

The leader saw her glance and grinned before speaking again. Four of his men dragged Elwy upright, still pinning his arms helplessly to his side.

The man waited while Elwy, his face a picture of anger and scorn, said, "That dung heap wants me to tell you he's come to burn the traitor's manor to the ground after he slaughters all those who would help him. Just as he did to the Hortons."

"He would murder other Welshmen?" Liliana crossed her arms, trying to remain calm.

The leader listened while Elwy repeated her question in Welsh, then he spoke again.

"He says," Elwy translated with more than a hint of contempt, "that we are not true Welshmen—we're traitors and deserve to die." Elwy let loose with a string of Welsh oaths directed at the rebel leader, which earned him a blow to the mouth. Blood began to trickle down Elwy's chin, but he ignored it and did not take his scornful gaze from the man. Indeed, he looked at the outlaw as if the man was a fly he would like to squash.

Liliana straightened her shoulders, new respect for Hu's friend making her braver. "Does he understand the consequences of what he means to do?" she asked coolly when the leader faced her. "That my father would never rest until he and all his men were captured and executed? That the king, hearing of this, would surely send more troops here? That the very people he thinks he will help by harming us will surely suffer tenfold for his stupidity and curse his name forever?''

Elwy translated everything, just as she said it.

When the leader spoke again, Elwy's eyes narrowed. ''He says he will never be captured and that the Welsh will sing his name forever because he dares to throw off the Norman yoke.''

The leader said something more, but Elwy remained silent. The leader hit him and barked a command. Still Elwy said nothing.

''What is it?'' Liliana asked. ''What is he saying?''

''It is not fit for me to repeat, my lady.''

The leader drew his sword and put the blade at Elwy's throat before speaking again, but Elwy only shook his head.

The leader put down his weapon and turned toward her. ''He is a brave man,'' he said slowly, his French better than she would have expected. ''A pity he will die.''

With that, he spun around and thrust his blade into Elwy's chest.

A strangled, horrified cry burst from Liliana's throat. Elwy stared in disbelief at the growing stain of blood on his tunic. Then he pitched forward and lay on the ground.

The workmen, their faces filled with anger, at once gave a savage cry, seized their tools to use in place of weapons and fell upon their captors.

Liliana took a step toward Elwy, but before she could reach him, the outlaw lunged for her. She tried to pull away from his grasp.

But he was too strong.

* * *

Hu looked at the body of Priscilla Horton. Sometimes in death there was peace on a person's features, but not so with her. Her lips were drawn back in a snarl like a wild animal's, as if she had died spewing forth hatred and bile.

He picked up a half-burned blanket and covered her with it. It seemed the least he could do.

With a sigh, he surveyed the ruin of Horton Hall. Nothing remained but a shell of blackened timbers, where they had found parts of a skeleton. It was probably William Horton.

Hu's men, who had gone to search for any survivors or witnesses, returned. They all shook their heads, and Hu could only hope that the servants had escaped.

But not for long. The last of his men arrived, to tell them about the bodies down by the river.

When Hu went there, he found Ralf among them, his throat slit and a piece of parchment clutched in his bloody fingers.

Hu gently pulled the paper free, then stared at it in horror. It was a charcoal drawing of his manor's temporary defenses. Hu muttered a curse, at Ralf and then himself.

Mott, who had been waiting quietly beside Hu, suddenly got to his feet, his nose quivering. Then he began to bark and dashed off through the trees.

Hu gasped, looking in the direction his dog had gone, then at the drawing in his hand. "What have I done?"

He ran to his horse and mounted quickly. "Back! We must go back!" he shouted as he spurred the animal to a gallop. His men were too surprised to move at first, until they saw the new plume of smoke rising in the distance.

Liliana struggled in her captor's embrace, twisting away from his lustful lips and hate-filled eyes. As fighting continued in the courtyard between her men and his, he dragged her into the hall and shoved her against the wall. "Don't fight me," he whispered, pressing a heated kiss to her cheek. "Beg me to spare you and I will let you live."

"I would rather die than submit to dung like you," she answered scornfully. "And I will *never* beg."

If Ivor had been as intelligent as he believed himself to be, he might have realized that a woman as beautiful as Liliana had been fighting unwanted advances for a long time. Her knowledge of men's weaknesses was good, and she used it now, bringing her knee upward with considerable force.

For an instant Ivor let go of her, which gave her a chance to break free and run toward the door. Outside she could see men fighting, and the barn was aflame, but before she could get over the threshold, Ivor grabbed her gown, tearing it and bringing her painfully to her knees. He pulled her inside as she tried to crawl away.

He hauled her to her feet. "Much as I like you on your knees, Norman, I want you to see my Welsh face."

When he bent to plunder her mouth again, she struck at him with all the force she could muster, which in her state of fear, rage and determination was substantial.

He tried to grab her hand, but she twisted away and made for the kitchen corridor.

Ivor ran after her. He was not about to let this prize slip through his fingers. He wanted to hear her beg for mercy, the arrogant Norman bitch.

Liliana dashed along the short corridor, spurred on by panic and the sound of the Welshman following her. She entered the kitchen and ran to the carving board. Once there, she grabbed the biggest knife she could find.

Then she heard the sounds of muffled crying. Glancing over her shoulder, she saw Jhone and the other women hiding behind a pile of wood.

She had to protect them as well as herself. She dashed to the door. The Welshman was close behind her. She rushed into the courtyard and saw most of the rebels riding out of the gates.

"Ivor! Run, man! Morgan's coming back!" one of the rebels called as he scrambled to mount his horse.

"Come back!" the leader shouted, running past her toward his fleeing comrades. "Cowards! Fools!"

"Ivor!"

The cry pierced the smoke-filled air. Liliana turned to see who had shouted. The man stood motionless, just inside the gate, a sword in his hand, his face bloody and bruised. His shoulder was wounded and his tunic was soaked with blood.

Ivor halted. "Thought I killed you, Dafydd."

"Not yet." Suddenly Dafydd ran at Ivor. Liliana moved quickly away as he raised his sword to strike.

Ivor parried the blow, then drew his dagger and jabbed. Dafydd fell, but he took Ivor down with him.

Ivor struggled to his feet. A growing stain of blood marked his chausses at the thigh. "I'll leave you here, Dafydd, with your Norman friends." He darted a look at Liliana and smiled icily. "Another time, my lady. Another time."

He limped quickly to his prancing horse, mounted and rode out the gate.

Liliana's whole body began to tremble as she stood there, the knife still in her hand. Dense smoke obscured her vision. Someone nearby shouted for help. Animals escaped from the barn and ran around the courtyard in wild-eyed panic.

Ignoring everything else, she let the knife drop and walked toward Elwy, lying on the ground. She knelt down. Gently, tenderly, she cradled his head in her arms and looked at the homely yet so dear face.

"Now you will sing with the angels," she whispered as she closed his eyes.

Jhone leaned against the side of the hall. No sound escaped her lips, but tears ran unheeded down her cheeks.

Hu's horse galloped through the open gate, and he was out of the saddle before it stopped. The courtyard was in a smoky uproar, with animals running loose, the maidservants helping moaning men, and the rest of the laborers carrying water from the well to the barn in a frantic attempt to put out the fire.

In the middle of it all, through the haze, he saw Liliana kneeling on the ground, holding Elwy in her arms.

He ran to her, noting with horror her torn gown wet with blood, her disheveled hair and her cut lip. "Liliana! Are you hurt?"

She lifted her sooty, tear-streaked face. "He's dead," she said woodenly, as if she still could scarcely believe it. "Dead."

Hu couldn't breathe. Not Elwy. Sweet Jesus, not Elwy.

She bowed her head and her shoulders began to shake. A deep sob burst from her throat.

"Did they...hurt you?"

Still bending over the body in her arms, she shook her head. "They came when you had gone. The outlaws." She looked at him. Her expression grew hard. "The ones you were always so sure were gone! You ignored my fears, my warnings! You left us here, with so few to protect us!"

Hu felt her words like a sword thrust to his heart.

"Elwy's dead because you thought—thought!— there was nothing to fear."

Liliana gently placed Elwy's head on the ground and rose to her feet slowly. "Your first duty should have been to protect your own land. Your own people. Your own wife."

His anguish turned to anger as she stood in the courtyard, upbraiding him like a delinquent child while his truest, best friend lay dead at her feet. "Don't you *dare* tell me my duty!" he shouted.

She glared at him, her face growing red. "I will if I am right! And I was. I am. Aren't I?" She went on, her words propelled by anger and the aftermath of fear. "You ignored me. I should have thought you would at least want to protect this estate you seem to care so much about."

"Of course I should have been here!" he shouted back. "Do you think I don't know that? You're *right*—because you always are, aren't you, Liliana? Always so sure and certain that you know everything!"

He turned on his heel and looked at the men who were staring at them. "The man who killed Elwy. What did he look like?"

"It was the man who stopped us in the forest that day," Liliana said accusingly.

Hu began to walk toward his horse.

"Where are you going?" Liliana demanded. "You're not leaving us here again?"

He looked at her, his eyes full of cold fury in his pale face. "I am going to find Elwy's killer. You enjoy giving orders. You can manage here, surely."

Liliana moved toward him, suddenly afraid for her husband. She had seen enough of Ivor to know that he would fight ruthlessly, and Hu, whatever he might believe, was still weak from his illness.

His brow furrowed and his voice was ominous when he spoke. "I am doing my duty—to Elwy. Do not try to stop me."

"Don't leave us again," she cried, truly desperate. She tried to think of something that would make him stay. "If you leave, I'll go to my father for protection!"

He raised one eyebrow but his expression remained hard and distant. "You have threatened to leave me before, Liliana, and you did not. Must I remind you that it is your *duty* to stay, wife?" With that, he mounted his horse and rode out of the gate.

Liliana watched him go, her shoulders sagging, fearing that she would never see him alive again.

Surely Hu would return safely from searching for the rebel leader. The Welshman had probably disappeared into the wilderness of the mountains.

She remembered how Hu had fought in her father's tournament. If Hu did find the rebel, her husband would defeat him. Even if he was not yet fully recovered.

Slowly she became aware that other people were nearby. Many others. Maude. Sarah. Jhone. The laborers. All staring at her.

How long had they been there? Long enough to hear them arguing? Long enough to hear her husband's harsh words?

And the expression on their faces! Didn't they see that she was right? They looked as if they held her to blame, but she had warned Hu that it was a trap. Did they think it was her fault he had abandoned them again?

Liliana lifted her chin. Hu had belittled her opinions time and again, refusing to see that she might be right and him wrong. He had berated her in front of everyone and ignored her plea that he stay.

She was Lady Liliana Morgan, and no man could shame her in front of the villeins when she was in the right. Not even Hu.

"Carry Elwy inside," she ordered. She would see that his body was cared for properly. And then she would leave, as she had said she would.

* * *

Hu searched the ground in front of him, following the trail of hooves in the mud. Ivor Rhodri had to be wounded to be so careless.

He forced himself to keep his mind on what he was doing and on what he would do to Ivor when he found him. He would not think about Liliana's accusations, or that she had threatened to leave him.

He would remember Elwy, dead in the courtyard.

He spotted a man lying on the ground near a thicket, a sword nearby and his chausses bloody.

God's teeth, he hoped he wasn't too late and Ivor ap Rhodri already dead.

Hu dismounted and approached the man cautiously, sword drawn. Ivor didn't stir.

"Getting sloppy," Hu said. He kicked Ivor with the toe of his boot, then tensed and waited for him to strike back.

Ivor rolled over and stared at him.

"I've come to collect the *galanas* of my friend," Hu said.

Ivor sat up. His hand moved toward his sword, until he saw that Hu's foot was already on the blade.

"The blood-price?" Ivor asked softly. "How much do you want, traitor?"

"Your life is the price I set."

Ivor rose slowly. "If you can take it, traitor."

Hu nudged the sword's blade toward Ivor with his toe.

Ivor bent down to grab the hilt, but as he did so, he pulled a dagger from his tunic and lunged at Hu. Hu sidestepped him and knocked the weapon from his hand. Ivor raised his sword, but Hu slashed at the blade with all his strength. The sword fell into the bushes. Ivor scrambled after his dagger, lying close by.

Hu tossed his sword to the ground and jumped on Ivor, wrestling him to the ground and pinning him there.

"I am going to kill you, Ivor Rhodri," he panted, staring into the man's scowling face.

Ivor's lips twisted into a mocking grin. "Dog of the Normans, kill me then, if you have the courage to do it."

Hu picked up Ivor's dagger, and with one swift, sure slash, slit the man's throat.

Chapter Seventeen

Liliana straightened abruptly as Maude entered the bedchamber.

"Has my husband returned?" she asked, trying to keep any emotion at all from her voice, although she felt a nearly overwhelming mixture of relief, joy and dread to think that Hu was home.

"Not yet, my lady."

Liliana turned away quickly and busied herself with closing and fastening the lid to a small chest. "Where are your things?" she asked after a moment. "We must leave at once. We shall have to travel in the dark as it is."

"I'm not going with you," Maude announced grimly.

"You are my maidservant," Liliana replied. "You go where I go."

"I'm staying here to wait for Gareth to come back."

Liliana pressed her lips together. It was quite obvious that Maude did not approve of what her mistress was about to do—but she was only a servant. What did it matter what Maude thought?

"Have they carried Elwy to the chapel?"

"Yes. Father Alphonse will say a memorial Mass in the morning."

Liliana stared at the floor. She did not want to miss that, but she had said she would go, so go she would. "Take this to the wagon," she ordered.

"Very well, my lady." Maude lifted the chest and walked toward the door. She hesitated on the threshold. "Safe journey, my lady," she said softly, and then she was gone.

Liliana grabbed her cloak and drew it on. At the door she paused for a moment to glance around the room. She didn't want to leave anything important.

Her gaze came to rest on the bed, and against her will she remembered Hu in his sleep, with his tousled hair and boyish face. The way he smiled at her in the pale light of morning. The way he kissed and caressed her at night... the way his body felt against hers...

She shook her head. Naturally he was wonderful in the bed. It was his actions when he was out of the bed that caused all the trouble.

She was going home to her father. *He* treated her with respect and let her run the household as she saw fit. He listened to her advice, too, more than Hu Morgan ever had.

She told herself it would suit her well if Hu Morgan never came near her again. Yes, it would.

When she went outside, Jhone stood beside the wagon, a bundle in her hands. "I have heard that Maude is staying here," she said quietly. "If you please, my lady, I would be happy to take her place as your maid."

Liliana studied Jhone's inscrutable face. "I would be pleased, too," she said. "But this is your home."

"That does not matter." Pain flickered across the woman's eyes, and Liliana realized the attack had upset even the usually placid Jhone.

Liliana glanced toward the wagon and the small group of men she had insisted accompany them, then nodded as she went toward her horse. "Get up on the wagon, then."

She mounted and turned to the driver. Jhone sat beside him, her face grave and her back stiff.

"Follow me," Liliana said.

Cold, hopeless despair settled over Hu as he stood on a low rise that overlooked the road and watched the wagon with its driver and passenger, the small escort and the blue-cloaked rider going slowly on their way.

Liliana was leaving, and she looked to be heading toward her father's castle. He should have known that she would do as she had said.

He should let her go. Just take Ivor's body to his manor and not bother any more with Liliana and her orders and her pride. He had apologized to her too many times already. Let her apologize to him for her accusations and arrogance.

He would concern himself with his manor, his livestock and building a fighting force. Ivor was dead, but there were other rebels in the hills, and he would be ready for them.

Other rebels in the hills. Liliana was heading for the forest with only five men to protect her. Gritting his teeth, he pulled the body from his horse and mounted.

"Stay," he commanded Mott, who sat obediently beside Ivor's lifeless body.

He nudged his horse to a walk, and proceeded to follow the cortege at a discreet distance to insure that Liliana arrived at her father's without coming to harm.

Not that she seemed to care what happened to him. She had gone without even waiting to make sure he returned safely. Obviously she did not love him as much as he had believed.

And what would she tell her father? Surely Lord Trevelyan would agree that he had been doing his duty by going to help the Hortons. Who would have guessed that the attack on the Hortons' manor was a trap to render another estate vulnerable?

Liliana had.

No doubt she would make sure her father heard that. She would probably also complain that her husband was an unprincipled, ignorant oaf unworthy of her, which had been his fear when they first married.

He should have paid attention to the fears in his heart. It suddenly seemed that the reward of the manor was not worth the pain he was feeling now for marrying Liliana. And if he had not wed her, it might not have been too difficult to forget her.

It would be impossible to forget her now. And soon, if Lord Trevelyan took the manor, he would only have his memories . . . and his pain.

Lord Trevelyan looked up from the chess game he was playing with his guest and stared at the cloaked figure standing in the entrance of his hall.

"Liliana!" he cried, hurrying toward his shivering daughter. "What's happened?" He looked past her. "Where's Hu?"

"At his manor," she replied calmly. At least, she supposed he was there now. She had seen him on the ridge. It had taken a great deal of self-control to keep from calling out to him, to see for herself that he was unharmed. He had simply sat there, watching. Letting her go on her way. "The Hortons were attacked. They are dead."

"Oh, dear God!" Lord Trevelyan embraced his daughter, then led her closer to the roaring fire blazing in the hearth, silently cursing himself for not insisting that Morgan have more soldiers. But his first concern was for Liliana. She was pale and had dark circles of exhaustion under her eyes but, he noted with relief, she did not seem to be injured. "So he sent you here for safety? That was wise of him."

He saw Liliana looking at his guest and said, "May I present Lady Jane Cotterill."

Liliana made a slight curtsy while her father gave a few brisk orders for mulled wine and some fruit.

He gestured for Liliana to sit down. "Now tell me what happened."

"The attack on the Hortons was a trap. To get Hu and his men away. When they left, the rebels came to our manor. They were...not successful in their plan to burn our manor to the ground."

"Thank God!" Lord Trevelyan said fervently, but he still eyed his daughter anxiously. "Was anyone—"

"Elwy. Elwy was killed."

"That's terrible. I can understand why Hu would want you to come here."

"It was my idea." Liliana didn't say anything more. It was very late, and she was very tired. She only wanted to make her way to her old bed.

Where she had spent her wedding night.

She banished such thoughts as Jhone and the driver came inside, each carrying several items of baggage. They looked at Liliana expectantly.

Liliana beckoned to one of her father's maidservants, who had just arrived with some heated wine. "Show them to my room," she said. "Jhone, I will need the things in the small chest first."

She glanced at Lady Jane, who looked to be slightly younger than her father. She had pale blue eyes, now full of sympathy, and a mild, pleasant countenance.

In a way, Liliana was glad her father had a guest. She was in no mood to give explanations or relate what had happened between herself and her husband, not even to her father. He would not expect her to with Lady Jane sitting there.

"I hope you don't mind that I came for a visit," Liliana said, suddenly aware that her father had not asked Lady Jane to leave them alone.

Her father smiled at her, but he didn't meet her eye. "Naturally I am happy to have you. It will be good to have you home again." He cleared his throat. "However, I was not expecting you until Christmastide, so you may find things a bit...disrupted."

Liliana reached to pour some wine for her father's guest when with another unpleasant shock of surprise, she realized that Lady Jane had leaned forward for the same purpose.

It had always been Liliana's place to act as hostess. She looked sharply at her father, who reddened. "I was planning to tell you when you came at Christmas," he said. "Lady Jane and I are going to be married. In fact, I was planning to journey to her manor tomorrow."

Liliana forced herself to smile, but inwardly she felt the ground under her feet give way. "Oh," she murmured, "please, don't let me interfere with your journey. Maybe I will visit Lady Eleanor for a while—"

Her father cleared his throat. "Lady Eleanor's daughters, with their husbands and children, are expected soon for the Christmastide."

"Then I shall stay here, if I may."

"Of course, Liliana," her father said with a warm smile. "This is your home."

Liliana's first thought was that it was no longer her home. The way Lady Jane was already acting as lady of the manor, the undeniable fact that her father was less than pleased to see her, and even the alterations in the furnishings, all showed quite plainly that much had changed.

"You look tired, my dear," Lady Jane said sympathetically. "It has been a long ride for you—"

"Yes, it has." Liliana stood up. This had been the longest, most difficult day of her entire life, and she wanted—no, needed—to get away by herself, back to her old room. Surely *that* would not be changed since her wedding night. "Sleep well, Lady Jane. Good night, Father."

"We will talk more of this in the morning," he said kindly.

Liliana nodded, but she couldn't deny that she was beginning to dread the necessity of explaining her actions to her father. Not that she expected him to question them. Surely he would not wish to see her humiliated. Not by her husband. Not by anyone.

In the darkness, Hu entered his courtyard, walking beside his horse, which once again carried Ivor's body. The barn was a smoking ruin, but he saw that his men had managed to round up the livestock.

A few of the men gathered silently around him, eyeing his horse's burden.

"Where's Elwy?" Hu asked softly.

"The chapel."

"I will watch the body."

The other Welshmen nodded, and said they would join the vigil that night, too.

Hu gestured toward Ivor. "As for this one . . . Bury him. I don't care where."

He turned away and saw Maude standing in the yard. He was surprised, for he had assumed the woman sitting on the cart had been Maude.

"We've got a prisoner," Maude said, gesturing toward the hall. "One of the rebels."

Hu frowned and nodded, then paused before going inside. "Who was the woman who left with my wife?"

"It was Jhone."

"Oh."

Maude put her hand on his arm. "That fellow there—" she nodded at Ivor's body "—he was wounded?"

"Aye."

"The prisoner's the one that did it. I saw them fighting."

Hu gave her a sidelong glance. "Why? Who is he?"

She shook her head. "He won't say a word, not to anybody. He's hurt bad, my lord, maybe dying."

"I will see if he will talk to me."

Hu marched into the hall. A man lay on a bench near the hearth, his body still, the rising and falling of his chest barely perceptible.

Hu approached him and stood for a moment looking down at the young man. He was dark-haired and dark-skinned. Welsh, surely. His shoulder was wrapped in a bandage, but blood was seeping through it.

Hu nudged the fellow, who slowly opened his eyes. "Who are you?" he asked in Welsh.

The man did not speak.

"It's like that, is it?" Hu said harshly. "Well, Welshman, you're not going to tell me why you fought Ivor Rhodri, either, then, are you?"

The man shook his head.

"You could have been attacked by those rebels, too, I suppose."

The man remained silent and gazed at Hu impassively.

"Nevertheless, you will no doubt be interested to know that Ivor Rhodri is dead. I cut his throat."

The fellow's dark, fearless eyes widened, but only for an instant.

"Look you," Hu said suddenly, kneeling down beside him. "Welsh and Norman have got to learn to live together. The Normans are too strong to push out now. But we Welsh are strong, too, in our own way. Fighting isn't going to accomplish anything but getting the Welsh killed, man."

The man frowned scornfully and finally spoke with great effort. "I would rather die than submit to Norman rule."

Hu sighed and stood up. "Then you give me no choice. You will remain my prisoner until Lord Trevelyan can pass judgment on you."

"If you are truly a Welshman," the young man whispered, "you won't let me die in a Norman prison, or on a Norman gibbet." His words were spoken slowly, reasonably, proudly and without pleading. "Morgan, take me up to the hills and leave me there. Let me die with the music of the wind in my ears and the land I love beneath me."

Hu looked at the Welshman. The fellow was weak and losing blood. Surely he could not survive if they left him out on the hills, just as he would surely die in Lord Trevelyan's castle.

This man had fought against Ivor, for whatever reason. Would it be so terrible to let him have the death he asked for?

Hu nodded slowly, and the man smiled.

The next morning, before Lord Trevelyan left on his journey, he listened to his daughter detail her reasons for leaving her husband. On the surface, they seemed valid enough. Hu would not listen to her. He didn't do as she suggested. His arrogance had contributed to their vulnerability to attack.

However, Lord Trevelyan knew his daughter. He could easily imagine how she would announce her opinion, with no room for differing ones. Her suggestions had probably sounded more like orders, which a proud man like Hu Morgan would eventually find intolerable. To be sure, Hu should have listened more to Liliana. She was an excellent judge of people, and if she had suspicions, they were worth paying attention to.

Obviously Hu had not yet realized that. Given time, he would.

"So when he shouted at me like that, in front of the servants and everyone else, I really had no choice but to leave," Liliana finished. Her tone was slightly defiant, and he knew that she wanted nothing more from him than reassurance that her husband was all in the wrong, and that she had done the correct thing.

Unfortunately, he did not believe the problems in their marriage were all Hu's fault, nor did he believe that their marriage was a disaster. He had seen his daughter and her husband together and believed he had never seen a happier couple. These two stubborn, equally proud young people simply had to learn to compromise.

Lord Trevelyan looked at her as she waited expectantly for him to speak. She was so sweet and vulnerable in her own way. Part of him, the doting father, wanted to tell her she was right and that she could stay for as long as she liked. But the other, wiser part told him that if he gave in now, she would never reconcile with Hu and would probably become a bitter, lonely woman.

He sighed softly and said, "Of course you may stay, Liliana." He rose from his ornately carved chair.

"Thank you, Father," she replied, standing.

He gave her a shrewd glance as they walked the length of the great hall. "Sometimes it is wise to admit defeat."

Liliana's lips pressed together, and he knew that he had said enough.

Chapter Eighteen

A fortnight later, Liliana was working on a tapestry. She had started it after her arrival at her father's castle, and with the abundance of spare time she had as a guest, had nearly finished it.

"Tired, my lady?" Jhone asked quietly. She sat nearby, sorting the different threads by color.

"Only my eyes," Liliana replied, rubbing them. "I...I haven't been sleeping well lately. It must be the different room."

Not the loneliness she felt, she told herself, or her dismay that Hu apparently did not care enough about her welfare to find out if she had arrived safely. He had not even sent a messenger to inquire.

Whatever her father thought, she had been right to leave Hu. She should have left him in the beginning, when she had feared that Hu did not truly care for her.

For a little while she had permitted herself to live in a dream. A very pleasant dream, some of it... But she had awakened from it now.

"It is unfortunate that your father decided to make such extensive changes to the bedchambers."

"Yes." Liliana's needle pierced the taut cloth.

"Perhaps you should stop sewing for a little while," Jhone said, glancing at the tapestry. She stifled a gasp and turned her head quickly away.

Liliana gazed at her usually serene servant, then down at the portion of the design she was embroidering. It was a banquet scene, with noblemen and noblewomen dancing to the music of minstrels. One of the musicians had dark hair and a rather large nose. She realized he looked very much like Elwy.

Liliana put down the sewing and voiced a regret that also disturbed her slumbers. "I wish I had attended the Mass for him." She looked at Jhone. "*You* could have."

Jhone regarded her steadily. Once again, her face was impassive, but Liliana saw that her eyes glistened with unshed tears. "No, I could not." Her gaze faltered, and Liliana suddenly realized she had been blind to Jhone's suffering. Or too selfishly involved in her own troubles.

"I would have...disgraced myself," Jhone finished quietly.

"I am so sorry, Jhone!" Liliana whispered, taking hold of her maidservant's hand. "I didn't know—"

"Nobody did, my lady. Not even him."

"There may be someone else someday," Liliana ventured.

"No." Jhone's tone was one of absolute finality. Her features softened a little. "I know you cannot understand, my lady, but I loved him with my whole heart. There can be no one else to fill that part of me now."

"I know how to love..." Liliana flushed hotly when Jhone's face betrayed skepticism. Liliana stared at her. "By what right do you dare to question my feelings?"

"You left your husband."

"I had to! You heard the way he spoke to me! You know how he ignored our fears! I tried to warn him, but he wouldn't listen."

"He loves you."

Liliana didn't respond. She turned away as tears filled her eyes. She loved him, too. At least as much as Jhone had loved Elwy. She had been miserable since she had been away from Hu, and in the long, lonely hours of the night, she had cursed herself for a fool. With her arrogance and stubbornness and hasty words, she had ruined her marriage to the best husband a woman could ask for.

She had tried to convince herself that if she went back to him, she would seem weak. That her dignity and honor demanded she stay here.

What was more important, she asked herself, her pride and her dignity, or being with the man she loved with her whole heart? The man she was certain loved her just as much.

"Oh, my *dear!* I came as soon as I heard!" Averil Beaumare exclaimed as she rushed into the hall. "How very unfortunate for you!"

Liliana gritted her teeth and rose from her chair. She might have known Averil would come. Like a vulture, she would rush to see the carnage of a ruined marriage and sympathize over the corpse.

"We were staying at the Cotterills' when your father arrived. He's most concerned for your welfare, so naturally I told him I would come at once to comfort you."

Jhone stood up and moved her chair for Averil.

"I appreciate your solicitude," Liliana replied stiffly.

Barris sauntered in. He nodded absently, looking around the large, comfortably furnished hall. "Very cold, this weather, very cold."

Liliana turned to Jhone. "Please get us some wine," she said. "And have a boy fetch more wood for the fire."

Jhone nodded and silently went out to the kitchen.

"Barris," Averil barked as she sat down without even bothering to remove her heavy, dun-colored wool cloak, "have the baggage taken care of." Averil leaned forward after Barris had sauntered out again. She put on her most sorrowful face. "I must say, Liliana, that you are looking far from well."

"I am tired, that's all."

"He didn't . . . beat you?"

Liliana would have been hard-pressed to say if Averil's eyes gleamed more from the firelight or her avid curiosity. "No," she said firmly.

"Well, my dear, I have to say I think you were lucky there. I didn't want to say anything when you were so pleased with the marriage, but everyone knows these Welshmen are *barbarians*."

If she thought only of Ivor and his like, Liliana might have agreed. But she thought instead of Hu, Elwy and their friends' easy banter, the traditions they maintained, the intricate and lovely songs they sang. She knew better, but she also knew it was useless to try to explain to someone as firm in her opinion as Averil.

As she herself had been at one time.

"What is your father going to do about your husband?"

Liliana looked at her. "What do you mean?"

"Why, everyone expects that Sir Hu Morgan will find himself without an estate."

Liliana toyed with a loose strand from the tapestry in the basket beside her. She, too, wondered what her return to her father might mean for Hu. Whatever happened, she had decided to ask her father to let Hu stay his ally. The estate meant so much to him.

"Justly so," Averil announced, obviously taking Liliana's silence to be agreement. "The fellow didn't deserve the honor in the first place. He may be fine as a tournament fighter or a soldier, but he has no idea of the proper notions of etiquette. That gown of mine was completely ruined by his stupid prank."

Liliana subdued a brief smile at the memory of Hu's trick. Yes, he was a little lacking in what Averil would consider the "proper notions of etiquette," but Liliana had been noticing, now that she was back among "mannered" people, how constrictive those notions could be. "Barris, of course, thinks his manners perfectly acceptable. He insisted on visiting him on the journey here, but I—thinking of you, my dear—refused to stay longer than the morning."

"You saw him this morning?"

"For only a few minutes, I assure you. No man can treat one of my dearest friends so foully that she is forced to go back to her father without expecting to be censured by me. And I must say, Liliana, that you should consider yourself blessed for coming back here. That hall is a pigsty now, and it was never much before."

Liliana shifted slightly. "How is...everyone?" she asked with a fair attempt at disinterest.

Averil gave her a very shrewd look before shrugging her shoulders. "Well enough, I suppose."

"What do you mean, well enough? Is anyone ill? Is Hu?"

Averil smiled smugly, and Liliana knew her curiosity was no longer a secret. But she didn't care. She wanted to know about Hu.

"No one is sick, I don't think, but I must say that servant of yours... What was her name?"

"Maude."

"Maude is not much in the way of maintaining a household. The rushes were disgusting, and the tables... Well, I'm sorry to tell you this, Liliana, but the hall looked like the worst kind of tavern."

Liliana guessed that Averil was no more sorry about being the bearer of such tidings than she was to be rich. In a way, though, she supposed she had herself to blame. She *had* gloated over her young, handsome husband, so was it any wonder Averil was enjoying her particular form of revenge?

"And Hu?" she asked, swallowing more of her pride to find out what she really wanted to know.

"Slovenly, my dear. Absolutely slovenly. I don't think that cook is doing her job at all, and—" she leaned closer and dropped her voice to a whisper "—the smell! He said something about tending some sick sheep, and I can well believe it!"

"He cares very much about those sheep. They were a wedding gift, and he hopes to do well with them at market."

If Hu was tending the sheep, Liliana thought, Gareth must not have returned yet. What if something had happened to him on his journey, as Hu had feared?

"Really? I wouldn't know about such business matters. I'm sure, Liliana, that your father is pleased to have you home to supervise his servants again."

Liliana said nothing as a maid brought in three goblets and a vessel of wine on a silver platter. In truth, her father's household had been managing very well without her. So much so that she had the distinct impression her presence was rather resented by the servants.

As the long, lonely, tedious days had passed, she had come to see that she was out of place here, as Hu must have felt out of place among the Normans.

Averil sipped her wine and once again assumed a conspiratorial whisper. "And about that Maude, I believe she is with child. Perhaps you were wiser to leave Hu Morgan than you knew," she added significantly.

Liliana didn't bother to hide her smile. "Maude loves a young shepherd named Gareth. I'm sure he is the father of her child."

Averil looked a little nonplussed, but only a little. "Well, far be it from me to tell you otherwise," she said lightly. "But she *is* rather attractive, and you know what they say about the Welsh and their lack of—"

"You must be very tired, Averil."

Barris came inside. "Holy Mother, it's freezing out there. Ah, wine!"

He came toward them, grabbed his wife's goblet and took an enormous gulp. "When do we dine?"

"Thank you for reminding me," Liliana said, rising quickly. "I must see to the preparations. I will send Jhone to show you to your chamber."

Averil stood up, too. "Thank you, my dear. And I must say, I think you did the best thing, running away from that intolerable situation."

Liliana paused and looked at Averil. "Thank you for coming," she said, with such sincerity that Averil almost regretted having been so happy to hear about the unfortunate Morgans.

"Hu?"

Hu grunted a response as he knelt, examining the ram. It was sick, that much was certain, for it had been off its food for the past few days.

"*Hu!*"

"God's teeth, what—" He glanced up, then got quickly to his feet. "Gareth! At last! Worried sick I've been."

"You look plenty healthy to me, and me going all that way to fetch Mamaeth."

"I got better."

Gareth grinned. "Then I'm letting *you* tell that to Mamaeth."

"She came?"

"Aye, and the baron, too."

"Sweet Jesus!"

"Now go tell them they made the journey for nothing while I take a good look at that ram."

Hu wiped his hands on some straw and brushed down his hair. His chausses were filthy from the stable, and his tunic not much better.

He did not hurry out of the half-rebuilt barn. It was not going to be easy to tell them he had recovered on his own.

And they would surely want to see his wife. He had no great wish to have them know she had left him.

He frowned. Never, since the day she had ridden out of this gate and back to her father's, had she even sent a messenger to inquire if all was well.

He had hoped she would come to the memorial Mass for Elwy, but she didn't. It was as if she was trying to forget she had ever been married.

Yet if that was so, why hadn't Lord Trevelyan come? For days Hu had expected to see his leige lord ride through the gate to demand that Hu vacate the property at once, oath or no oath.

Why hadn't he? As Hu lay in his lonely bed at night, he sometimes dared to hope that Liliana meant to come back to him. That the love he felt for her was returned.

But as the days had passed, that hope had started to dwindle.

Nonetheless, when he entered the hall, he forced himself to smile. "Emryss! Mamaeth! Happy I am to see you."

Mamaeth, looking even more wiry and wizened than he remembered, turned her beady black eyes on him. "You're not sick," she accused. It had been years since he had seen her, and he had forgotten how little innate respect she had for men she had known since they were children.

"I'm much better."

Baron Emryss DeLanyea, leaning his weight on his good leg, also gave him a shrewd look with his remaining eye. "Seen you looking healthier, though, boy."

"Thought you'd mend," Mamaeth said briskly. "Didn't come for that. Came to see your wife. Gareth tells us she's some beauty, which is good. Judging by this hall, Hu, she's not a deft hand with the servants. Now, where in the name of Jesus is she?"

Hu coughed awkwardly. "She . . . she went to visit her father." Emryss's raised eyebrow made Hu blush, but he acted as if nothing was amiss. "Please, sit down and have some ale. Maude!"

Osyth appeared in the kitchen door. "Maude's gone out to the barn," she said, her eyes widening at the sight of the visitors. Hu glared at her, and she added a hasty, "My lord."

"Bring us some ale and see that chambers are prepared for my guests."

"Yes, my lord."

Mamaeth sniffed loudly. "The way you smell, I don't blame your wife for leaving."

"I was looking at one of the rams."

"Not sick, I hope," the baron said.

"I'm not sure. I'm glad Gareth's back."

"Is she with child?" Mamaeth interrupted.

"Who?"

"Your wife, of course."

"No."

"Why not? Not taking after Emryss there, are you?"

Emryss grinned. "Not Hu, I don't think, eh?"

"Why did *you* come?" Hu asked the baron bluntly. Between his concern for his livestock, his lack of sleep and the need to keep the truth of his ruined marriage from his old friends, he had little patience left for banter.

"Since I couldn't come to your wedding, I decided to come now that the leg is better."

"Oh."

"What happened to the barn?"

"Rebels. They killed Elwy."

"Oh, blessed Jesus, no!"

"God in Heaven!" Mamaeth whispered.

Hu nodded grimly. "They attacked another manor not far from here first, to draw us away. I left Elwy and a few of the men here." His voice dropped to a whisper. "I should have been here to defend my manor. They tell me Elwy didn't even have a chance to fight."

Emryss glanced at Mamaeth, who sat as still as one of the stones of the walls, then at Hu. "What else could you do, boy? Not a seer. Come, you," he said gently to Mamaeth, helping her to her feet. "Us for a rest, is it, and then more talk after the evening meal. Right, Hu?"

"Yes, Emryss. Sorry I am to have to tell you."

"Me, too, boy. Me, too."

Later that night, when the evening meal was over and the servants had taken down the tables, Hu and Emryss sat together near the hearth.

Hu sighed and leaned back in his chair. "It is easy to forget that Mamaeth is an old woman. I should have found an easier way to tell you about Elwy."

Emryss nodded thoughtfully. "Death is always hard to hear about, to see and to talk of," he replied. "But Mamaeth is a strong woman. She will be herself in the morning." After a short pause the baron spoke again. "The rebels—think you they will trouble you again?"

"I don't know. I killed their leader."

"Thought you said you were gone when they attacked."

"He was wounded and got away. I followed his trail and . . ."

"And?"

"When I found him, I slit his throat."

If Emryss was surprised by the hard edge to Hu's voice, he kept it from his face. "Deserving it, sounds like. And the rest of his men?"

"They ran away."

Emryss nodded. "Not wanting to find myself facing a mason in a fight," he remarked calmly. "No doubt their leader found that out."

"That was the strange thing," Hu said pensively. "It wasn't one of my men that wounded him first. It was one of them."

Emryss looked a little surprised, then shrugged his broad shoulders. "Rebels fight everyone, even their own, I suppose. Did that fellow get away, too?"

"Yes. No. I don't know." Hu regarded Emryss steadily. "He was badly wounded. I thought he was dying, so when he asked me to take him up to the hills to die, I agreed. I went back the next day, but he wasn't there."

"Maybe his friends came and took the body."

"Or maybe I made another mistake," Hu replied bitterly.

Emryss frowned. "Do you think you did wrong to take him to the mountain?"

Hu thought a moment, then answered honestly. "No, no, I don't. There was something about him . . . Something that made me wish we were not enemies." He looked at Emryss, a half-Welsh, half-Norman lord. "Will there always be fighting over the land like this, Emryss?"

Emryss sighed. "Hard to say, Hu. Maybe not, if the Normans change their ways, or the Welsh."

"What are we to do, then? Keep fighting?"

"Is that what you want?"

"All fighting leads to is death."

Both men sat wrapped in their thoughts for a long moment. Then Hu spoke quietly. "What can a man do, but make his own way and do his best?"

"What, indeed," Emryss replied.

"I wish my wife understood that."

"She doesn't?"

"No."

"But you understand her, do you think?"

"She's proud, and stubborn, and arrogant, and gives orders like a—like a . . ."

"Like a Norman."

Hu eyed him warily. "Aye, like a Norman."

"Well? What else were you expecting from Trevelyan's daughter? Is there nothing in her favor?"

"She's beautiful."

Emryss shook his head. "That's not what I meant, and you know it."

"She can be quite . . . affectionate. And pleasant to be with."

"That's good. Known plenty of Normans who would die before they would smile."

"She's good with the servants."

"That's a rare quality, too."

"She did a lot of the whitewashing for this hall. Not very well, I grant you, but she tried."

"Now *that* I find hard to believe. Lord Trevelyan's daughter whitewashing?"

"I assure you, it's quite true." Hu smiled at the memory of Liliana's splattered face and her laughing eyes as she recounted her instruction.

"It sounds as if you like her."

"I do."

"Does she like you?"

Hu looked away. "She used to."

"Used to?"

"After the rebels came, she accused me of leaving my manor, and her, too vulnerable." He stared at the floor. "I did."

"You underestimated your enemy." Emryss shifted his crippled leg. "We've all done that. Why didn't you just say so?"

Hu stood up and began to pace impatiently. "I did, but I was also angry and upset and sick to death of apologizing to her. She was wrong to accuse me, Emryss."

"Yes, she was. So now you hate her."

"God, no!" He halted. "That is the worst thing of all, Emryss." His voice dropped to a whisper. "I love her. I can't stop loving her."

"Ah, like that, is it?" Emryss nodded sagely. "Mysterious thing, is love. Do you think she hates you, then?"

"How am I supposed to know that? As you said, I am no seer."

"You could ask her."

"And swallow my pride yet again? No!"

Emryss rose. "I'm tired, and all this talk of love is making me wish I had stayed home with my wife. Sleep well, Hu."

Hu nodded. "Sleep well, Emryss."

As Emryss passed by Hu, he paused for a brief moment and looked at the boy he had known for many years. "Never thought it was your way to give up, Hu," he said.

Hu stared at Emryss as he limped from the hall. Give up? Emryss thought he was giving up?

Was he?

Hu closed his eyes, remembering the night his grandfather had been killed and he had hidden in the bushes. He had promised himself afterward that he would never again retreat from a fight.

And yet here he was, giving up his wife and hiding in his manor because he was—what? Afraid? Afraid that Liliana didn't love him after all?

She did. She had to. He loved her, and he was sure she loved him.

Standing in his lonely, empty hall, Hu Morgan made a decision. He would stop sulking here. He would go to her and demand—ask—that she come home with him.

And he would not give up until she agreed.

Chapter Nineteen

In the courtyard of Lord Trevelyan's castle, Liliana mounted her horse despite Derrick's clear misgivings. "But my lady," he pleaded, his breath like smoke in the cold morning air, "we should have a larger escort."

"You said you could only spare this many men with my father away," she replied, folding her cloak more tightly about her.

"That's true enough—"

"So these men will have to do. I have complete faith in your abilities, Derrick. And I simply cannot wait."

"What message shall we leave for your father, my lady?" Derrick asked resignedly as he gestured for one of the senior servants to come forward.

"Tell Lord Trevelyan his daughter has gone home. And tell him I hope his marriage is as happy as mine."

Derrick smiled briefly. He was happy for her, and yet he still feared that there might be outlaws in the forest. However, he had known Liliana all her life, so he also knew there would be no use trying to deny her request to escort her to her home. He could only hope Lord Trevelyan would understand.

Derrick mounted his horse and led the small cortege under the portcullis, through the outer wards, along the main street of the village that surrounded the castle and into the forest. He could hear Liliana and her usually silent maid—a most admirable young woman, really—talking as they rode along in the growing light of the early morning.

The ground beneath their horses and the wagon was frozen and the trees bare, so he hoped he would be able to catch sight of any outlaws who might be waiting in ambush, although it seemed as if the Welshmen had vanished into the early morning mists. Lord Trevelyan had ordered his men to patrol these woods all the way to the edge of Hu Morgan's manor, and no one had reported seeing anything amiss.

Lord Trevelyan had ordered his patrols to move beyond the border and into Morgan's land, but that was to be kept secret, so that Morgan would not feel insulted. It was just that Lord Trevelyan wanted to be absolutely certain the risk to his daughter and her husband was alleviated, at least for the time being.

Nonetheless, Derrick watched warily and kept alert for any unusual sound. When they were in the deepest part of the forest, he suddenly signaled a halt.

"What is it?" Liliana asked, looking around her nervously.

Derrick twisted to look at her. "I'm not sure, my lady."

Then she heard it, too. The thundering sound of a horse's hooves on the frozen road.

Liliana glanced nervously at Jhone. "Perhaps we should have waited, as Derrick suggested."

Before Jhone could answer, a lone horseman appeared, riding swiftly toward them.

Liliana stared, then smiled, rose in her stirrups and let out a surprisingly loud cry of her own. "Hu! It's Hu!"

Derrick looked at her in amazement. Liliana fought to keep the smile off her face, then gave up the effort.

Her husband pulled his horse to a flourishing halt. His face was serious, but his eyes—Liliana's heart leaped with happiness to see them.

"Well met, my lady," he said gravely. "May I have a word with you?"

"Of course," she replied, her tone equally grave despite the joy in her heart and the excited throbbing of the blood in her veins.

Hu dismounted and came to help her down from her horse. When he touched her, it was all she could do to keep from embracing him fiercely. But they were not alone.

He took her hand in his and led her a little distance from the others. "Liliana—" he began, turning to look at her.

"Hu, I apologize," Liliana interrupted. She looked into his face, determined to say what must be said. "I didn't understand how things were for you. I was too proud and too stubborn."

"Liliana." He put his hands on her shoulders.

"I swear to you, I will try not to be so arrogant or so sure my opinion is all that matters. I shouldn't have berated you that way, either. I know that now. I was upset and angry—"

He gave her a little shake. *"Liliana!"*

Startled, she stopped. He smiled slowly. "As much as I'm enjoying your apology, there is something I must say, too. I was wrong. I should have listened to your advice."

"Oh, Hu..." She put her arms around him and reached up to kiss him. His arms moved slowly about her as their lips touched for what became a long, lingering, wonderful kiss.

"Liliana," Hu whispered huskily, his lips trailing across her cheek to her ear, "you do...love me?"

"Yes, Hu, yes! With all my heart," she answered softly. "Now take me home."

He lifted his face and looked at her with a strange expression. "Are you begging me to let you come back?"

Liliana frowned and pulled away, disappointment sweeping over her. If he thought he was having some kind of triumph over her... She loved him, yes, but she would never beg. Never!

She gazed at his merry dark eyes and began to smile as a sudden delightful suspicion bloomed in her mind. "Where were you going, my lord?"

He chuckled softly, pulling her against him and holding her tight in his arms. "Oh, Liliana! I've missed you. I need you. I want you to come home with me."

She smiled at him and saw the happiness shining in his eyes. "Do you love me, Hu?"

"Yes, wife, I do. With all my heart. Let's start afresh. No apologies, no recriminations."

"Yes."

He bent to kiss her again but paused, glancing at the group of people on the road waiting for them. "What will they think?"

"I don't care," she murmured as she arched against him. He loved her, and she loved him, and that was all that mattered.

"I must apologize again for sending for you. We really thought Hu was seriously ill," Liliana said to Mamaeth as they finished the evening meal. Hu sat on her left, the baron on her right, and Mamaeth was beside him.

Maude, delighted to have Gareth home with her, had been excused from her duties when Mamaeth had pointed out that the girl was truly ill, although it was because she was with child. Nonetheless, Maude had insisted on joining everyone in the hall and had fussed over Gareth so much she only giggled once. Halfway through the meal, Liliana realized that the young couple were no longer in the hall.

Jhone, once again in charge of the servants, gave no indication that anything important had happened in her life in the past weeks. Liliana, however, knew the woman's secret sorrow and hoped that Jhone would someday find a husband worthy of her. In the meantime, they would be good friends.

Osyth and Dena scurried about like happy rabbits, and it occurred to Liliana that she might have some work to do to restore a proper sense of decorum, provided she really wanted to.

"Hu was always one to take a terrible fever," Mamaeth said briskly. "Expected it even if he had a splinter, me. Still, I'm not sorry we came. Wanted to see how the boy was doing."

Liliana glanced at Hu's scowling face and smiled impishly. "I'm glad, too. I want to hear more of what Hu was like as a boy."

"No, you don't," Hu said.

"Yes, she does," the baron said, his face bright with laughter. His iron gray hair hung down to his broad shoulders, and his smile was so infectious that Liliana soon ceased to notice the terrible scar that marred his face. She had also seen the older man jump from his horse with astounding alacrity, and could understand why Hu had laughed at her notion of the baron as a feeble old man.

"A lovely boy he was," Mamaeth said, "despite Emryss's efforts to corrupt him, dragging him about to tournaments. Stubborn, though—oh, a terrible creature he was for that."

"I must confess that he learned such regrettable behavior from me," the baron said mournfully. "When I got back from the Crusade, Hu followed me around like a lost puppy for days. It probably started then."

Liliana had to smile at Baron DeLanyea's contrite expression.

"Are you two quite finished?" Hu asked pointedly.

"Oh, I hope not!" Liliana said. She was enjoying herself immensely. She didn't think it would be possible for her to be any happier than she was at this moment, now that she was home with Hu.

"You're not with child," Mamaeth suddenly announced in a disappointed tone.

The force of her personality was such that Liliana blushed and felt ashamed, until she saw Hu's grin.

"Not yet," he said meaningfully.

Liliana flushed hotly, even though her thoughts had been tending in that very direction. She had wanted nothing more than to be alone with Hu ever since she had returned home.

"You must forgive Mamaeth," the baron said with just the hint of a smile on his lips. "She likes children."

"Huh!" Mamaeth snorted. "Some."

"You know you would dote on any baby of Hu's."

"Well, and what if I would? But if he's going to sit here swapping stories all night, I don't see much chance of him having any. No being like Emryss and wasting time for you, Hu Morgan. I want to see your children before I die."

"Wasting time?" the baron grumbled. "Made up for it, haven't I? Roanna's with child again, too."

"Good thing," Mamaeth replied sharply, and those at the head table began to laugh.

Hu rose with lordly dignity, his face serious. "I shall endeavor to comply with your request, Mamaeth, provided my wife is willing."

There was a time Liliana would have died rather than take part in such levity on such a subject, but now she, too, rose with a great display of dignity and a bow in her husband's direction. "As a dutiful wife, my lord, I shall do my humble best to please you."

Hu looked at Liliana. She looked at him, and they both knew the time for teasing was past. With a pagan shout, Hu grabbed Liliana, threw her over his shoulder and carried her off toward their bedchamber.

"Hu!" she gasped when he kicked the heavy door shut. "Put me down! I can't breathe!"

Hu, panting as well, did as she requested. Then he turned to her, his eyes filled with undeniable desire.

The strength of her feelings and the knowledge that they were finally alone made Liliana suddenly feel as timid as she had on their wedding night. Her knees trembled, so she sat down and picked up her hairbrush.

"We should see that Maude and Gareth marry," she said with a tremor in her voice, well aware that Hu was watching her.

"Should we?" he asked, coming to take the brush from her hand. He sounded so calm that Liliana hoped she hadn't imagined the ardor in his eyes.

He began to brush her long, unbound hair, stroking the golden locks with his lean, strong fingers as he did so.

"Yes. They must be married, for the child's sake." She closed her eyes and enjoyed the sensation of the brush strokes and his hand.

"That's the Norman way," he said quietly. "Welsh don't care so much about the legalities. Supposing we let *them* decide the way they want to take, my lady."

Liliana opened her mouth to protest, but closed it with a smile. "As you wish, my lord."

She stood up and turned to him. "I missed you, Hu," she whispered.

He smiled, his eyes filled with love, and put his arms around her. "And I missed you."

She gave him a sidelong glance, all too mindful of the heat growing in every limb. "Just in bed, I suppose?"

He shook his head and his breath caught as her hand slipped inside his tunic. "Not *just* there."

They heard a scratching at the door. "Mott," Hu said, twisting to open the door. He paused and looked at her. "He can sleep out there, if you like."

Liliana shook her head. "Mott sleeps where you do."

Hu grinned boyishly and let his dog into the bedchamber. Mott went over to the wall and lay down, wagging his tail.

"Now, where were we?" Hu said as he closed the door again.

"Talking about how much you missed me."

He lifted her hand to his lips and began to kiss each finger. "Wasn't it how much *you* missed *me?*"

"Something like that," Liliana agreed.

"Shall we go to bed, wife?" He began to kiss her neck, his hands tangling in her thick hair. Quickly his fingers loosened her gown.

"Please, Hu, yes," she moaned softly.

With a deep chuckle, he picked her up and carried her toward their bed. When he set her down, her gown slipped from her shoulders. She gasped and her hands gripped his forearms as he kissed her breasts through the thin fabric of her shift.

She could not wait, but tugged his tunic over his head impatiently.

"It's cold, wife," he said, laughing again and throwing back the covers on the bed.

She hurriedly removed the rest of her clothes and joined her naked husband in the bed, snuggling against his warmth. "Not here, it isn't."

He began to caress her slowly. "You're right. I'm burning—and not with fever." He moved so that his body covered her.

He kissed her forehead. Then her cheeks.

"I had an interesting conversation with Mamaeth while we were overseeing the meal," Liliana whispered.

"Not more stories about me, I hope?"

She pressed her lips to his throat. "No, about me. She is most concerned that I am not with child. She offered me plenty of advice."

He looked at her skeptically. "First Lady Eleanor, now Mamaeth. Needing some privacy about such things, I think."

She grinned mischievously at him. "I wouldn't want to *arrogantly* assume I know everything, especially about that."

He grinned back and sighed. "Well, what did she say? Drink some ghastly potion by the light of the full moon?"

"No." Liliana gasped as he bent to move his tongue over her hardened nipples ever so lightly.

"I don't believe we need any more advice," he murmured.

"I think you are right, my love."

* * * * *

COMING NEXT MONTH

#227 MARIAH'S PRIZE—Miranda Jarrett
In this installment of the *Sparhawk* series, a desperate Mariah West convinces jaded Gabriel Sparhawk to captain her sloop, never guessing at his ulterior motives.

#228 THE HIGHLANDER—Ruth Langan
Scottish chieftain Dillon Campbell abducted Lady Leonora Wilton as an act of revenge against the English. But one look into Leonora's eyes and it became an act of love.

#229 SIMON'S LADY—Julie Tetel
The marriage between Simon de Beresford and Lady Gwyneth had been arranged to quell a Saxon uprising, yet the Saxon bride has much more than *peace* on her mind.

#230 SWEET SONG OF LOVE—Merline Lovelace
When knight Richard Fitzhugh was called to battle, he left behind a meek child bride given to him by the king. So who was the curvaceous beauty who now greeted him as *husband?*

AVAILABLE NOW:

Fifty red-blooded, white-hot, true-blue hunks
from every State in the Union!

Look for MEN MADE IN AMERICA! Written by some of
our most popular authors, these stories feature fifty of the
strongest, sexiest men, each from a different state in the
union!

Two titles available every month at your favorite retail
outlet.

In July, look for:

ROCKY ROAD by Anne Stuart (Maine)
THE LOVE THING by Dixie Browning (Maryland)

In August, look for:

PROS AND CONS by Bethany Campbell (Massachusetts)
TO TAME A WOLF by Anne McAllister (Michigan)

You won't be able to resist MEN MADE IN AMERICA!

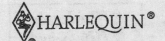

**Harlequin Books requests the
pleasure of your company this June
in Eternity, Massachusetts,
for WEDDINGS, INC.**

For generations, couples have been coming to
Eternity, Massachusetts, to exchange wedding
vows. Legend has it that those married in
Eternity's chapel are destined for a lifetime of
happiness. And the residents are more than
willing to give the legend a hand.

Beginning in June, you can experience the
legend of Eternity. Watch for one title per
month, across all of the Harlequin series.

**HARLEQUIN BOOKS...
NOT THE SAME OLD STORY!**

Looking for more of a good thing?

Why not try a bigger book from Harlequin Historicals?

SUSPICION by Judith McWilliams, April 1994—A story of intrigue and deceit set during the Regency era.

ROYAL HARLOT by Lucy Gordon, May 1994—The adventuresome romance of a prince and the woman spy assigned to protect him.

UNICORN BRIDE by Claire Delacroix, June 1994—The first of a trilogy set in thirteenth-century France.

MARIAH'S PRIZE by Miranda Jarrett, July 1994—Another tale of the seafaring Sparhawks of Rhode Island.

Longer stories by some of your favorite authors.
Watch for them this spring, wherever
Harlequin Historicals are sold.

ᗞᴇꜱᴛɪɴʏ'ꜱ ᴡᴏᴍᴇɴ

Sexy, adventurous historical romance at its best!

May 1994
ALENA #220. A veteran Roman commander battles to
subdue the proud, defiant queen he takes to wife.

July 1994
SWEET SONG OF LOVE #230. Medieval is the tale of an
arranged marriage that flourishes despite all odds.

September 1994
SIREN'S CALL #236. The story of a dashing Greek sea captain
and the stubborn Spartan woman he carries off.

Three exciting stories from Merline Lovelace, a fresh new
voice in Historical Romance.

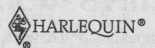

Fifty red-blooded, white-hot, true-blue hunks
from every State in the Union!

Look for MEN MADE IN AMERICA! Written by some of
our most popular authors, these stories feature fifty of
the strongest, sexiest men, each from a different state in
the union!

Two titles available every other month at your favorite
retail outlet.

In May, look for:

KISS YESTERDAY GOODBYE by Leigh Michaels (Iowa)
A TIME TO KEEP by Curtiss Ann Matlock (Kansas)

In June, look for:

ONE PALE, FAWN GLOVE by Linda Shaw (Kentucky)
BAYOU MIDNIGHT by Emilie Richards (Louisiana)

You won't be able to resist MEN MADE IN AMERICA!

HARLEQUIN®

Don't miss these Harlequin favorites by some of our most distinguished authors!
And now, you can receive a discount by ordering two or more titles!

HT #25551	THE OTHER WOMAN by Candace Schuler	$2.99	☐
HT #25539	FOOLS RUSH IN by Vicki Lewis Thompson	$2.99	☐
HP #11550	THE GOLDEN GREEK by Sally Wentworth	$2.89	☐
HP #11603	PAST ALL REASON by Kay Thorpe	$2.99	☐
HR #03228	MEANT FOR EACH OTHER by Rebecca Winters	$2.89	☐
HR #03268	THE BAD PENNY by Susan Fox	$2.99	☐
HS #70532	TOUCH THE DAWN by Karen Young	$3.39	☐
HS #70540	FOR THE LOVE OF IVY by Barbara Kaye	$3.39	☐
HI #22177	MINDGAME by Laura Pender	$2.79	☐
HI #22214	TO DIE FOR by M.J. Rodgers	$2.89	☐
HAR #16421	HAPPY NEW YEAR, DARLING		
	by Margaret St. George	$3.29	☐
HAR #16507	THE UNEXPECTED GROOM by Muriel Jensen	$3.50	☐
HH #28774	SPINDRIFT by Miranda Jarrett	$3.99	☐
HH #28782	SWEET SENSATIONS by Julie Tetel	$3.99	☐

Harlequin Promotional Titles

#83259	UNTAMED MAVERICK HEARTS	$4.99	☐
	(Short-story collection featuring Heather Graham Pozzessere, Patricia Potter, Joan Johnston)		

(limited quantities available on certain titles)

	AMOUNT	$	
DEDUCT:	10% DISCOUNT FOR 2+ BOOKS	$	
	POSTAGE & HANDLING	$	
	($1.00 for one book, 50¢ for each additional)		
	APPLICABLE TAXES*	$	_____
	TOTAL PAYABLE	$	_____
	(check or money order—please do not send cash)		

To order, complete this form and send it, along with a check or money order for the total above, payable to Harlequin Books, to: **In the U.S.:** 3010 Walden Avenue, P.O. Box 9047, Buffalo, NY 14269-9047; **In Canada:** P.O. Box 613, Fort Erie, Ontario, L2A 5X3.

Name: _____

Address: _____ City: _____

State/Prov.: _____ Zip/Postal Code: _____

*New York residents remit applicable sales taxes.
 Canadian residents remit applicable GST and provincial taxes.